women within

a novel by

anne leigh parrish

The final approval for this literary material is granted by the author.

Second printing

ISBN: 978-1-61296-839-1
PUBLISHED BY BLACK ROSE WRITING
www.blackrosewriting.com

Printed in the United States of America
Suggested retail price $18.95

Women Within is printed in Adobe Caslon Pro

To John, Bob, and Lauren

women within

part one

chapter one

The Lindell Retirement Home was lovely. Wide lawns could be reached through automatic glass doors at the end of every hall. Secluded patios with benches and flowering plants made for pleasant sitting in the warm months. The common areas were full of natural light and good quality art, often by a resident's own hand. Some wings had an aquarium or well-populated birdcage, and one, Skilled Nursing, offered a very large stuffed dog that on occasion brought a smile to the faces of the dementia patients. The overall impression was one of calm, poise, and comfort.

Within the rooms themselves, there was less comfort. Aging wasn't easy. Memory was unsure, especially with the help of certain frequently prescribed drugs. Physical discomfort was quite prevalent, for which, ironically, fewer drugs were prescribed.

Constance Maynard, age ninety-two, knew this well and would have shared her complaints, had she cared to. At the moment, she just wished Eunice and Sam would ease up a little. They were attempting to wash her feet by putting them in a plastic tub full of warm, soapy water. Constance thought the task should be simple enough. She didn't see why it required four hands to manage it. They always teamed up when any sort of bathing or dressing was needed. Weren't they the oddest pair? Fifty-something Eunice and twenty-something Sam. One, slight and wiry, the other, a linebacker. *Big and Small. Short and Tall. Who's the fairest of them all?*

That was her sleep aid talking. The young doctor who came around told her rest was essential. Who was he kidding? Any moment now she would enter the realm of eternal rest. She should have the luxury of lying awake all night if she wanted to. Night was the traveling time. The time of seeing.

Eunice, the little one, knelt and lifted one gnarled foot out of the water, ran a scratchy washcloth between the toes, and lowered the foot back into the tub. The same was done to the other foot. Constance observed her feet with dismay. They certainly weren't anything to brag about.

·   ·   ·

They had been once, small and shapely, so pretty in heels, worn out by years of walking back and forth before a blackboard, teaching morons the lessons history had to offer. Years of dull faces; years of dull minds. Engineering students needing to fulfill their liberal arts credits; fools who had no idea what to study and who got assigned to her lecture by that toad, Harriet, in Registration.

"Miss Maynard's class is too hard for me," whispered more than one curly-haired girl. Just there to get a husband and start cranking out imbecile children. The so-called research papers they wrote were scandalous. No matter how many times she went over proper footnoting procedure, their sources (if they were actual sources) went uncited. Her remarks were harsh and often caused tears. The Dean scolded her. She could be hard on the men, that was fine; they were serious, hoping for a bright future. The women, well, what could you expect? Constance fumed. And then, she was blessed when Angela Lowry signed up for her class. Angela had a first-rate mind and was eager to learn. She'd read everything on the War of the Roses. Her final paper was good enough to be published. When Constance checked one of her beautifully cited reference materials, she discovered that Angela had plagiarized a man writing two decades earlier, Dr. Harold Moss, at Harvard. She invited her to come to her office.

"I think you know why you're here," Constance said. She had brewed a cup of tea, hoping it would soothe.

"You caught me." Just like that. Angela didn't even blink. What color was her hair? Like the inside of a yam, a pale orange. Her blouse was white with small red buttons, and embroidered roses on the collar. She had big hands that looked raw, as if she washed them a lot in harsh soap.

Angela had wanted to test her professor, to see how good she really was. Hence the intentional plagiarism. Constance knew that was nonsense. The girl got stuck for time and panicked. Then she tried to talk her way out of it. Constance admired her moxie.

Was that a word anyone used anymore, moxie?

. . .

They were still fussing with her feet. Sam trimmed her nails. Eunice was talking.

"He says I'm kind," she said. Her hair was bushy, copper streaked with gray.

"Aren't you?" Sam asked. She had a pleasant voice for such a big girl.

"Never thought of myself that way before. Gullible, yes."

And then to Constance, "You're all done, dear."

"Can't you see I've still got the other one to do?" Sam asked.

"Right."

Snip, snip, snip. Constance jerked her foot back.

"You need to hold still," Sam said.

Sam clipped the last nail, on the little toe of Constance's right foot, then wheeled her from her bathroom back into her bedroom. Eunice spread a blanket across her lap. The blanket didn't quite cover her feet, which were now slippered, yet distinctly cold. She could never be comfortable when her feet were cold.

. . .

"You are, I can tell."

"I am what?"

"Getting cold feet."

Constance held her cocktail and looked down. A smell of lilac came in on the breeze lifting the gauze curtains in the study. Lilac was her favorite flower. They might have made a pretty wedding bouquet.

She could feel William watching her. She smoothed one sleeve of her dress with her free hand. She brought the glass to her lips, then lowered it.

"William—"

What had she told him on that long-ago afternoon? What reason did she give?

There were too many to count. They rolled through her mind, as her gin and tonic warmed in her hand. The breeze was a comfort, then it died, the curtains stilled, and she found her voice.

"I can't."

9

Nothing more was ever said between them. Not even when she returned the ring. She thought he might remark on that, at least. Choosing it was probably their most intimate moment. What he had first presented her with was a thin band that had belonged to his mother. The look on her face—shock that he would take such a step at all—was misinterpreted. He chided himself for not understanding how badly she would want her own ring, not one someone else had worn, however happily, for over forty years.

At the jeweler's he talked her into a larger diamond than she thought appropriate, or which looked good on her hand.

"Isn't it rather … ?"

"Tasteful and grand?" he'd asked.

"Vulgar," she wanted to say, but didn't.

Of course, it was beautiful. Diamonds always are, and this was quite a good one. E color, very, very small inclusions, round cut. Two point three carats.

"It suits you, darling," he whispered, under the jeweler's approving gaze.

They met at Brown. Her field was history, his, philosophy. He was impressed by her academic ambitions, that she'd attended Smith College, that she was petite and self-possessed. He was no doubt used to women who swooned over his attention and the prospect of marrying his money. William was rich in that quiet, understated way people tend to find so attractive. He never called attention to his wealth. He dressed modestly. It was the family home that gave it all away. Abundant opulence. The silent, invisible servants. His aunt's cool assessment of Constance, and then her grudging acceptance. Since his mother's death, his Aunt Helen had run the show. William's father made himself scarce. Like Constance, William was an only child.

He didn't seem entirely surprised by her refusal. Her letters to him the summer before, written from London, had been cool and objective, unlike his, which were warm and intimate. In one, he'd even begged her to return early so they could be together. She said she couldn't just yet because she still hadn't found a good topic for her doctoral thesis. In truth, she'd already settled on the fifteenth century English queen, Anne Neville.

That era's military campaigns and shifting factions were interesting enough, she supposed, but they were the stuff of men. She wanted to study the women. Marriages were political and strategic. Love, if it came, was after the fact. Anne Neville was a perfect example. She was married off at fourteen to a French prince who was killed trying to invade England. Then the widow of a dead traitor, she threw herself on the English king's mercy. For her trouble, she was placed under the king's guardianship, shut away, and urged to join a convent so the king could retain control of her fortune. Her only recourse was to marry the king's brother. *Such a rotten deal*, Constance always thought. *Trading one prison for another.*

· · ·

Eunice straightened the sheets on Constance's bed while Sam removed dirty clothes from the basket in the closet. She put the clothes in a bag marked with Constance's name and pulled the drawstring tight.

"Plans for the weekend?" Eunice asked her.

"Going through old stuff in the attic with my mother."

Sam's tone said it was really the last thing she wanted to do.

"Hm. You could tell her you're sick or helping out a friend. Use me as an excuse, if you want to."

"I can't do that. She depends on seeing me. She's—you know, *needy.*"

Constance nodded. Sam noticed.

"But you've never met her, Constance. You must be thinking of someone else," Sam said.

· · ·

Constance's family fell apart when she was nine. They lived in Los Angeles. Her mother had dreams of stardom that never came true. Her father worked as a bookkeeper for a number of small businesses—a plumbing company, which Constance remembered him praising for paying their bills on time, also a small theater troupe where Constance's mother had had several auditions, then one modest part, then poor reviews and a gentle invitation to leave the cast. It sat badly with her. She stayed home, a cigarette in her hand, circles below her eyes, stains on her bathrobe.

Constance was in awe of her mother because she had attempted something brave that other mothers didn't, which made her failure more acute. When her mother made a new career out of disappointment and sloth, she lost interest in Constance. Constance escaped the pain of her rejection through books, into the world of knights and ladies fair. All those lovelorn women left to worry and wait while the men had their fun fighting. What

11

did they do to pass the time? They reveled in the quiet and calm, no doubt, and kept busy with embroidery and weaving. The noble women would have held fine linens and lace; the servants sat at looms crafting tapestries to soften and warm stone walls.

Constance learned the art of needlework from her downstairs neighbor, Mrs. Pauline Lester. Her hands were gnarled terrors, yet quick and precise when wielding a needle. She sewed the most beautiful things! Fields of ornate flowers and birds, a young girl with flowing blond hair that made Constance despise her own raven curls, a small white dog sleeping on the threshold of a charming cottage in the woods. Constance began with a simple patterned canvas, following the outlines faithfully, crying when she erred and had to pull the tender thread from where it didn't belong. The world of her imagination, populated with dreams and the fabric in her own hands kept her going, far from the sour mood of her mother and the stony silence of her father.

It was decided that Constance's mother suffered from a nervous condition and needed to be in the company of people better able to help her. Constance waited with Pauline while her father put her mother and her one suitcase into the car and drove away. He was gone a long time. When he returned, he stood visibly straighter. His voice had a lighter tone. Soon, though, the task of caring for his young daughter weighed him down again.

Constance's father had been raised by his stepmother, then widowed and living in upstate New York. The stepmother was notified of the change in circumstance, and Constance was packed off on a train across country, alone, with her name and destination typed on a piece of paper and attached to the lapel of her coat with a safety pin. Her shock at the upheaval of her world was deep. What occupied a still deeper space within her was the splendor of the passing landscape. The desert seemed a glorious and terrifying place! She'd seen it before, of course, in little excursions with her parents before her mother cracked up. Pauline used those very words to a neighbor in her kitchen when she thought Constance was still embroidering in the living room, out of earshot.

It was as apt a term as any, Constance thought.

The woman who received Constance into her Dunston home on a still spring night was as solid as a rock. Lois Maynard would brook no nonsense, she informed Constance as she led the way up the dim stairway. But she would reward good behavior. Constance could be sure of that.

In the years that followed, Constance was seldom punished and seldom praised. She was surprised to find how little she minded it. She adored school and excelled in all her subjects.

"A natural scholar," more than one teacher said. When she wasn't at her books, she embroidered. The owner of the yarn shop in town, Mrs. Lapp, smiled when she came in.

"It's not the same shade of red," Constance said. Mrs. Lapp stared at her sympathetically. To her, Constance was an unfortunate case. The grandmother—stepgrandmother—was well known. Her house, a mansion, really, was clearly visible on its high hill, particularly in winter when the trees bared. Not much of a life for a child, living in a cold place like that, Mrs. Lapp thought, though Constance was nearly thirteen at that point. She was small for her age, and had given up hoping she would be taller.

Mrs. Lapp checked the skein Constance had taken from the peg on the wall, then consulted her inventory book and assured Constance that the lot number was the same. Constance gave her what remained of the skein she'd used to embroider a row of roses. Mrs. Lapp took both skeins to the glass-topped door where the sunlight poured through.

"How right you are! The new is slightly more brown, isn't it?" Mrs. Lapp asked.

Even so, there was nothing to be done. Mrs. Lapp suggested that Constance use the new wool in a corner, somewhere the eye wasn't instantly drawn. Constance had already thought of that.

• • •

"It's nice to see you smile," Eunice said. Constance was not aware that she was smiling. She wanted a skein of that red wool—the proper color. She needed to finish her embroidery. She loved it so. She pointed to the table by her bed. The lower shelf had her rolled-up canvas. Eunice brought it to her, set it in her lap, and then she and Sam went on their way.

chapter two

Four days after arriving in London, in the summer of 1946, Constance met Jean-Phillippe at the home of Professor Eric Spalding in Mayfair. Professor Spalding was a colleague and an old friend of Constance's thesis advisor at Brown, Professor Reynolds. He'd offered her a room in his large home, promising to keep an eye on her during her time there and to assist her with locating some primary sources for her thesis. Professor Spalding poured her a cup of tea from a lovely Limoges teapot he said he'd obtained before the war, and suggested that to really know one's subject, one should visit where she grew up. In Anne Neville's case, this was Middleham Castle in North Yorkshire. As the trip took shape in her mind, Jean-Phillippe was introduced as a new houseguest, also a student of history, just arrived that day from France to study the reigns of Henry the Seventh and Henry the Eighth.

She may have fallen in love on the spot. Even years later, she wasn't entirely sure. All she could recall was that the focus of her scholarship—her academic drive—vanished in the moments they first stood chatting politely in the drawing room about the English countryside. Jean-Phillippe was not a tall man, though easily several inches taller than Constance, who suddenly no longer regretted being short. He was broad in the shoulders. His teeth were bad, which she found endearing. When she spoke, he looked at her closely, his eyes never leaving hers, as if she were the only thing in the world that mattered. In time, she learned this was merely a habit. She saw him do that with other people, especially young ladies, and it galled. He wasn't a wolf, or a cad, just a man in love with the effect he had on women.

Before she realized any of that, however, he suggested that they go visit Middleham Castle together. Though it didn't bear directly on any of his own work, he thought such a visit would be most amusing. She must bring a notebook, camera, and sturdy shoes. Despite her fascination with him, she found his suggestion condescending. She knew perfectly well how to prepare for a trip. Yet she responded as if his words contained a rare and remarkable genius. She hated herself for feeding his ego, even as she came to adore him that much more.

The afternoon they arrived, the sky threatened a drenching rain. Constance had no umbrella. She'd been distracted at the last minute back in London, unable to find her purse, which she'd left in her room hanging on the doorknob. They walked through the ruined castle in silence. The place was theirs alone, except for a black and white dog who appeared at the top of a tumbled-down stone wall and barked once at them, then trotted off.

Their conversation stayed on neutral ground. Had he ever visited the States? He had, once to see friends in New York before the war. Could he ever see himself living there?

"New York, certainly. A marvelous city. You are from there?" he asked.

"No, upstate. Then college in Massachusetts. Returning to Rhode Island at the end of the summer."

"Rhode Island. Is it anything like the Island of Rhodes?"

She didn't respond. He lit a cigarette and offered her one. She shook her head.

After that he spoke about Professor Spalding, his taste in furniture and art, the questionable skills of his cook who never failed to serve watery potatoes and tough beef. Constance hadn't found the food distasteful. She was grateful for a free place to stay. Her room was at the top, under the roof, in what had once been maids' quarters. It faced the garden and was full of light. Jean-Phillippe's room was below ground, also in the quarter of former servants, and accessible by a set of stairs descending from the street.

Jean-Phillippe continued his assessment of Professor Spalding's home. The hot water took a long time to come up, there were water stains on the ceiling in the upstairs bath, the window in his room didn't close all the way, allowing a near-constant draft that he was certain would end up in his chest. Constance had never heard a man complain so much about domestic matters. She wondered if he were a homosexual. When she turned her ankle on a broken bit of stone, he caught her securely, then kissed her hard. She didn't wonder anymore. He released her and continued walking, as if the moment had never happened.

She behaved as calmly as he, feeling anything but. Their tour of the ruins came to an end. The rain picked up, and they walked briskly down the road to the nearby town of Middleham and a tavern called *The Duke of York*. The place was empty, except for one table by the windows occupied by two white-haired men bent over a chessboard. Jean-Phillippe suggested a whiskey. Constance accepted. He helped her remove her coat and asked the barmaid if he might drape it over the empty wooden bench in front of the fire. The barmaid did that for him, brought the drinks, and asked if they wanted anything to eat. Jean-Phillippe ordered a sandwich. Constance asked for nothing. She was unable to keep up her end of the conversation.

He talked on, about his childhood, his family, his studies. He became flushed from the whiskey. She hadn't touched hers, then drank it quickly. The burn it left in her throat was unpleasant. She asked to be excused for a moment. She went to the washroom and stood, gripping the sink, and splashed water on her face. She heard a radio playing in the room on the other side of the wall. The sound led her down the hall to a small private parlor where the same barmaid was pouring tea for an old woman. The old woman sat with a blanket on her lap and something she was sewing in her hands. The barmaid asked Constance if she'd gotten turned around and come there by mistake.

"Oh, no, I'm sorry. I didn't mean to intrude. I heard the music. It sounded so lovely," Constance said. It was a piano piece by Brahms. Classical music had been a favorite of Lois Maynard's. Constance knew a lot about the major composers, thanks to her. The old woman looked up at Constance with watery eyes. Their color was arresting, a cobalt blue. There was a chalky quality to them, too, as if for her, light had dimmed. She was beautiful, Constance thought. Calm. At peace.

"This is my grandmother," the barmaid said.

The old woman said something in what Constance recognized as Gaelic. There had been an Irish student at Smith, and she rambled wildly in her native tongue when upset. The old woman lifted her hand, and Constance shook it. Her palm was smooth and soft.

"She wonders if you'd like to sit with her for a bit," the barmaid said.

"Oh, I can't right now. I've got to get back to my friend."

The barmaid nodded. "Well, I best get back, myself. Never does to leave them too long on their own. They'll be wanting something. You'll come again, I hope?"

"I'm afraid I won't be able to. We're just here for the day."

The old woman's hand was still in Constance's. The other rested on her needlework. It was a painted canvas that had been unrolled and sewn carefully. The stitches were even and regular. Some, though, were messy and skipped a space or two. It was proof of the old woman's failing eyesight, Constance thought.

Constance and Jean-Phillippe took rooms at the local inn because Jean-Phillippe complained of not feeling well. In the morning his head hurt, his muscles ached. He blamed the poor weather. Constance could sense in his voice a condemnation of her for the outing, which he himself had suggested. She poured him a cup of hot tea. He accepted it without a word. He sat before the fire in his room, a shawl around his shoulders, slumped and small.

The moment she was free, she returned to the tavern. Someone else was serving the patrons, a man this time. Constance explained that she'd been invited. He merely nodded at her and went on wiping down the bar.

She found the old woman and the barmaid again in the private parlor. The barmaid explained that serving in the tavern wasn't her regular job, that her uncle, the man Constance had passed on the way in, had been sick the day before.

"My name's Tess. Didn't properly introduce myself before. This is Maeve," she said. Both women wore wool sweaters and skirts. Maeve had several thin silver bracelets on each arm that jingled as she raised and lowered her cup. Her hearing was keen, Constance observed. The sound of muffled laughter from the dining room next door caused her to turn her head in that direction.

Constance said that she was staying on a few days because her friend was under the weather, and hoped they could direct her to a nice ladies' shop because she'd brought no change of clothes.

Tess recommended a place called *Lady Alice*, then suggested that the owner of the inn, Mr. Townsend, might be able to lend Constance's friend something, because the gentlemen's shop carried very substandard merchandise, though as she recalled, the friend was on the short side, while Mr. Townsend was not. Constance said nothing. Tess sensed her unease and continued to talk. How did Constance like England? Was it so very different from America? How had people over there handled the war and the rationing? Did Constance have any brothers who'd enlisted and met with misfortune? Here Tess paused. Her expression said someone close to her had been lost. Maeve put her gnarled hand on Tess's smooth one. The quiet went on for a few moments more.

"That's a lovely piece of work you have there," Constance told Maeve.

Maeve nodded and said what must have been "thank you."

"She has no English?" Constance asked.

"Oh, she speaks it as well as you or I. But in the last few years she's returned home, as it were. She's lucky I understand her. No one else seems able to," Tess said.

Constance picked up the end of the tapestry. It had been years since she'd held needlework. Maeve handed her the entire length of canvas. Constance unfurled it. It measured roughly one foot high and two feet across. Only the first third had been sewn. It depicted the stages of a woman's life, from left to right, entitled Girlhood, Betrothal and Marriage, Motherhood, and lastly, Widowhood.

"She received it when she was young and put it away. Lately, though, she's wanted to get at it," Tess said. She poured Constance a cup of tea.

Maeve said something.

"She's says you're welcome to try, if you like," Tess said.

"Embroider, you mean?"

"Yes."

Tess handed her a woven wooden basket full of yarn. There was a small package of steel needles.

Constance politely declined, made small talk, finished her tea, and went back to the hotel. Over the next few days Jean-Phillippe lay sick, cranky and needy by turns. He begged Constance to sit in the chair by his bed and read from a volume of Tennyson poems. But he soon grew tired after only one or two and dropped off. Constance had cabled to Professor Spalding about the illness. The local doctor had looked in and confirmed that it was influenza, and that no secondary infections had yet taken hold. Continued rest was called for, but within the week, the doctor said, he should be well.

Mrs. Townsend, whose husband owned the inn, along with her daughter helped see to Jean-Phillippe, freeing Constance to visit Tess and Maeve. She worked on the tapestry. It was lovely to feel her hands push and pull. She delighted in the area she filled in around the bride at the altar.

Then one morning Jean-Phillippe finally sat up in bed and complained about his soft-boiled eggs being cold. He didn't thank Constance for bringing them. He asked if more wood could be brought for the fireplace. Constance went down and made the request to Mrs. Townsend.

That afternoon, unhappy with the new skirt and blouse she'd bought because they were both too big, she sewed in silence, alone then with Maeve since Tess was needed once more in the pub.

"Your life will contain none of these," Maeve said in clear, though heavily accented English.

"I'm sorry?"

Maeve waved her hand over the tapestry. Constance sewed for a few minutes more. She considered Maeve's odd statement. Tess returned, and Constance made her good-byes. She and Jean-Phillippe were returning to London the following day, she said. Maeve asked Constance, once again in Gaelic and translated by Tess, to bend down so she could receive a kiss on her cheek. Constance did so. Maeve said something else.

"She wants you to have it," Tess said.

"The tapestry? Oh, no, I couldn't."

"It's no use to her anymore."

Constance accepted the rolled up canvas, which she carried under her arm back to the hotel, glad the day was dry, for a change. Back in her room, she spread it out on her bed and studied the piece as a whole. She could distinguish her stitches from those added by Maeve before her eyesight dimmed. An experienced needle worker could always see a different hand. In one corner were stitches that were different still, which meant that someone else had worked on it, someone other than Maeve.

Constance learned that she was right when she got a letter from Tess, which Maeve had dictated. It began with an explanation that her address had been obtained from the hotel where she had stayed with Jean-Phillippe. Maeve wanted to share the tapestry's history. It came to her from a woman who had employed her as a chambermaid right after the turn of the century. At the time, Maeve had been in love with the footman (this was a large Irish country estate). The footman wasn't interested in her, and Maeve had tried everything she knew to change his mind. *I thought if I did what I ought not to do, he would be gallant and offer to marry me.* She cut to the chase. She offered herself to him, and he turned her down. Naturally, she was devastated. Though she always thought of herself as strong and capable, the footman's disregard caused her to unravel. She could not contain her misery, and one day her mistress, Lady Norbury, summoned her into her private parlor and demanded to know the cause of her constant tears.

At first, Maeve thought she would keep quiet, not wanting Lady Norbury to think her wanton and unsuitable for her position in the household. But Lady Norbury was an intelligent woman, and rightly suspected that her troubles were romantic in nature. She asked Maeve to sit and compose herself. Then she asked if she knew how to embroider. Maeve did. Lady Norbury gave her the tapestry and told her to sew a few rows to calm herself. Maeve continued where Lady Norbury had left off, with the young girl dressed in white, preparing for her First Communion. Maeve worked row after row. It was effortless, and did in fact bring a sense of peace. She even went so far as to suggest that it was the memory of herself at that age, full of hope and the will to do God's work, that soothed her soul.

He would have made you very unhappy, Lady Norbury said after a time. Maeve didn't need to ask to whom she referred. She didn't believe her words, but soon the footman was discovered to have been involved in the theft of Lady Norbury's prize silver candlesticks, and went to prison.

Constance put the letter away.

For the rest of the summer she spent her days reading at the library, taking page after page of notes. Soon she felt as if she'd exhausted anything of interest about Anne Neville, who turned out not to be such a compelling figure after all. She wrote of her concerns to her thesis advisor, who responded by saying that perhaps she should focus her efforts on a woman who played a more significant role.

Constance considered. She needed a figure she admired. Elizabeth Cady Stanton came to mind. In high school, Constance had gone on a field trip to Seneca Falls and learned about the early efforts to get women the vote. Another possibility was Carrie Nation, wielding her axe. Then there was Margaret Sanger, though she was still living, which made her less appealing as a research subject, from a strictly historical perspective.

Constance put forward the first two, saying she understood that this would represent a major shift in her area of expertise. Professor Reynolds was firm. *Do not discard the point in history that you have already begun to investigate. Changing course now will make you appear flighty and unreliable as a scholar.* Constance was taken aback. Would he have said the same to a man? Surely not. Was it that he found it inappropriate to shed light on an attempt to give women political parity? Or, in Nation's case, to deny men the pleasure of drink? Frustrated, sometimes to the point of tears, Constance returned to the War of the Roses.

It was Jean-Phillipe who suggested Margaret Beaufort. He was familiar with her from his own work, because she was the mother of Henry VII. Constance dug in, and soon discovered that Margaret was driven to secure her son's place on the throne and devoted her entire life to that one result.

Mothers made sacrifices for their children all the time, didn't they? So what about this particular story bothered Constance so much? That one of the most powerful women of her day was only as valuable as the man or men she supported? Constance thought that the woman she should write about was Anne Boleyn, for whom Henry VIII established the Church of England so they could marry. But no, she was really just another victim in the end when she couldn't bear a living son. Her daughter, though, Elizabeth I, bowed to no man. Now there was a fine topic!

But Professor Reynolds again discouraged her. *Stick to your chosen time period. Build on what you have.*

So, she did.

While she worked diligently, sometimes frantically, over the remaining weeks, Jean-Phillippe spent his time wandering the city rather than on his own research, and returned late, drunk, often with the smell of cheap perfume.

They encountered each other one morning at breakfast. Professor Spalding had gone out, and they were alone. Jean-Phillipe accused Constance of shunning him, and that this was the cause of his bad behavior.

When she didn't answer, he said, "Here I am, trapped under the same roof with the cruelest of women, one who intends to break my heart. It is unbearable."

Constance dropped two lumps of sugar into her cup and stirred her coffee. The clock on the wall clicked out the seconds. The silence went on. And as it did, Constance felt as if she were moving away, further and further into herself. Before, such a transit was always toward a greater darkness. Now it was toward light.

She knew he was insincere; she also knew that he was unaware of it. He truly believed he was in love with her. He *needed* to believe it.

Just as she had needed to believe that she was in love with him. On some previously unknown level within her, she feared she was incapable of love, and so sought it, or invented it.

"I could never make you happy," she said.

"I do not require happiness. But I do require love."

"Are they not the same?"

He laughed. "How little you know of the French!"

She smiled. "No doubt."

His mood had improved in those few moments, yet there was still hunger in his eyes. Constance excused herself and went to her room, where she sewed a few rows of the tapestry, something she did each morning before leaving for the library. She had recently progressed to Betrothal and Marriage. The generic young girl who'd taken her First Communion was now a taller, though unremarkable, young woman looking down at her left hand, where an equally uninspiring kneeling male figure had just slipped an engagement ring on her finger.

Now, nearly seventy years later, she held the canvas in her lap and went on remembering until her head drooped, and she was asleep. Eunice removed the canvas, then she and Sam got her into bed without waking her, courtesy of her sleeping pills, and left her to rest, dreamless.

chapter three

The offer from UCLA was not the one she wanted. She'd hoped it would come from an Ivy, but those all went to men. They had to be paid back for their service in the war, didn't they? She was lucky to receive an offer at all really. Women who held PhDs were strange creatures. No one seemed to know what to do with them.

That's what Lois Maynard told her, at any rate. She still lived in the big house in Dunston. Constance had visited her there, after leaving Providence on her way west. Lois had grown frailer, though she still moved deliberately and in a way that suggested a larger person. Her hair was completely white now, pinned up and held with lovely silver clips.

Constance asked if she were lonely, living by herself. Lois stared at her probingly. Constance understood. They'd never been much for direct speaking. Day after day of polite and distant interaction. The crises, such as they were, easily met. A hand on her fevered forehead, syrupy elixir dispensed; a quiet voice in response to tears caused by a playground slur, the command to always rise above.

"I'm an old woman, and many think that an old woman shouldn't live on her own. Your father, for one," Lois said.

"You're in touch? I had no idea."

"Not for quite some time. Then he called just the other day, before you arrived."

Constance had had very little contact with her father over the years. He'd visited her once, when she was thirteen. He'd praised everything about her in a way that suggested he didn't—and wouldn't—worry anymore about her. Constance hadn't assumed that this would come to mean he'd take no further interest in her. Before the visit, there had been letters and telephone calls, more at first, then dwindling to only on her birthday. Lois always said he was busy, and wasn't the kind of person who tended to communicate all that well.

Even as a child, Constance had understood that her feelings were being spared. From her mother she'd heard nothing, which was easier to accept, given her situation. Sometimes Constance had wondered if she were still crazy, or whatever the precise nature of her illness was, then she stopped thinking about it. She came to love living in Dunston and enjoyed Lois's slowly increasing generosity. She had nice clothes, went to Smith, then to Brown, then abroad without having to pay for any of it herself.

"What did he have to say?" Constance asked.

"Your mother remarried."

Constance's parents had divorced not long after she left Los Angeles. News of it had come in one of her father's early letters. *I'm afraid we split up*, were his exact words. Another letter informed her that her mother had left the rest home and was working in a new theater troupe, managing costumes, never on stage herself. His tone was almost kind, as if he felt sorry for her. He'd called her, *the poor dear.*

Lois suggested that they move to the screened-in sun porch. The summer day was hot and humid. The dining room they'd been in was paneled with dark wood. That, along with the heat, made it particularly oppressive. They sat side by side in dusty rocking chairs. Lois set herself to a slow rhythm of back and forth. Constance sat still.

"Why would he make it a point to tell you? That doesn't make any sense," Constance said.

"He called to ask for money. He's given up the bookkeeping business, apparently. The moment I agreed, his mood improved. He went on and on. Your mother was just one of many things he mentioned."

"But why are they even in touch? They've been divorced for years."

"I guess they ran into each other. He was a bit vague about that."

The new husband owned a grocery store, Lois said. Constance's mother went in to buy a loaf of bread. One thing led to another, as it does with lonely people. The husband was a widower. He had no children. He wanted children.

"Which brings me to the second bit of news. You have a baby sister. As of about two weeks ago," Lois said.

Constance did the math. She was twenty-six. Her mother had had her before she was even twenty, but she was still pretty old to have another baby.

"It doesn't seem like it would have been possible," Constance said.

"She's not young, it's true. But the baby's healthy. It's really a miracle, when you think about it," Lois said.

The tone in her voice made Constance see how much she must have wanted a child once. Her late husband—Constance's grandfather—was said to be a cold person. Yet he required companionship. After his first wife died, Lois was the answer, especially when Edgar, Constance's father, grew up and went west. Lois was a widow in her forties when they met and married; he was at least fifteen to twenty years older still. A child wouldn't have been a good idea, even if it could have been possible, physically.

So many solitary people, and now this baby, this sister! Constance didn't know how she felt about it.

"I got the sense that your father hoped you would see him—all of them—once you get yourself settled in L.A.," Lois said.

"I can't imagine why I would."

Lois closed her eyes for a moment, as if fatigued.

"Just try to remember that family is family," she said.

"I don't think of them as family at all."

"No. I suppose not."

Constance remembered being very young, holding her mother's hand, having her hair brushed, her face washed, her feet helped into socks and shoes. Her mother's touch had been soft. Then it turned rough, and then was absent altogether. She tried to imagine the woman her mother was now. Did she look at her baby's face and remember Constance at that age? But there was no point in thinking about any of that. No point at all.

A blue jay soared from the top of a pine tree at the edge of Lois's yard. Its color was startling, and caused a sudden surge of joy in both women. They watched the bird light on one branch, then another, then lift off and disappear into the stand of trees separating Lois's yard from her neighbors. Neither was thinking any longer about Constance's mother and father, or of Los Angeles. They were firmly in the present, wishing for the bird to return, then resuming other trains of thought when it was clear that it would not.

"Do you ever think about visiting England again?" Lois asked.

"I'll be able to, when I get my first sabbatical."

"You enjoyed your summer there."

"I did."

"Your letters were amusing, all about that horrid little Frenchman and Professor Spalding."

Constance cast her mind back. She'd wondered from time to time how

Jean-Phillipe was getting along. He'd promised to write and never did. She never wrote, either.

"I enjoyed the story about getting a fancy piece of needlework from that old woman."

"It was a nice surprise."

"Do you still have it?"

"Yes."

"Here, with you?"

"Yes. Would you like to see it?"

"That would be splendid."

Constance climbed the stairs to her old room, opened one of her two suitcases, and reached down below all the summer blouses she had carefully folded, thinking how warm it would be in her next home. The canvas was rolled and slightly mashed from being transported. She tucked it under her arm and returned to Lois. She sat and unrolled the canvas across her lap. In that white summer light the gray wool she had used for a baby's blanket took on a pearl-like luster. She had never noticed that before. The wool was new and not particularly high quality, an ordinary two-ply, but she saw then that one of the wrapped threads had more depth than the other. She couldn't imagine how such an effect had been achieved. She had learned how wool was spun. She'd observed it years before, on a farm there in Dunston, and again in England when she took herself alone on a day trip to Colchester. A miracle of nature, clearly. It pleased her enormously.

Lois examined the canvas.

"Quaint," she said.

"More like propaganda."

"Aren't you cynical!"

"Well, honestly."

"If you think it's silly, why do you work on it?"

"I like to embroider."

"Might I try a row or two?"

"Of course."

Lois's fingers were twisted with arthritis, yet she sewed well. Constance had never seen Lois hold a needle and thread before. She mentioned this.

"Oh, I'm an old hand at this sort of thing. I was responsible for many seat cushions, in my day. All that fine work, just to receive someone's posterior."

She worked the baby's cradle slowly and carefully. She examined her stitches. She seemed satisfied.

"I'm tempted to jump ahead," she said, pointing to the empty figure of Widowhood.

"I don't have any black yarn."

"When you get there, let her wear red. Why not?"

A pleasant breeze brought the smell of freshly mown grass from somewhere, yet did little to ease the heat. Even so, Lois shivered. She ran the needle through a bare patch of canvas to secure it until next time, and looked at Constance.

"You know, I've been thinking. I've spent an awful lot of time here in this big old house. Drafty in winter, too close in summer. I might just take a trip out to see you when you get settled. Wouldn't do a bit of harm to shake myself up a bit."

Lois looked quite pleased with herself. The thought of travel, for the first time in years, certainly since Constance had come to live with her, had brought color to her face. Constance could see the much younger woman she once was, and that she'd been lovely.

chapter four

Eunice helped Constance into a clean dress and combed her hair. Then she checked her nails and gave them a little trim. She wiped her nose. She straightened the room, made the bed, and emptied the trash basket, though it contained little.

Eunice worked alone. Sam was somewhere else. Constance was glad. She preferred Eunice. She was quiet and delicate. A deep thinker, that one. Wasted on caring for the elderly certainly. But maybe she saw it as her life's calling. That was hardly likely though. Only a fool would love touching old bodies.

"Why are you smiling?" Eunice asked.

"Just thinking about old bodies."

"I see."

"You think I'm off my rocker."

"Just full of surprises."

Constance had refused her prescribed sleeping pills six days before. Her mind had been slow to clear at first. Now, she felt like herself again. Saucy, someone to be taken seriously, or at least not quickly dismissed.

"Give me that mirror, won't you?" Constance asked.

Eunice gave her the hand mirror from the top of her dresser. Its face was dusty. Constance asked Eunice to clean it for her. Eunice wiped it with a rag she had in her pocket.

"Thanks," Constance said.

She supposed the wrinkled, blotchy mess in the glass belonged to her. Mirrors were evil things. You had to confront the relentless process of time. Nature was so cruel. Surely, at the end, though, there was mercy? She passed the mirror back to Eunice.

"She'll be here soon. You just sit there and enjoy all this lovely sunlight until then, okay?" Eunice said.

Constance didn't want to see her. She had no choice. Meredith had requested a formal evaluation. She wasn't sure that Constance was still capable of rational thought. The meeting would begin with a social worker. Depending on her recommendation, a doctor might also be consulted. Constance could ask to see her files and the notes from her quarterly care meetings, which she no longer attended though it was still her right to. They might give a hint about what the staff thought of her mental acuity, which was a lot better now since she was off the pills. That decision came upon her suddenly one morning at breakfast as she stared stupidly into her oatmeal, the tapestry in her lap because Eunice had let her take it with her just that once, and was met with concern from the nurse who came around every evening with the medications cart. They'd always been optional and could be discontinued if she wanted. And now, she wanted.

Meredith wasn't young, though sixty-six wasn't as old as it used to be. She wore it well, Constance supposed. She was fashionable, in a quiet, understated way. In her career as a financial planner, looking successful was important. She had a number of elegantly cut jackets and slacks. There was often a silk scarf, a broach on the lapel, a heavy bangle bracelet. Makeup was minimal, hair was short, more gray than white. People trusted her. She gave an impression of wisdom coupled with serenity.

She wasn't wise. She formed attachments with some of her clients, usually men, though sometimes a woman, that were not of a romantic nature so much as a form of psychological dependence. She wanted friends. Most people were confused by being asked over to dinner or to the movies or to go along to the mall to pick out a pair of shoes for an upcoming conference. Nearly everyone begged off, made a polite excuse, or simply didn't return her call. As far as Constance knew, Meredith had never lost a client after displaying her social neediness, but then she couldn't be certain.

Nor was she serene. She had a sharp edge. Old disappointments could suddenly surface, and she would talk bitterly about things she'd been denied or missed out on. These included a father, siblings, joining the Girl Scouts, learning to ride a horse, knowing her way around a kitchen, even how to iron. The makeup of the family Constance hadn't been able to help. Everything else had essentially been up to Meredith to ask for, or show an interest in. Constance didn't offer things because she assumed if Meredith wanted anything badly enough, she'd have made her desire known.

Constance was dead sure that Meredith wanted this evaluation so she could be put in charge of her money. The current arrangement was that the manager at the bank drew up a small number of monthly checks and brought them by for her to sign. These were to Lindell for her rent, a donation to a homeless shelter, and another to an organization that helped women become small business owners in Africa. There had been no irregularities; the account was never overdrawn. The bank saw to that. It wasn't, therefore, a question of competence, but of access. Meredith wanted a peek at Constance's accounts. She wanted to know what was coming to her when Constance died. Why couldn't she wait? How much longer did she have anyway? She was already vested to make medical decisions for her if things got dire. Now she wanted a power of attorney, to write checks herself.

But then, it was possible that Meredith wasn't acting out of greed, but a sense of duty, affection, even. She was capable of that. A tender heart had once been hers.

What was that silly little dog's name? The one that limped, and then had to have the offending limb removed? There had been a series of pets, then little friends from school to whom Meredith clung in a way Constance couldn't bring herself to discourage, then that piano teacher she was absolutely agog over. Mr. Brian. An older man, but with a youthful attitude. Meredith was a poor student, but she imagined that she would blossom under his kindly gaze. She always described the way he looked at her. With something more than an interest in her musical development.

The poor child. How lonely she had been! Constance had been aware of it, yet wouldn't let herself be moved. Youth was naturally a lonely time. Hers certainly had been. Later, after graduate school, when Lois opened herself in a way that brought Constance in, she wasn't lonely. Those had been good years. Lois moving to Los Angeles had been strange, at first, then very welcome. They spoke often of the house back in Dunston. Lois never could bring herself to sell, and so rented it to an endless stream of professors and their children, who left marks on the walls; on the furnishings; and, on the slanted ceiling of one upstairs bedroom, a series of dates written in pencil, a child marking time, as if wishing it to pass more quickly, often with a short statement: *Ma says no more baseball until the math grade comes up. Feb 5, 1952; Debbie won't give me the time of day, Nov 9, 1954.* When Lois died, at the age of 92, the house came to Constance. She still owned it, still rented it out.

Lately she'd had the idea to turn it into a center for women who needed basic life skills: how to apply for a job, what to wear for an interview, how to balance a checkbook.

· · ·

Constance noticed Meredith's shoes first. They were new. Loafers, probably hand-stitched. And she'd changed her perfume. Today it was floral, very Lily of the Valley. Last time it had been spicy, earthy, not like Meredith at all. Constance allowed her gaze to travel upward. The trousers of Meredith's linen suit were crisp, unwrinkled—an enviable state, she thought, since linen was so hard to wear. Her necklace was long, genuine pearls, no doubt. And what's this? Blond highlights? No more iron gray. This was a woman with big plans, clearly. She'd practically given herself a makeover.

Constance felt a little guilty at that. Meredith's self-esteem had never been good.

"You look well," Meredith said. She sat in the room's only chair, a rocker with a bright yellow cushion tied to the seat. Her hands, with painted nails, lay lightly on the arms.

"You, too."

"Thanks."

Constance let the silence stretch. It was up to Meredith to take the lead.

"You know why I'm here," Meredith said.

"To see if I need a padded cell."

Meredith stared at her hard.

"There's something different about you," she said.

"Yes. I'm not all doped up on those sleeping pills."

"You're not taking them?"

"That's what I just said."

"You can't just stop something that's prescribed."

Constance looked her in the eye.

"I'm going to check with Dr. Morris, if that's all right with you," Meredith said.

"Be my guest."

Constance wheeled herself to the small table by the bed, where the tapestry lay. She put it in her lap and made her way back across the room. The effort tired her. Her breathing slowed, and she unrolled the tapestry to

31

see where she had left off.

She patted her chest to feel for the reading glasses that hung from her neck on a chain decorated with plastic pearls. The chain had been a gift from Meredith on her last visit. Constance put on her glasses, flexed her stiff fingers, and sewed. Her goal was to finish the tapestry before she left this world. She wouldn't make it. There was an entire section on the right-hand side still empty. She'd have to give it to someone else to work on. Not Meredith, though. Meredith wouldn't know what to do with it.

"So, you've taken it up again," Meredith said.

"Obviously."

"You're in a mood."

"Liked me better when my head was full of cotton?"

"Let's change the subject."

"Very well. Why don't you tell me about your trip?"

The whole thing had been a disaster, Meredith said. First, the limo driver had been late picking her up, and she'd had to really hustle through the terminal. It didn't help that the stupid TSA people wanted her to have a full-body scan and then a pat-down, too. Something must have looked odd in the X-ray.

"Did you ask what it was?" Constance asked.

"Of course not. That would only have taken more time."

Then the man next to her wouldn't stop talking. He was also flying out to visit family, whom he hadn't seen for a long time. The thought of it both upset and thrilled him.

"Classic case of ambivalence, I told him," Meredith said.

"Uh-huh."

Constance went on sewing. Meredith said nothing further. She was no doubt thinking about the meeting with the social worker. Constance could tell her not to worry. But, why should she? Meredith had made that bed, and she was going to have to lie in it.

"Can I get you anything?" Eunice asked. Constance hadn't heard her come in.

"We're fine, dear," Constance said.

"I wouldn't mind a cup of coffee, if it's not too much trouble," Meredith said.

"Sure." Eunice left.

"They're not supposed to wait on you. This isn't a hotel," Constance said.

32

"She offered, didn't she?"

"She was just being polite."

Constance returned to the tapestry. Her thread was running short. She needed to pick through the sewing basket and find the red she was using for the flowers the widow bent to lay on her husband's grave. The basket was on top of her dresser. She didn't ask Meredith to get it. She sat, with idle hands, until Eunice returned with Meredith's coffee, and then asked *her*. Eunice brought a small side table and set it next to Constance's chair. She put the basket on the table within easy reach. Eunice noted that Constance had taken up her embroidery again after a long time of just looking at the tapestry or holding it in her lap. In spite of not being interested much in food these days, she had a greater energy to her that didn't seem just the result of having a clear head.

"How long?" Constance asked Eunice.

"I'm sorry?"

"Until we get this stupidity underway."

"Oh, right. Well, the social worker's probably already down in the conference room. But if you'd rather she come to you, that's fine, too."

"Ask her to come here," Meredith said. She had put the cup of coffee on the floor by her chair.

"No, don't be ridiculous. I'm perfectly capable of going there. If you don't mind helping me," Constance said. The remark was to Eunice, not Meredith, who fell in line behind as Eunice pushed her down the hall. Constance had put her sewing basket on her lap along with the tapestry.

The conference room had a long table with ten or twelve chairs. Constance never understood why the geniuses at Lindell thought so many people would ever gather around it. A display of power was at odds with the soothing mood they tried to create at every turn. For a while, in the beginning, she had been cheerfully enveloped by it.

When she first arrived, Constance had had her own cottage and lived more or less independently. She cooked for herself. She was surrounded by her own things. One day she slipped in the shower and had to use the pull cord in the bathroom to summon help. Nothing had been broken, but at the time she was eighty-seven, and it was decided, with minimal input from her, that she should move into one of the assisted living wings in the main complex.

She resisted. Meredith, as her next of kin, was consulted. At the time,

Meredith was still a few years from retirement and working hard in L.A. She told Lindell to do what it thought best. The assisted living wing, despite the cheerful decoration and bland furnishing, forced a firm level of anonymity, a loss of self, as if one were being absorbed by the very walls and olive carpeting that in some rooms had a faint smell of urine. Personal belongings weren't exactly discouraged, they just proved inconvenient. The maintenance staff was stretched thin; pictures couldn't, therefore, be hung right away and were left leaning against the wall week after week, month after month, until some cheerful aide suggested that it might be better just to stow them away for now. Constance could have hired a handyman but found she had no interest. She had her car and could use it when she wished, but that didn't entice her either. Age had gotten the better of her; she was ready to sit and struggle with the crossword, watch television, wander the halls, say hello to her neighbors who were as adrift as she, find a level of peace in all of that, until one day, and much to her surprise, her spirit rebelled.

She packed a bag with clean underwear, pantyhose, her favorite red sweater, a shower cap, toothbrush, reading glasses, three hundred dollars from a large envelope she kept on the top shelf of the closet and which, for some reason, she trusted the staff not to discover and pilfer, and left. She was supposed to check herself out. The rules requested that she let the receptionist at Lindell know where she was going and how long she was likely to be away. She went out a side door, nowhere near the front desk, which meant a long walk around the back of the building to the carport where her late model Mercedes was parked.

It was October. The trees were aflame with brilliant color. Proof of life about to pass, that was already passing, added to her restlessness. She'd had no idea where she intended to go, but once on the highway, she kept to the road on the east side of the lake. Mile after mile, hillside after hillside, she put Lindell behind her. After a while it occurred to her that she had failed to make a plan. All her life she had made plans. She couldn't recall a single instance of acting wholly on impulse. Except in the matter of Meredith. She hadn't considered the problems that bringing her home would entail. She'd listened to her heart, and while she never really regretted it, she could cite a great many times when further deliberation would have helped.

Such as when her next-door neighbor stopped her as she wheeled the baby proudly down the street.

"And whom do we have here?" she'd asked. She had a purse with a scarf tied around one of the straps. She wore a straw hat. She had lipstick on her teeth.

"This is my little Meredith," Constance said. The words sounded so strange! She'd never spoken them before.

"Why, where's her mother? Are you babysitting?"

"I'm afraid you don't understand. I just brought Meredith home." That quick glance to her ringless left hand. The sly smirk. Constance bore that silent, smiling condemnation beautifully.

It happened again, over and over, as Meredith grew up. Constance shed the stigma; Meredith couldn't. She suffered. Constance told her to rise above it, be her own person, not one defined by anyone else. Money helped. Lois bought them a pleasant ranch-style home in Beverly Hills. The other girls at Meredith's private school were aware that she had no father and were too well bred to ever mention it. If she'd ever gotten close to any one of them, made a best friend, the subject might have been broached. Sometimes she pretended that her father had been killed in the war or a traffic accident or, once, by carjackers who stopped him late one dark night. No one believed her. Constance was candid about never having been married. It was just one of those things! The jaunty toss of her head didn't quite work, and even she felt like a failure then.

The truth, when it came, was hard. A crushing scene, played over and over. So, Constance was a liar. Fine. It became its own rhythm. In with the truth, out with the lie. In, out. Mechanical, like breathing in an iron lung.

Constance knew she'd done wrong. But she'd had her reasons. Women were always so badly treated, so harshly judged, so she lived the lie and defied it every day.

And the day she took off in her car, what was she defying then? That she was no longer young? That was as good a fight as any. Better, really, so she kept driving. But then she needed to stop for gas in a little town she didn't recognize, not that she would have, necessarily. She wasn't usually one for exploring out-of-the-way places. The trouble was that she was quickly overwhelmed and disoriented. Later, she had to admit that she really didn't know where she was, though the explanation she made to the folks at Lindell was that she'd gotten tired.

She told the man to put gas in her car, and then she sat down on a wooden bench. The station was attached to some sort of country store with weathered wooden boards and a pair of double hung windows in front. The bench was placed between the windows, a few feet from the entrance. A number of people passed by on their way in and out. Finally, the station attendant approached her and told her how much she owed for the gas. Constance realized that she'd left her purse in the car, and told the attendant so, but didn't rise to get it. She went on sitting. He offered to bring her the purse, probably thinking how silly he'd look carrying it. Constance didn't reply. She was looking at her hands, which trembled. After the police arrived and took it upon themselves to look through the bag for someone to contact, Lindell was called and a social worker dispatched. It took over an hour for her to arrive, driven by another staff member so the social worker could take Constance's car back to town. At first, Constance was asked to ride with the other staff member, a woman she didn't recognize, who turned out to be one of the housekeepers, but Constance said she wanted to stay in her own car. In the interim, she remembered how she'd gotten there, but not having known for that slippery interval of time was horrible. She submitted to her fate, which was a series of scans to see if she'd suffered a stroke. Nothing could be found. She was allowed to remain in assisted living, but if she wanted to go out again, it was urged that she take someone with her. She never wanted to leave after that. She rode the bus provided by Lindell into town if she needed an outing.

It was a sudden infection in her back—a disk—that required IV antibiotics for four months that made relocating to the nursing wing necessary. There, she was truly trapped, not only by her lack of will, but by her stupid body. She grew combative, hence the dispensing of daily sleeping pills. Rather than making nighttime an oblivion, with a mellow carry-over effect through the daylight hours, they made her jagged within, woeful, bent once more on escape, though to what, where, or whom she had absolutely no idea.

The social worker who joined them in the conference room was the same woman who'd driven Constance's Mercedes back to Lindell that gorgeous fall afternoon five years before: Angie Dugan. She'd been firm and cheerful, yet didn't treat Constance like a child, the way so many at Lindell did. She'd tried to draw Constance out in conversation, probably as a way to assess her mental state, but when Constance didn't care to talk, she let it go. She'd grown plumper. Her manner had matured. She smiled pleasantly at Constance, though not at Meredith.

They sat at the end of the table nearest the door. A chair was removed so that Constance could be wheeled into the space it had occupied. Meredith sat opposite Constance. Angie Dugan was in between. Eunice also took a seat, though she hadn't been invited to.

"Ms. Maynard, before we get started, I wanted to bring up the matter of your prescription. It says here that you've stopped taking your Ambien. Is that right?" Angie asked.

"Yes. They made me groggy and stupid."

Constance spoke firmly, and with flair.

"And how long ago did you stop taking the medication?" Angie asked.

"Just about a week."

"A week ago tomorrow," Eunice said.

"I see." Angie looked at the forms in front of her for a moment. "Dr. Morris has made a notation here that suspending the medication is acceptable as long as you don't have difficulty getting enough rest at night."

"If I'm not sleepy right away, I watch television. Quietly, I might add. So far, no one has complained," Constance said.

"They're all pretty hard of hearing in that wing," Eunice said.

"Exactly."

"Are you sure he said it's all right?" Meredith asked.

Angie Dugan regarded Meredith at some length. "I'm positive. Of course, you're free to ask him yourself, if you're concerned," she said.

Meredith removed a tissue from her handbag and wiped her nose. She suffered from seasonal allergies rather badly, Constance now recalled.

"Well, now, Ms. Maynard, do you know why we're here today?" Angie asked.

"Meredith would like to be given control of my bank accounts."

"That's not it at all! I just think I could be useful to you," Meredith said.

"How are banking matters currently handled?" Angie asked.

"Mr. West comes by once a month with my checkbook. He fills out however many checks I need to write, then I sign them. Though it was someone else last time. I think Mr. West had gone on vacation," Constance said.

"And who reviews your statements?"

"He does, I suppose."

"You don't see them?"

"He told me he'd look them over for me. There are very few transactions."

"And do you have holdings separate from your bank accounts?"

"Of course."

"Who manages those?"

Constance gave the name of her investment company. She heard from it quarterly. She wasn't sure where the statements were. She'd been keeping them in a file. Now that she was more alert, it shouldn't be too hard to find them, if Ms. Dugan needed them for any specific reason.

"I don't need to see them, no. As long as you're satisfied that everything's being handled properly."

"So far, so good."

Angie turned to Meredith. "Can you elaborate on your cause for concern about your mother's business affairs?"

"I'm not concerned. I'm just trying to help. If she prefers I don't, that's fine."

"Normally when a family member calls for an evaluation of mental faculty, there's a specific reason. Was there some recent incident, some behavior that worried you?"

Constance could see Meredith remembering an afternoon several months before. She was surprised that she recalled so much of it herself. Meredith had come to tell her that she was retiring at last, and planned to move to Dunston and live in Lois's old house. Constance couldn't believe she'd be happy there after living all her life in a city the size of Los Angeles. Meredith was adamant. She needed a change of scene. Her tone alarmed Constance. She was running away from something. It couldn't be a man; it never had been. A woman was just as unlikely. Had she done something illegal? Embezzled someone's life savings? Constance asked her point blank.

"Nice to know you still think so highly of me," Meredith had said. Spring sunlight had poured in the window of Constance's room. It wasn't flattering to Meredith in the least. She looked old and worn out. Constance pretended to be confused about the house, saying someone was living in it and couldn't be put out. At the time, the house was vacant, which she knew full well. So did Meredith. The pretense was possible because she hadn't taken the Ambien the night before. Some crisis had kept the nurse from completing her rounds before Constance shut off her light for the evening. If she believed in divine intervention, she'd have thanked the higher powers. As it was, she put it down to a random moment of serendipity on the part of the universe.

"It's about our house, you see," Meredith told Angie.

"My house," Constance said.

"The last time I was here, she didn't remember that the house was unoccupied."

Angie straightened the papers in the small portfolio she'd brought into the meeting.

"I see. Ms. Maynard, how long has it been since you've been in touch with your home's property manager?" she asked Constance.

"Not since the last tenants left. There's no reason for her to be in touch with me unless there's a problem I need to know about. The next morning, I did remember the house was empty, but by then Meredith had gone back to California. We didn't speak about it after that."

Angie closed the portfolio.

"I'm satisfied that Ms. Maynard's affairs are being handled properly. I'm concluding the meeting."

Meredith put the tissue back in her purse. She didn't look upset, as far as Constance could tell, but she'd always had a good poker face.

Back in Constance's room, Meredith read email messages on her cell phone. Constance sewed several rows of the tapestry. The light softened. Eunice came to say she was going off shift. Would they come down to the dining room, or would they prefer something brought to them there?

"You always go out of your way," Constance said. It had taken a few minutes to replace her thread. It was long enough that she had to extend her arm quite a bit as it moved in and out.

"It's no trouble."

"We'll make our way down."

"Good night, then."

Meredith continued to stare at her phone. She stepped out into the hall to make a call. Her voice receded as she strolled further away from Constance's door. Constance wondered if she'd just keep going, right through the exit and into her rented car. It would make things easier, really. But then Meredith returned, looking a little happier.

"My house sold," she told Constance.

A house Constance had seldom been invited to, though it was less than a mile from the home Meredith had grown up in. Extravagantly decorated with gilded mirrors and French provincial furniture. Fussy décor, so at odds with Meredith's severe demeanor.

"Congratulations," Constance said.

"After I finish everything up, I'll be back here in a couple of weeks."

"Looking for a new place?"

"I'd still like to have your old house for a while. Give myself a chance to settle in."

"I'm turning it into a community center for women."

"A community center?"

Constance explained. She suggested that Meredith might volunteer her time, teaching the fundamentals of money management. Meredith appeared stricken.

"Is such a suggestion beneath your dignity?" Constance asked.

"Of course not."

"Then why all the gloom?"

"I just wish you thought I was doing the right thing."

"By moving here? That's not for me to say, is it?"

There they were again, Meredith needing approval and Constance maintaining a neutral position. In the last year of her life, Lois had told Constance she needed to give Meredith more guidance.

"Look, I don't know what you hope to accomplish by living in Dunston. It's a charming little town, and I'm sure you could make some friends if you tried. It just seems like such an unnecessary upheaval," Constance said. She ran the needle in and out, in and out. As always, it calmed her. She felt optimistic. She might complete the tapestry, yet!

Meredith stood and closed the door. Constance continued to sew. Meredith sat back down. She removed a silver flask from her purse. Constance stopped sewing. Meredith saw where she was looking and explained that she had learned the value of having a small amount of whiskey on hand for difficult moments. Constance wondered what sort of moments she meant.

"You're upset that they're not going to put you in charge of my money," Constance said.

"No."

"Isn't that why you're moving here? To try again, once you're closer?"

Meredith unscrewed the lid of the flask but didn't take a sip. Constance could see her mind wander. She was far away.

"Do you remember that blue dress? The one you bought me for my high school graduation?" Meredith asked.

Constance thought hard for a moment. She recalled pretty little stars around the waist.

"I don't know why they held it inside. It was stifling. I could see you fanning yourself with the program, way up in the bleachers," Meredith said.

"Strange thing to remember."

Meredith took a sip from the flask.

"Everything changed for me that day," she said.

They'd gone to lunch after the ceremony, in a private dining room at the Beverly Hills Ritz-Carlton. They ordered champagne and lobster, which required tucking the heavy white linen napkins into the necks of their dresses. Meredith had been accepted to Berkeley that spring, and was saying she wasn't sure any longer that she wanted to leave L.A. She had one friend who was going to defer college for at least one year, though the girl's mother was against the idea. Meredith had had a manicure the day before, and her fingernails were perfectly round and polished with pale pink that reminded Constance of a hue her own mother had worn years before. The color hadn't suited Constance's mother at all, nor did it suit Meredith. It was a frivolous shade.

Meredith went on talking about the friend and the friend's mother who apparently wanted her out of the house for reasons Meredith didn't understand. They'd never gotten along, but the friend didn't make a lot of demands and was no doubt easy to live with. It was the mother who caused problems by insisting on strict behavior and firm routines, which the friend accepted and performed faithfully. Meredith's conclusion was that the mother was just plain mean, probably frustrated with her own life, as so many women were seeming to be then (this was 1966), and took out her unhappiness on the friend.

"Do you know what I told her? That she should have a mother like mine."

"I'm not your mother."

It should have been more gracefully handled. She'd planned to tell her for a while. Why had she been so blunt? Because the moment arose, and she took it.

Meredith seemed suspended, her lifted glass in hand, as the color drained from her face. Constance could see a thought taking shape. She'd just been told a joke, and the punchline was about to come. There was also understanding, her entire life finally making sense, an explanation of why their relationship had been so formal and cold, why it had never felt *right*.

Constance began at the beginning. Her mother—Meredith's mother—had a history of mental illness. She'd been away for a huge part of Constance's own childhood. After remarrying and finding she was pregnant, she thought—hoped—she might be able to take care of a child the second time around. And she tried hard, she really did, but babies are demanding and soon it was clear that she couldn't take the strain. Constance wanted Meredith to know that it broke her mother's heart to give her up. The truth was that she was relieved, as she no doubt had been the first time when she went away and Constance got packed off to Lois's.

The husband—Meredith's father—didn't think he could cope on his own. What really happened was that he begged Constance to get involved. He came home from work every day to a wailing baby for whom his wife had done little, if anything. Sometimes she wasn't there, and the baby was all by herself, her diaper filthy, she hungry and miserable. He didn't know anything about how to take care of her.

"And I do?" Constance had asked him. He'd assumed, of course, that because she was a woman she possessed solid maternal instincts. Nothing could have been further from the truth. Constance was just as at sea but refused to let the baby suffer any longer. With Lois's help and assets, a series of competent nurses and nannies came to populate Meredith's childhood.

Not long after, the legal formalities were seen to and Meredith was formally adopted. Her father called from time to time but offered no help and never asked to visit. The parallel to Constance's own life was both marked and painful. History was repeating itself. Meredith and Constance were not only connected by blood, but by a sad thread of Fate that determined that they both would be abandoned and overlooked.

The champagne glass was still aloft, the bubbles gently rising. So was Meredith's color. Constance thought she might cry, but Meredith was too well bred to cause a scene.

After a moment, Meredith said she was grateful for her explanation, and telling her such an important fact on this momentous occasion. The steely cynicism in her voice sounded so natural, as if it came easily, that Constance felt suddenly that she didn't know Meredith at all. She'd been calm and quiet her entire life. Her few outbursts had been caused by ordinary things: a bee sting, breaking a doll, falling off of her bicycle. One incident, though, when Meredith was ten years old, came unexpectedly to mind.

Lois, then 85, was frail physically, though not mentally. Her words had become sharper than before, her patience, which had grown over time, vanished. Meredith had roller skated over the bare living room floor on her way to the back door, where she planned to go carefully down the short flight of stairs to the concrete path that ran from the back of the house to the front and then met the wider sidewalk where she could sail along freely. Constance didn't know if she'd done this before—skate in the house. Lois apprehended her, grabbed her by the shoulders, and told her she was a rude, clumsy, stupid girl. Lois and Meredith typically avoided one another. The house was large enough to make that easy. Lois was often in her own room, watching television. Sometimes she joined them for dinner; usually she didn't. And here she was, shouting at Meredith, holding her in place. Meredith shouted back, called her an "old witch," and then spat in her face. Lois had been too shocked to do anything further at that moment, though a number of things would have occurred to her. Smacking Meredith across the face with her cane, which she'd left propped against the wall, perhaps. The cane rested. So did Lois.

Meredith, meanwhile, skated for a long time to calm herself down, then snuck silently into the house past the cook and housekeeper and hid in her room until Constance knocked on her door. She'd come home to a changed atmosphere—something thicker in the air. She looked in first on Lois. The hallway of her private wing was lined with heavy carved pieces, offset with several Van Gogh replicas and their brilliant, racing colors. Constance opened her door after one quick, soft knock. Lois was watching television. She nodded pleasantly, benignly, yet with a deeper light in her eyes that Constance knew meant, *You should go see about Meredith.* When she turned back to the television abruptly, Constance knew something unpleasant had taken place, which she had seen coming for a long time. A young girl, an old woman, an uneasy warp and woof.

She made her way along the long sunlit hall, and turned the corner to the one containing both her and Meredith's room. The sorrow and rage in Meredith's face as she lay on her bed, and pretended to be engrossed in her comic book, were clear. The moment soon forgotten. Until then, over that elegant lunch.

Meredith asked Constance why she'd pretended, why she hadn't just told the truth. Constance had asked herself the same thing many times. So had Lois. In fact, Lois had cautioned her against playing the part of Meredith's mother.

"Why put yourself in a bad light? You know how people are. Do you want them thinking you're a common strumpet?"

In fact, she did. Accepting condemnation was her way of protesting the narrow roles women were allowed to play. She'd dug very deeply into the life of Margaret Beaufort and other noble women of her day. Once married, their use was reproductive. If they were barren, or didn't produce sons, they were discarded. Here was a chance for Constance to stand against the notion that a woman's highest and best use was as a wife and mother. Twentieth century mores didn't emphasize the value of sons over daughters as much, but women were still tightly slotted and controlled.

Some of her colleagues were more understanding than others. A few regarded her with suspicion and contempt, but in time that faded. She was a good scholar, an excellent teacher, thorough and dedicated. She was often excluded, however, from social gatherings. Those she hosted herself were occasionally avoided, but less so. She knew how to give a good party. Lois could always be counted upon to be gracious, even charming. When Meredith was presented, always briefly, right before her bedtime, her shyness was appealing, even winning.

Constance wanted Meredith to be strong and refuse to be defined by anyone else. The trouble, she then saw, was that *she* had defined her, given her a false identity. The truth she'd clumsily shared now required her to assume a new one. It occurred to her that if Meredith were a stronger person, less frail, she might have walked out of Constance's life and never returned. Maybe she had considered it for a moment. Maybe she wished she had. Maybe she still did.

"And you're about to tell me that this change was for the worse," Constance said.

Meredith shrugged. She capped the flask and put it back in her bag.

"Who knows what life would have been like if I'd never known?"

"No point in speculating on a thing like that."

"Can't help it. I remember things at odd moments. A lot more these days. Since I retired, I guess."

"You need a pastime, a new avocation. Which is why the community center is such a wonderful idea, if you'd only deign to consider it."

"Stop it, please."

"All right, all right. But you see my point."

Meredith looked at the tapestry. Her expression turned sour.

"It's absurd, isn't it? This notion of the ideal woman's life," she said.

"I think of it as an irony. Especially in my hands."

"Because none of these roles applies to you, is that it?"

"Only Motherhood. And please don't say what you're thinking."

Constance looked closely at the sewn images. Each face was serene, pleasant, bland. That was the real role history wanted women to assume—the embodiment of peace. Women should be passive, and wait to be asked. Women who asked first were thought to be unfeminine, unnatural, predatory.

"What on earth are you thinking about?" Meredith asked her.

Constance shook her head. She was tired then. It would take too long to explain.

chapter five

Darren Stiles was a colleague. He was also a widower. His wife had died years before, when she was still a young woman. Childbirth took her. Within only a few days, the child died, too. He relayed these facts without an ounce of self-pity, and Constance admired him for that. She told him about the difficult lunch she'd had with Meredith the week before. And then, once again on impulse, she told him her true relationship to Meredith. He looked into the glass he'd been sipping from, which held one of Constance's excellent martinis. Rather than asking why she'd taken on such a burden, he said, "That must have been very hard."

Constance realized she'd expected praise, not sympathy. She wasn't used to sympathy. Darren, it turned out, had loads of sympathy, always offered quietly, gently. At the moment, Meredith was up in Berkeley for the summer, in advance of her autumn enrollment. She was staying with a friend. Her departure had been abrupt. Constance wondered if the rift would become permanent. With Lois gone, she had no one to confide in. Despite her popularity in her department, with her students and her colleagues, she had a hard time making and keeping friends. She confided easily in Darren. He never seemed unsettled by it, as she was sure any number of other men might have been.

He didn't think Meredith would remain silent. She needed time to absorb what she'd learned, that was all. Constance should find a way to occupy herself in the meantime. Darren was sailing to Europe the following week. He took Constance completely aback by inviting her to go with him. He'd reserved a state room. It was expensive, but he couldn't bear smaller quarters. There need be nothing physical between them, if that were her preference. Sharing the bed might be pleasant enough.

He smiled at her. He had dash. Her opinion of him shifted entirely in his favor. Her affairs with men tended to be short-lived and sordid. She usually sought professors in other departments, the most passionate of whom had been Saul Frank, a physicist. After him, she slept with a number of other scientists, met in the faculty dining hall, the university country club, even the paddock where, on a mad whim, she learned to ride horseback. One of her conquests had been married, and the wife voiced her suspicions loudly enough so that for a brief, difficult time, Constance had feared for her job. Though she wasn't let go, it was suggested by her own department chairman, a kindly man who wore a three piece suit even in warm weather, that she was doing herself no favors having that kind of liaison, given the circumstances of her daughter's birth.

Darren stayed for dinner. She served vichyssoise, followed by cold lamb and small roasted potatoes. She apologized for having no dessert. He didn't usually care for dessert, and said he'd gotten out of the habit of eating it. The way he studied her linen tablecloth at that moment told her that dessert had been something of a tradition, when his wife was alive.

"I don't know how I feel about traveling with a man possessed by a ghost," she said. She apologized at once, saying she was seldom so bold.

"I don't believe that of you for a moment. A woman who martyrs herself must be bold at heart."

She finished her wine. It was a good Pouilly-Fuissé.

"Rather a strong word, don't you think?" she asked.

"It suits."

She supposed it did, though she'd never looked at it that way before. For years she thought her decision was either incredibly brave, or reckless, depending on her mood. What she did know then, and hadn't really faced, was that the decision had harmed Meredith.

"It's not right, to ask a child to assume your mandate, is it?" she asked.

Again, Darren studied the tablecloth.

"I think we're all duty-bound to keep those close to us from harm," he said.

He wasn't talking about her, he said, but of himself. His wife had been a frail woman, and the doctors advised her not to have children. He was willing to live without the activity that brought them about. She wanted one, though. She wore him down. He relented.

"It's a normal thing, to want to sleep with one's wife," Constance said. She wondered, suddenly, if her death had ruined him in some fundamental way that would make him a bad companion. She had no reason to think so, but now that she was more attracted to him, his ability to respond was key.

"Yes."

The evening took on a golden tone. The patio glowed. The smooth stone was a delight under her stockinged feet. She danced before the lavender hedge, her empty glass in hand. He sat in his chair, tie loosened, neither approving nor disapproving, it seemed to her. Just an observer. But then he stood, took her hand, and danced too, humming a familiar tune she couldn't recall the name of.

· · ·

Being again on the open sea reminded Constance of her voyage over twenty years before. Then, she travelled alone. Now, sharing Darren's stateroom made her feel deliriously grand. They did not have sex until the last day, as if the time up until then was a trial, an experiment in how well they got along. In the morning, Darren studied her across the table. Clearly, her physical passion had surprised him. When she looked up, he had trouble meeting her eye. But when he finally did, the warmth of his expression pleased her.

Their destination was France's Loire Valley and the resplendent castles therein. Seeing them had been Darren's lifelong dream. How glad he was to have Constance by his side! Sharing their beauty with her made the experience so much better. He became a different man as they walked slowly through the great rooms, apart from the larger tour group they'd initially joined. He was openly joyous. His field was the reign of Louis XIV. When he was writing his thesis, he'd had no money to travel abroad. He'd had to content himself with books that held crucial information, but had in no way prepared him for the magic of actually standing before the bed in which some French nobleman had slept.

Constance thought of the women. Their part in preserving the peerage was always the same. They rocked the cradle, but seldom ruled, and though they may have advised and guided, it was always in private. They almost never sat in counsel, held office, presented bills. This is what she had tried to make Meredith understand as she grew up. She spoke often of the scant opportunities available to women even then, in the middle of the twentieth century. Constance bought her a copy of *The Feminine Mystique*, which lay untouched on her dresser. Her secret fear was that Meredith would marry a man who demanded that she play the traditional role of staying home, cooking, cleaning, and raising children. Not that the lesser chores would necessarily fall to her. Meredith would be in an income bracket that made maids, cooks, and nannies possible. If Lois were still alive, and knew of her specific concerns, she'd tell Constance she was being narrow-minded. Lois, herself, had lived a quiet, domestic life. She took care of one husband who sadly had died young, then a second while raising the child from his first marriage. She never seemed to mind. She hadn't been trapped by anyone's view of her—a goal Constance had always put in front of Meredith, who was simply too fragile on an emotional level to feel the wisdom of those words.

And would the truth have changed her? If she had known she was a sister, not a daughter, would she have become a bolder spirit? The ceiling of the chamber in which they stood, side by side, was painted navy blue and emblazoned with tiny gold stars. Constance gazed upward and implored them for an answer. None came.

At the end of a narrow corridor, they entered a grand chamber with a magnificent carved fireplace. It was easy to imagine the leap and dance of flames, and servants bearing plates to and from the immense wooden table. The sound of their footfalls echoed as they strolled, held in a state of reverence, the past a palpable, living thing all around them. Beyond the fireplace a large tapestry hung on the wall, behind a velvet rope so visitors would not be tempted to touch it. Constance, though, needed to touch it, if just for a moment. She asked Darren to stand guard.

A woman stood in a bright clearing, with trees all around. She stared quietly at the ground, hands clasped as if in prayer. She was waiting for something, clearly. Her dress had tones of red and gold. The wool was surprisingly coarse. One of the fibers felt particularly sharp, and Constance wondered if someone had left a needle behind. She withdrew her hand and leaned back, certain that she'd taken a very long time to inspect the fabric, and then to brush it with her fingertip. Darren assured her that she'd been quick. He moved off, making for a wide doorway leading to another chamber, then turned when he realized that Constance was still staring at the tapestry. He came back and placed his hand lightly on her elbow. She knew he wanted her to leave then, to go where he wanted to go and see what he wanted to see.

She stood still. He asked if she were well. She said she needed just one more moment, and to go on ahead. He cautioned not to touch the tapestry without him being there to alert her if someone came into the room.

49

"I'm all through with touching," she said.

Over dinner, he asked her why the tapestry had fascinated her so. They ate in the back garden of the auberge they would spend the night in. The light faded slowly; a duck quacked in the distance, perhaps on its way to the small lake nearby. Other birds quickened the hedge bordering the garden. The fish course had been eaten, a beef dish was then being presented by a serving girl with scars on the backs of her hands. Constance suspected her attendance at a Catholic school, where liberal punishment with rulers was allowed, even encouraged. After she withdrew, Constance explained.

"It's what the women did. The weaving, I mean," she said.

"Ah. You and your women."

"Men warred, conquered, stole land, plowed it, and so on. Women wove."

"A very useful skill, given how cold these castles are."

"The servants wove, I should say. Their mistresses embroidered. Being skilled at needlework was considered a very fine trait."

Constance was aware that her face had flushed. She hoped Darren would blame it on the wine.

"Are you fond of it, yourself? Embroidery?" he asked.

"Oh, yes."

She had the Stages tapestry with her in their shared room. She wondered if she'd be in the mood to work on it. She hadn't for some time. She'd packed it at the last minute. She couldn't bear to be parted from it, even though it remained rolled up.

"My mother was quite keen on needlework, though I don't think she used a canvas to embroider. Just a plain piece of fabric. What's that called?" he asked.

"Cross stitch, maybe. Or crewel work."

"I think it was crewel."

"Hm."

Artisans at their looms. Great ladies at their smaller stands, pushing their needles in and out, in and out. Life's rhythm.

"You're a million miles away," Darren said.

"I'm sorry."

They ate in silence for a time. Neither felt the need to bring up a new topic, or to continue on the previous one. Dessert consisted of stone fruit in cream. Darren suggested a cognac. Constance agreed and asked if they might take their glasses with them while they wandered around the grounds before turning in.

"That's a lovely idea," he said. He signed the check. They hadn't talked about money. He was clearly spending a lot, and Constance felt bad. Though to offer to share expenses might insult him. It was a matter she'd have to return to later, for further consideration.

The air had cooled. The stone path along the auberge led through a patch of woods, then arrived at a clearing where a stone bench had been installed so visitors could sit and contemplate their good fortune. Or so this was how Constance understood its presence. The remaining sunlight streamed at an angle, and gazing at it, feeling remarkably clearheaded despite the bottle and a half of wine with dinner and now the cognac warming her throat most pleasantly, she realized that before her was the scene from the tapestry. Who was the woman? There'd been no information, nothing tacked to the wall beside the piece to explain what it depicted. She thought of the hands that wove the fabric. She looked then at her own. Age had begun to show. The veins had thickened. She lifted her glass from where she'd set it on the stone at her feet, and drank gratefully. Tonight was the night. She would sew again.

In their room, Darren stood on the balcony, watching the night. He was restless. The calm Constance enjoyed as she worked the stream flowing past the cave was made opposite in him. He smoked a cigarette, and then another. He sat in one of the two chairs placed side by side, then stood once more. He entered the room and sat at the desk. He attempted to write a letter, to whom Constance had no idea. He put the crumpled paper in the fireplace, then lit it. Constance lifted her head and watched the few thin flames rise, then die down.

No sooner had she resumed sewing, there he was, directly in front of her, begging her to listen to what he must say. Reluctantly, she put the tapestry in her lap. He sat.

When he was young, before he met his wife, he'd made a mistake with a woman. She was a college student in Michigan. He was too. That's where he was from, Michigan. He wasn't sure if he'd ever told Constance that or not. In any case, he fell in love with her. Even then, he was the kind of man who fell in love easily. Surely, Constance must have noticed that.

She didn't want to hear about love. It was always a pointless subject to discuss. Love required action, not words.

He continued. He assumed this woman cared for him, too. She gave all the signs. She smiled every time they met. She laughed at most things he said, and he began to wonder, under her warm approval, if he weren't more interesting than he thought. He came from a large family and was often overlooked in favor of his two older brothers, and three younger sisters. A middle position is always hard, and he hadn't realized until then just how ordinary he'd always felt. After a few months he was ready to propose marriage. He saved his money, took her to an elegant restaurant. They drank a lot of champagne, and afterward, back at her rooming house, she invited him to her bedroom. He'd never seen the inside of it, and assumed that she was ready for the physical side of things, even though he had failed to get the words out over dinner, the proposal still unspoken.

She wasn't ready. She refused to sleep with him. If he hadn't been drunk, he might not have been so demanding. She stopped struggling early on, which at the time he took as her assent. Afterward, he fell asleep. When he woke up, she was gone. She'd returned home. He had a letter from her father saying he was in full possession of the facts of his daughter's situation and hoped that Darren understood that the right thing must now be done. Since he wanted to marry her anyway, being presented with this mandate was providential. Then he realized that the girl didn't want to marry him and never had. Darren assumed she was pregnant. She wasn't pregnant, though in time he learned that she said she was, to further the pressure brought on Darren by the father.

"But you said she didn't want to marry you. Why would she want her father to say that you must?" Constance asked.

"Because she wanted me to come to her on bended knee, apologize, then beg for her hand, just so she could turn me down."

"Sounds fair."

Darren lifted his head. His eyes were unkind.

"You raped her," Constance said.

"I didn't know I was raping her. I thought she wanted me to make love to her."

"You mean 'with' her."

"What's the difference?"

"If you don't understand that, then I've severely misjudged you."

He put his head in his hands. She could see he was all in. She told him to get undressed and get into bed. No good would come of his being exhausted the next day. They were due to leave the auberge and visit another castle quite a few kilometers to the south.

He was asleep at once. Constance was wide awake. She was troubled. Why had Darren told that story? As a way of garnering sympathy? To bring them closer together by baring his soul? When he commanded her attention, she'd been afraid that he was going to ask her to marry him, though in retrospect, that would have been too soon, despite the fact that there they were, alone together, traveling as man and wife, despite how supposedly progressive the Europeans were about such things.

On their last day in France, as they prepared to go north into Belgium for their final two days because Darren longed to see Bruges, Constance returned from a damp morning walk to find him bent over her tapestry, which he'd unrolled and laid across the bed.

"Oh," she said.

"I hope you don't mind. I was just curious about it since you'd worked on it that other day, and then not again since."

"I've gone years in between."

She put her purse on the bedside table. She checked herself in the small oval mirror on the wall. The rain hadn't caused her hair to frizz. She wore it short those days, as was the style.

"The stitching has pulled it out of shape," Darren said.

"What are you talking about?"

"Look." He held it up, his hands far apart.

Constance saw at once what he meant. She had never secured it to a frame to keep the canvas taut. It leaned, like an old barn in a field. She took it from his hands, began to roll it up, when he took it back from her, not altogether gently.

"There's a name on the back," he said.

"Where?"

He showed her. It said, *Gerrard et Fils.* In red ink, no less, at the far left corner.

"Must be the manufacturer, or whoever designed the image," he said.

Constance looked closely. Why had she never noticed it? The back was always of far less interest than the front, but it felt odd, even so.

Darren was clearly delighted. He was younger then, full of energy. His short-sleeved plaid shirt added to the effect.

"Don't you find it a bit fascinating? I mean, we're historians, after all, and here's a little piece of history," he said.

"It's not very old. Made in the last century, at the earliest."

"Where did you get it?"

She sat on the bed and explained about her trip to England, going north, the tavern, Tess, Maeve, the letter about Lady Norbury and Maeve's time there.

"An Irish manor. Good stuff!" he said.

Constance reclaimed the canvas. She vowed not to work on it again until she was back in her own home, comfortably alone.

"Don't you want to find out more about it, though?" Darren asked. He sat on the bed next to her.

"It's a pastime, that's all."

"I wish you could see your face when you're sewing."

"Why? What does it look like?"

"Beatific."

"Oh, nonsense. Let's go eat lunch."

Darren didn't bring up the tapestry again. He grew quiet, preoccupied, though not necessarily downcast. Constance didn't mind. She preferred to think her own thoughts. She wondered how Meredith was getting along. She'd written her several postcards detailing what they'd seen. She assumed Meredith would take in stride that Constance was traveling with a man. She would disapprove, naturally, but her disapproval would be unvoiced.

Their three-week itinerary was then at an end, and Constance was looking forward to the voyage home. Belgium had been disappointing. The hotel there had had narrow stairs and a shared bath down the hall, much lower quality than places they'd occupied in France. Constance understood that Darren was being more careful with money. On the first night out, she asked him to be honest with her about his situation.

"It was a small inheritance, that's all. My father died last spring," he said.

"Oh, I'm so sorry! I wish I'd known!"

"It's fine. We didn't get along. In fact, he hated me."

"I'm sure that's not true."

"It's true."

They were walking on deck. The wind had quickened. The sea became restless. Its gray was tipped with white caps. Constance felt insignificant in a way only an ocean could make her feel.

They linked arms.

"How can one hate one's own child?" Constance asked.

"The same way one hates anyone, I suppose. Hate is hate."

"And love is love."

She felt his affection in the distance he closed between them. When they were again in Los Angeles, preparing for the fall semester, busy with their own lives, she would miss him, she thought. In a way, she missed him already. They still shared a bed, but nothing more. That had been her choice. She regretted it.

She stopped walking, released Darren's arm, and gazed down into the troubled sea. The ship rose and fell with the waves beneath it, yet no rain fell.

"It'll be a rough night. You're not given to seasickness, are you?" Darren asked.

She looked into his face. It was a good face, displaying kindness and honesty. He'd been particularly honest in telling her about that girl. Might he be an asset? A refuge from herself?

"Marry me," she said.

His expression didn't change.

"Isn't that supposed to be my line?" he asked.

"Does it matter?"

"To some people."

"To you."

"Yes, a little."

"Well, then."

They went in to dinner, watching the wine in their glasses slosh, laughing at the crooked manner in which they and everyone else had to walk in order to avoid falling, then awoke to clear skies and flat seas. They never spoke of marriage again.

chapter six

The party was in honor of Constance's friend, Elaine, who'd been appointed head of the new Women's Studies Department. They'd met at the grocery store, of all mundane, non-academic places, and recognized one another instantly. Previous encounters were cheerfully recalled. The faculty lounge. The quad. The new students' orientation. Reaching for the same bag of apples became a touchstone.

Elaine taught in two departments, Sociology and Anthropology, what she called "soft sciences." She'd been on digs in the Southwest and once in Africa. Her articles on ancient burial rites were highly acclaimed.

Elaine was divorced, with two teenaged boys under her roof. Her ex-husband was in television and developed situation comedies that typically featured a strong male character and a silly female one. Elaine's blond hair rose from her head in an afro, though she didn't have a single drop of African blood in her veins. Some lovely fluke of nature, she called it. The hair on her sons' heads was straight and black, like their father's. She wore dashikis to class, which she found at a thrift shop. She doubted they were genuine. The colors, for one thing, were muted, compared to the vibrancy she'd observed in Kenya.

Despite her apparent passion for all things African, the curriculum she was to oversee was centered primarily on Europe and the United States. She was coordinating with a number of faculty members from both English and History, also Political Science and Fine Arts, as well as her own joint fields to develop a course of study that would expose students to the many roles women had played over time. The theme throughout was how consistently their contributions had been overlooked.

Many of those faculty members would be at Constance's party, including Darren. Ten years had passed since they'd gone abroad. They were cordial when they crossed paths at work. Sometimes he called and they went out for a drink. One rainy weekend he helped her with a leaky dining room window. He remarked that a house of that grandeur—as compared to his much smaller bungalow—should have been better built.

"Well, it's not," Constance had said, laughing as they soaked up the water with one clean towel after another. His gaze had lingered. Romance, though, was off the table.

Meredith was also due. Now twenty-eight, she worked for a financial advisor in Hollywood. Her passion for numbers was still surprising to Constance, though she'd majored in math at Berkeley, a field that wasn't all that welcoming to women. She understood investments quite well, particularly in terms of estate planning. Though Constance admired her perseverance, she couldn't imagine a more boring way to make a living. She kept that to herself.

Elaine wanted to meet Meredith. She was thrilled that Constance's daughter was making her way in a man's field. She loved Constance's elegant home, and spent as much time there as possible, an arrangement Constance often found inconvenient.

The truth was that Elaine was clingy. The face she gave the world was that of a tough, independent woman, a survivor, unflappable. Constance had been witness to a number of crying jags, usually after a few glasses of wine. Elaine's husband had left her nearly six years before, yet the event was painfully raw. Her unrelenting sorrow grated on Constance's nerves. She was brilliant at not showing it.

The other bone of contention between them, also unvoiced, was that Constance was jealous of Elaine's appointment. She was certain she knew more about women through time than Elaine did. During her almost thirty years teaching history, she had stressed one thing—women had never been given their rightful place. After the publication of her thesis, she'd presented a number of articles about English women during the War of the Roses, all exposing that shameful fact. Then she turned to America's own past and wrote *Silent and Unseen*, which began with the settlement at Jamestown and ended with the passage of the Nineteenth Amendment. It detailed the wives and daughters of landowners, merchants, and craftsmen, all living obscurely as befit the unchanging heritage of their sex. It had been poorly reviewed and never taken up as teaching text, which infuriated her.

She suggested the party not only to prove to herself that she could overlook a professional rivalry, but because she was bored. People made a wonderful distraction, in limited doses. She'd been much more aware of this since her tenant, Edna May, had moved out. Edna May was a college student, one of a series of young women who'd occupied Meredith's vacant bedroom. The rent Constance charged was minimal. The company provided by the students was just enough to fill a void but not enough to overwhelm.

Elaine arrived early. She was nervous about mingling with so many people, she said. She'd tried to get some work done around the house, but was a useless mess. Her boys were off with their father for the week. Constance knew she was feeling the solitude of her empty home.

Elaine sat while Constance worked. The caterers had brought too few devilled eggs, but too many fruit cocktails. Two telephone calls resulted in the vague promise that another tray of eggs was on its way. The shrimp was chilled and paired with red sauce. There were oysters on the half-shell, a platter of crudités and dip, pretzels, potato chips, cheese and crackers, and thinly sliced layer cake for dessert. The bartender had his station at the end of the living room. He'd already provided Elaine with two glasses of white wine. Constance watched her discreetly. She expected a flood of woe at any minute. To her surprise, none came.

Instead, Elaine talked about the program she was to develop. Wouldn't it be wonderful to contact women artists in the community; women authors; even a few actresses, assuming one could penetrate the veil of their publicity machines?

"Let them tell their own stories about competing in a man's world," she said with a slight slur.

"We could tell that tale ourselves, don't you think?" Constance asked. She'd just rearranged a vase of white flowers—carnations, roses, and daisies—a second time.

"Very true." Elaine glanced into the living room, which Constance took to mean her wanting another drink.

"I like your dress, by the way," Elaine said.

"Oh, thanks!"

The dress was pale lavender and sleeveless, which Constance could still carry off at her age. Her arms had always been thin. Elaine had fancied up her daily dashiki with a necklace of heavy wooden beads. Constance asked her if they were African. They were.

Meredith let herself in the back door. She was wearing a beige pantsuit, which Constance thought made her look much older than she was. She supposed it was intentional. To get people to trust you with their money, you had to look solid and serious, two conditions the young usually failed to attain. She kissed Constance on the cheek. Constance was sure her peach lipstick had left a mark, and reminded herself to go to the powder room before the guests arrived and check.

Constance introduced Meredith to Elaine, who stood and gave her a warm hug. Meredith was visibly taken aback, then recovered. Constance could bet hugging wasn't a known ritual in the staid offices where Meredith worked.

Meredith and Elaine fell into an easy conversation. Constance left them and went through the living room to make sure the ashtrays were clean, the nut bowls full, the bartender at attention and not helping himself to anything. She asked him to pour her two glasses of dry sherry, one for her, one for Meredith.

"You must be so proud of your daughter," Elaine said, then looked longingly at the servings of sherry Constance had brought in.

"Yes, she's quite a girl," Constance said.

"Is that for me?" Meredith asked.

"Of course."

"What is it?"

"Sherry."

Meredith, as far as Constance knew, was not fond of alcohol. The sherry was to keep her mood mellow. She tended to fall into herself when she visited home.

"A woman, managing money. Such empowerment," Elaine said, warmly.

"Well, I'm supervised. I don't have any authority to make investments, only to recommend them," Meredith said.

"But that will change, right? In time, when you have more seniority."

"That's the idea."

Meredith sipped her sherry. She seemed to like it. Constance could tell from the slight lift of one cheek, a gesture she'd seen many times over the years that expressed pleasure, which in another would be a smile, or laughter, a little gleam in the eye.

The first guests arrived, professors from the History Department, including Chairman Banks who made straight for the bar and asked quietly for a Scotch on the rocks. He surveyed the bottles on offer and appeared pleased at the presence of Johnny Walker Red. Constance knew that was his preferred poison. He'd always ordered it at the faculty lounge the few times they'd gone in together, at day's end.

As the crowd grew from small to modest, Elaine left her safe perch in the kitchen and made the rounds. Constance studied her. She was poised, spoke clearly, nodded to show interest, made eye contact unwaveringly. An excellent dissembler, Constance decided. No wonder she'd earned her appointment. The goodwill shown her spilled over to Constance herself. She was complimented on her home, though many people had been there before over the years; the food was enjoyed wholeheartedly; she was thanked for having thought to include them.

Some months before, Constance had installed the tapestry in a corner. She'd had a frame made and mounted on a stand. There was a chair in front of it, purely for show, because sewing had once again fallen by the wayside. Some guests admired it politely; one woman, the wife of a sociology professor, leaned in closely to examine the work, just as Constance had done to the tapestry on the wall of the French chateau. Constance became alarmed. She realized it had been stupid to display the tapestry in a public space. She hoped the woman (Nancy? Nina?) wouldn't touch it. Constance willed her to walk away from it, which she did easily enough when her name (Nora) was called by her husband, standing at one of the food tables.

Meredith had made a brief appearance and then took herself off somewhere, maybe to her old room. Constance hoped she wasn't suffering from some aching nostalgia. It had been hard for her to leave the house, though she'd really left it years before, when she began college up north. During those years, she'd returned for vacations, but the summers were always spent away. Even so, when Constance announced that she was renting the room out, Meredith's eyes had filled with tears.

Constance saw that her guests, maybe a total of twelve or thirteen people, had settled themselves comfortably in her large living room in small groups. Some were talking about an art show they'd been to, and the frenzied, abstract colors of a new Peruvian painter. Others described their summers, the trips they'd taken; one man had gone to Spain to visit a cousin he hadn't seen in decades.

Constance went down the hall from the kitchen. Her house was shaped like three sides of a square. The first wing held the living room, dining room, and kitchen. Meredith's room—the rented room—was in the adjacent wing. It was empty. So was Constance's room, the small den Constance used as an office, and the television room. She turned the corner to Lois's old wing, which contained a quiet sitting area and a large bedroom that Constance hadn't had the heart to redecorate or change even a little bit since her death almost thirteen years before. It was wasted space, to be sure, but then so much of the entire house was, with just Constance as the primary resident.

Meredith sat in Lois's green easy chair, the one she used to watch television from. Her legs were curled up under her, her eyes closed. They opened a moment after Constance entered the room. Maybe she'd been asleep.

"What are you doing in here?" Constance asked.

"Recovering."

"From?"

"All your guests."

"They're hardly a crowd. Come on, be sociable."

"You know I don't like talking to people I don't know."

"Oh, honestly! How do you handle your clients, then?"

"We only talk about money."

Constance lowered herself onto the window seat.

"And it's different when the conversation has a chance to be random, is that it?" she asked.

Meredith said nothing.

"Because you might get asked something you don't know how to answer?"

"You always said I didn't think very well on my feet."

"That's not true!"

Meredith shrugged.

Constance realized she probably had wanted to avoid the party altogether but felt it her duty to come for a little while, at least.

"Well, stay here then, if you like. I don't imagine it'll run on too much longer. Once the food's gone, people will drift off," Constance said.

Meredith nodded, and closed her eyes again.

When Constance returned to the kitchen, she was met by Elaine, who looked flushed and agitated. Even her dashiki was askew. She put her hand on Constance's arm and whispered, "He's here."

"Who?"

"Darren."

"Oh, I'm sorry I wasn't there to greet him. I had to go see what Meredith

61

was up to."

"Is she all right? I thought she'd left."

"She's in hiding. Gets a bit of stage fright around new people."

Elaine looked like she understood completely.

"Well, let's not keep Darren waiting," Constance said.

Why did his presence cause her to feel unmoored? It was a little bit like that day at sea, being tossed and rocked, never quite sure of where her feet would land next.

He had his back to her, talking to someone. Constance arranged her face to look its most pleasant and gracious. She approached steadily, ready to announce her presence with a light touch on his arm.

He was with a woman. Constance recognized her. She was a graduate student. She was tall, blond hair pinned up. She wore a white jumpsuit and high-heeled, gold-toned sandals. Her necklace was long, made of gold beads, and hung well into her cleavage. On campus she dressed much more conservatively: quiet pantsuits, jackets, and skirts. Constance couldn't recall her name. It was on the tip of her tongue when Darren caught sight of her and took her hand.

"We thought you'd run out on us," he said. He'd been drinking. She wondered where they'd stopped off. She smiled. Darren released her.

"You remember Gabrielle," he said.

"Of course! What a pleasure to see you. I'm so glad you could come!"

Gabrielle stared down at Constance. She smiled after a moment, as if she hadn't recognized her at first.

"We're just back from Las Vegas," Darren said.

"How exciting! I love Las Vegas," Constance said. The one time she'd gone, she'd been in the company of a lover. She'd bet over a thousand dollars playing blackjack and lost it all.

"We just got married," Darren said. His arm went around Gabrielle's waist tightly, pulling her off balance.

Words of congratulation flowed from those sitting down. Chairman Banks rose to shake Darren's hand and give his best wishes to Gabrielle.

"I've got a couple bottles of champagne around here somewhere. Let me just go and look," Constance said.

She was aware of Elaine watching her as she went at a calm, easy pace across the long room and into the kitchen. Then Elaine was next to her saying, "Oh, for God's sake! Can you *believe* it? What was he *thinking?*"

"I don't think a mental process was involved." Constance had the refrigerator open. She stared into it without seeing it.

"Men. One day they're geniuses, the next they're retards."

Elaine didn't usually speak so bluntly. Constance thought she was animated from the alcohol and having been the center of attention, if only briefly, among her colleagues.

"There's no reason to assume he's making a mistake," Constance said and closed the refrigerator. The two bottles of champagne at the back of the first shelf would keep. "I'm sure she's a lovely person."

"No, she's not. Don't you remember that business with Ned Price?"

"What business?"

"He was her thesis advisor. He ended up leaving his wife."

"You can't assume the two things are related."

"You're playing devil's advocate. I know you're trying to keep an open mind, because that's the kind of person you are, but I'm telling you, Darren did something really dumb, and he'll rue the day. You know it, too."

"Oh, come on. It doesn't matter what I know or don't know."

Some of her guests came into the kitchen to thank Constance and say good-bye. She protested that they were leaving too early, then said she understood and thanked them profusely for coming.

The party was down to the Chairman, his wife, Darren, and Gabrielle. Both couples were sitting easily on the large sectional sofa. Darren smiled when Constance and Elaine entered the room. He didn't ask about the champagne. He looked woozy. Maybe he was just deliriously happy. Constance had never noticed before how close together his eyes were or the how red his nose got when he drank. Even the sound of his voice as he described the houses they'd been looking at, since his was too small, grated. At the mention of each, Gabrielle gave an approving nod. She was flushed and a little glassy-eyed.

Meredith appeared. She looked composed. Whatever had assailed her was now past. She said hello to everyone and shook Gabrielle's hand. They were roughly the same age; another insult, Constance thought. Darren was in his fifties, as was Constance. He had a good twenty-five years on his new wife.

Elaine was in a chair across from the sectional, babbling at Gabrielle about home renovation projects. Gabrielle clearly wasn't listening. She turned to Meredith and said she'd heard that she worked in investments. Might she be interested in pointing her in a good direction?

"Investments?" Constance asked. All conversation ceased.

"Gabrielle's father left her a little something," Darren said.

The way Gabrielle patted his hand said she wanted him to change the subject.

"He was in real estate," Darren added.

"What's his name?" Meredith asked.

"Frank Hawkins," Gabrielle said.

"He built half the Sunset Strip!" Meredith said.

"That's right."

"Well. I'll speak to my supervisor. I'm sure he'd be happy to set up an appointment."

Elaine looked at Constance. One of her eyebrows was raised, as if to say, *He married her for her money!*

Certainly a possibility, Constance thought, then decided that Darren just wasn't that sort. Gabrielle was beautiful and elegant. Her talents as a scholar weren't bad either. Constance had never used her as a teaching assistant, because her field was early American history, but those who had said good things. Why would someone with her assets—both physical and financial—waste her time looking back?

That's what it meant to study history, didn't it? To look back? And what did all that looking back do? It never accurately predicted the future. The future always did as it pleased. Knowing the foibles of one's forebears made one cynical, even jaded. Constance wondered when that had happened to her. She'd begun with great passion for the past and the secrets it held. The dead were more real to her than the living. Her own life had contained ambitions and expectations, which were now played out. She had never felt so bitterly disappointed.

Constance drank a glass of wine, then a second, third, and fourth. The Chairman and his wife had left. They'd filled her ears with warm words, and admiration again for her charming home. Meredith asked her if she were all right. Constance waved her away.

As Constance sank, Gabrielle seemed to rise. She was alert, talking a lot, and paying Constance one compliment after another. Her home was lovely, her daughter was wonderful, her students were full of praise for her insights and compassion. Constance didn't know what she was talking about. She was a good professor, and a fair one, but hardly compassionate.

"And you have so many interests," Gabrielle said.

"Do I?"

"Your sewing. I understand you're very dedicated."

Constance caught Darren's eye. She hoped he registered the irritation she was trying to convey. His expression remained bland and pleasant.

"I only do it now and then," Constance said.

"Let's go take a closer look."

Gabrielle got up and walked across the room to the corner where the tapestry sat on its stand. The sound of her sandals was loud and firm, at odds with the mellow jazz Constance had playing on the stereo system. Constance went with her. She turned on the floor lamp next to the tapestry. Gabrielle sat in the chair in front of the stand and ran her finger over the tapestry, tilting the frame a little up, then a little down, to better view the stitched—and still bare—images.

Constance stood by. She felt like a servant, waiting for her mistress to give her an order. Gabrielle remained intent on the canvas.

"Such a sweet piece," she said.

"Yes."

"And the whole role of embroidery—generations of women sitting quietly, occupying their hands rather than their minds."

"I think that's the idea."

"It's only how it looks from the outside, though. When you're sewing, I'm sure your mind's not a blank."

"No."

Constance turned and looked behind her at her three remaining guests, hoping Gabrielle would take the hint and get up.

"My mother embroidered pillows and seat cushions. She wasn't very good at it actually. And I'm not even sure she took much pleasure from it. Her expression was always so fierce, as if the whole thing made her angry," Gabrielle said.

"Maybe it did."

"My father was the one who made her angry. She was jealous of his success. She was an ambitious person but didn't pursue what she wanted."

"And what was that?"

"Anything that didn't have to do with being a housewife."

Gabrielle sat back from the canvas. She was concentrating hard.

"It's aggressive, don't you think? Piercing something with a needle?" she asked.

"It's just a craft."

"While the men were hunting or fighting or engaging in politics or building a real estate empire, the women sewed and sewed, piercing, penetrating, as if they were men too, in that moment. Maybe it made them feel less excluded, or let them take a break from nurturing—which was their only valued role, right? Though I'd be the first to admit that's a bit of a stretch."

Constance had no words. Worried that her growing silence might be interpreted as astonishment, she walked quickly into the kitchen where she drank a glass of water.

Through the window over the sink, the backyard was illuminated by the exterior floodlights. It was deep and lush, a luxury of water stolen from the Colorado River, there in Southern California. It invited her to enter, wander, and collect herself. She'd had a stone bench installed, much like the one she and Darren had discovered in France, and it had been there that she'd conceived the outline of *Silent and Unseen*, and the "unyielding divide between the sexes," as one sour reviewer had put it.

In all the years she'd spent thinking and re-thinking what it meant to be female, she'd never once imagined the plain, simple, and blinding truth Gabrielle had just pronounced.

How could it be proven, or disproven? And did it need to be?

"What are you doing in here, all by yourself?" Elaine asked. Constance hadn't heard her come in.

"Just getting a drink of water."

"Well, they just left. I told them good-bye for you."

"What? Why didn't you come and get me? They must have thought me awfully rude!"

"Not really. Gabrielle said she had to go, that she wasn't feeling well."

"Oh."

"And naturally Darren jumped up and got her purse for her, and ushered her out like a little girl."

"Hm."

"Meredith is still here, though. She and Gabrielle certainly hit it off, didn't they?"

Constance took in Elaine's wide, flushed face. Her eyes were full of triumph and confidence. She'd had a good evening, clearly.

Constance excused herself so she could give the bartender his check. The caterers had returned as pre-arranged, and removed the remaining food and dirty dishes and silverware. While they worked, Meredith, Constance, and Elaine sat and recalled moments from the party, commented on how people looked and whether or not they'd enjoyed themselves, what the weather would be like the following day, and over the course of the coming season. The caterers left, saying Constance could expect a bill in about another week, then Meredith and Elaine also said good-night.

When Constance was alone, she went to the tapestry and sewed for at least an hour until her vision blurred and her needle hand ached.

It's only to pass the time, a way to endure loneliness, she thought. Nothing to do with men and women. Or with men versus women.

In, out, in, out, her needle went. From one painted patch to another. When she needed to, she plucked more yarn from the basket on the floor below the stand.

In, out, in, out.

chapter seven

Meredith didn't bring up the house again. She bought a small place on the other side of the faculty golf course, surrounded by trees and with a creek in back. She admitted that the quiet wasn't easy to get used to after living in Los Angeles her entire life. Constance understood that Meredith simply wanted to be near her. She forced herself to be pleasant when she stopped by, which she did several times a week.

Meredith sought out Eunice when Constance was sleeping, something she did more and more, even without the pills. At first Eunice said it really wasn't appropriate to follow her on her rounds through the wing, then relented. Clearly, Meredith needed a friend. Eunice invited her to an upscale coffee bar near Lindell. It sat in a new cluster of high-end stores.

Meredith blew into her coffee without taking a sip.

"Your mother seems comfortable at Lindell," Eunice said.

"She should be, by now."

"I mean that she's well settled. Some people never really adjust to leaving their own home."

Eunice's tone had become a little defensive, and she hadn't meant it to be. She just didn't know what else to talk about, and Meredith didn't have much to offer. Until she all of a sudden did.

Her mother was a deeply frustrated woman, she said, and it had taken years for her to realize that. She always acted as though she were satisfied with her career and that she loved teaching, but in fact she really didn't like it all that well. She said all the time that her students were stupid, with very few exceptions. And she was bitter about her thesis, even now, after all these years. She'd been talked into a subject she didn't really care for. She yielded under pressure, and had always regretted that decision.

After she retired, she tried writing a book about sex trafficking—could Eunice believe that? She didn't finish it. She began two others, Meredith didn't know what about. Then she volunteered at a shelter for abused women. Her mother, with her beautiful clothes, in a place like that. Meredith suggested, more than once, that she tone herself down just a little, and Eunice could imagine how *that* had been received.

One day, one of the shelter women really let her mother have it. Not physically, though it could very well have come to blows. Her mother had accused her of causing the mess she was in by choosing the wrong man. Well naturally this woman, with all her pent-up sorrow, let fly. Meredith wasn't sure, but she suspected that her mother was asked not to return.

"And then?" Eunice asked.

Her mother left L.A. and returned to her childhood home, which must have been very odd. She always said it was a relief, a welcome change, but she was a practiced liar, which Eunice would have no way of knowing, of course.

Meredith tasted her coffee. Eunice studied her hands, wrapped around the heavy mug. The nails on one hand were longer than the other, which struck Eunice as odd, given how meticulous the rest of her appearance was. But women could be like that, she'd found. They paid close attention to certain things and let others go. In Eunice's case, her blind spot always seemed to be her hair, which had retained its thick, springy texture as she'd aged. She washed it once a week and let it dry on its own. If she had to go outside, she pulled on a wool cap that had gotten some choice remarks from some of the residents. One man said she looked a gun moll. Eunice said she'd have to be in a dress for that to be the case, but he disagreed. All the sassiest women wore slacks in the thirties, he said. Eunice told him she was nothing, if not sassy.

Meredith said her mother had always taken the war between the sexes personally. When she was a young girl, her own mother…

She paused. She stared hard into her coffee cup.

"Her own mother what?" Eunice asked.

Got sent away, Meredith said, put away, was more like it. She was emotionally fragile. She'd wanted to be an actress and failed. It was hard on her, and she fell apart.

"That's harsh," Eunice said.

Meredith nodded.

"And hard for a little girl to see."

"Yes."

"So, what did she figure, your mom, about the whole thing? That a woman who tries to be anything other than a mother and a wife gets punished?"

Here Meredith leaned back in her vinyl chair and regarded Eunice across the wider distance she just put between them.

"I think she'd agree with that," Meredith said.

"You're a mom, a wife, or else."

"Yes."

"Well, she was a mom, at least."

Meredith got a queer look. Eunice became uneasy.

"What was your father like? She never said anything about her husband," she said.

"She never married."

"Wow. Can't have been easy, having a child out of wedlock in those days."

Again the queer, strained look. Not exactly sad, or angry, just stressed as hell, Eunice thought.

"There was a man she wanted to marry. He didn't want to marry her," Meredith said.

"Your father?"

"No."

"So, who was he? Or did she never say?"

"She never said."

"That's a hell of a mystery, right?"

"It is, indeed."

Meredith stood up abruptly and said next time, she'd treat.

Constance weakened. She spent more and more time in bed. She lost interest in food. Meredith grieved. Eunice understood. It was hard watching a relative go downhill. Meredith spent hours with Constance while Constance slept, and Eunice worked around her quietly, leaving her to her private thoughts.

part two

chapter eight

Eunice Fitch lived in a drafty clapboard house her parents tried miserably to make a home in. The roof, which sagged under time's weight and ravage, leaked—in Eunice's room, as luck would have it. The plaster softened, yielded, and dripped its steady measure of every passing cloud. Eunice's solution was to get a large pot from the kitchen and push her bed as far back as possible. During a particularly rainy season, when sleep failed to come and the new day began in a ragged state, Eunice moved to a small room at the far end of the hall where the roof, for the time being, held fast.

Her parents often left her alone at night so they could play cards with another couple down the road. Her companion was usually the black and white television set in the living room, two floors below the unsound roof. One evening, she was treated to a festival of silent movies. Background music played, piano and strings, cheerful or dire, by turns. Eunice tried to read the lips of the silent movie stars but found herself relying on the subtitles instead. She loved the subtitles. They summed up the action and gave the gist, just enough to go on. She loved the queer lighting, the fabulous twenties gowns, and most of all Lillian Gish. Eunice was enthralled by her courage and beauty.

She sought to perfect the burning gaze, the taut skin around her eyes, the firm jaw. All these conveyed anguish from the firmest part of her soul, and made for an elegant display of suffering when she got teased at school after she spilled her milk down the front of her ill-fitting plaid dress. Her reward for this brilliant performance on a spring day full of birdsong was to be called a retard by the tallest boy in class.

Next, she cut her hair in a bob. Her red curls and waves lay gorgeously on the filthy bathroom floor. Her mother was outraged. Several slaps ensued.

"What the hell's wrong with you? You look like an idiot."

Eunice's mother, Louise, was a small woman whose rage made her huge. Eunice ran to her father. He was planted in his easy chair, beer can in hand, watching a baseball game. He hit the mute button and looked at her with a blend of love and worry.

"You did that all by yourself?" he asked.

Eunice nodded, sending more strands of cut hair into her father's lap. He picked them up.

"You came into this world with a full head of hair. Did you know that?" he asked.

Eunice shook her head.

"Your mother snipped a lock of it, wrapped it with a little green silk ribbon, and put it in an envelope."

"Can I see it?"

"Oh, I don't know where it got to. She may have pitched it during one of her tidy up fits."

These occurred on an irregular basis. In fact, their house was pretty dirty most of the time because Eunice's mother was a cleaning lady for rich people and said she couldn't stand to bring her work home. Her father was a deliveryman for a liquor store. His job, like Eunice's mother's, also brought him in contact with the town's elite. He didn't resent them the way his wife did, but he, too, was jealous.

"Those folks drink first-rate hooch," he told Eunice more than once. "Just think of that!"

Eunice couldn't understand alcohol's wide appeal. She had learned over the years from watching her parents that drinking was entering a state of voluntary madness that seemed pleasant enough at first, until beer number three or four when her mother accused her father of something dire, usually of ruining her life, and threw something at the wall while he looked at the floor as if he wished it would open beneath him.

Eunice's father reached up and stroked her damaged hair.

"Such a shame," he said. His words made her feel much worse than her mother's well-aimed blows.

Her classmates, however, recovered then from the milk disaster, admired her new do. Sadly, she'd done a poor job. The back, in particular, was uneven. And since her hair was so thick and full of body, it stuck up in a way

Eunice didn't care for. Her Grandma Grace gave Eunice an Oreo cookie and told her not to worry, her hair would grow back. They were at her house, seated at her kitchen table in matching yellow chairs. The room was clad in faded floral wallpaper, the windowsill over the sink was crowded with flowering plants, and the ancient electric clock above the stove hummed happily to itself. Grandma Grace was in one of her many solid color dresses—this one pale green—an apron, and a pair of worn slippers. The only piece of jewelry she wore, a little chain with charms collected long ago, slid along her arm as she pressed a tissue to Eunice's nose and told her to blow.

Grandma Grace was Louise's mother. She was generally a cheerful person. Eunice's mother wasn't. Eunice didn't see how the two could be so different.

"Time, that's all. I had my trials in the world, like anyone else. I was pretty feisty, back in the day. You ask your mom. She'll tell you," Grandma Grace said.

Eunice never asked. She went on as she always did, and steered clear of her mother as much as possible.

Every so often, her mother would remember that she was there, living in the same house and eating at the same table. Her focused interest was terrifying.

"What happened to your report card? I didn't get a chance to see it," her mother said.

The report card in question contained the usual number of C's and D's. Eunice knew her mother didn't care about her grades. She did, however, care about making an effort to care, and this effort, more often than not, involved presenting herself at school and demanding to speak to one or more of Eunice's teachers, and once, to the principal himself. Eunice's mother accused them of treating Eunice unfairly.

"She's much more talented than she lets on," her mother told her math teacher, Mrs. Adams.

"Then she must apply herself," Mrs. Adams said. That same evening Eunice's mother called Mrs. Adams a "moron."

Her lecture to the principal, Mr. Delmon, was delivered on a plume of beer. Eunice had seen her mother come into the building and knew from her exacting gait that she was three sheets to the wind. Eunice managed to position herself discreetly in the main office, out of sight, but within earshot of the open door Mr. Delmon had been too surprised to close.

"Sheeza good girl. Mark my words. Iffa you wan my avice, lay the hell OFF," her mother said.

Eunice shared this with Grandma Grace. She shook her head woefully.

"No good loving liquor if you can't hold it. Don't even know where she got the habit. She never touched a drop living here with me. Your dad must have wanted her to try it," she said.

Eunice doubted that. Her father couldn't persuade her mother of anything.

Eunice's despair deepened. She stood before her mirror and peered into her own eyes until they filled with woe. She made it a point to stare at her mother until she saw it, too.

"What's the matter with you? Are you sick? Keep your distance, if you are," her mother said.

chapter nine

By the time Eunice was stumbling unwillingly through high school, it was Grandma Grace who had perfected the look of longing and pain. She'd broken her hip the year before, and been laid up a good six months, during which time a string of sullen and inept homecare workers came and went through her kitchen door. On her feet again, Grandma Grace was a changed woman. Gone were the brassy tone and sharp tongue Eunice had known all her life. What replaced it were long stretches of silence, accompanied by a furious gaze that bore through whatever it fell upon, even Eunice, who felt clumsy and inadequate. Once, she asked Grandma Grace what she'd done wrong.

"Who says you did anything wrong?"

"The way you look at me."

"I'm not aware of looking at you in any particular way."

Eunice knew Grandma Grace had meant no harm.

When the supply of care workers dried up, Eunice took over. Though she got around reasonably well, Grandma Grace was clearly terrified of another fall. So Eunice cleaned her house, changed the sheets on her bed, did the laundry, and even bought groceries when her father had time to drive her to the store, which had to be scheduled during the narrow window between the end of his workday and the start of his evening revelry. He roosted in their living room, watching the same television where Eunice had discovered Lillian Gish years before. Her mother claimed the kitchen table for her daily binge. Eunice passed by them, receiving scant acknowledgment, sometimes a request for another bottle of beer, a clean ashtray, or to take out the trash.

"What are you going to do with your life?" Grandma Grace asked Eunice one afternoon.

"I don't know."

"Nonsense. You're almost eighteen years old. You have to have some idea."

Eunice shrugged. She unpacked the two grocery bags she'd brought in. She now had a driver's license and used Grandma Grace's old Buick to go back and forth.

"How can I, when I'm not good at anything?" Eunice asked.

"You're good at taking care of people."

Eunice supposed that was true. She'd taken care of her parents for years. To fulfill her quota of mandated community service hours (this was a new requirement to graduate from high school) she volunteered at the Clearview nursing home where she read stories to dull-eyed old men and women, then wheeled them around the grounds to look at the flowers. And she'd been at Grandma Grace's side almost constantly, so much so that they'd talked about her moving in and leaving her parents behind.

"But it might not be the best work for a young woman. Not right off, anyhow. Go out and tool around for a while first."

It was 1976. The bicentennial had people on the road in record numbers. Everyone wanted to see America.

"I bet the world is pretty much the same everywhere as it is here," Eunice said.

"Maybe." Grandma Grace paused to shuffle the worn deck of cards she always had in the pocket of her sweater. She could play solitaire for hours.

"Besides, who would take care of you?" Eunice asked. She put a can of tuna fish on the counter as a reminder to herself to use it later to make sandwiches for lunch.

"I'll find someone."

They had this conversation about once a month, and it always ended with them dropping it until the next time.

"What about boys?" Grandma Grace asked. This was a new tack, and it caught Eunice off guard.

"What about them?"

"Don't you like any?"

"No."

Eunice had had a terrible crush on Brad Chalmers in her math class the year before. He was spectacularly handsome, and incredibly stupid. Whenever he spoke, people laughed, and the poor thing turned red. Eunice felt his pain. She, too, was sometimes laughed at. She decided that they were peas in a pod, two survivors stranded on the cruel island of Dunston High School, alone against the world.

"We can face it together, you know," Eunice once summoned the courage to tell him when she cornered him by his locker.

"Face what?" he asked. Up close she noticed that one nostril was smaller than the other, there was a pimple on his chin, and his breath smelled like an old shoe. She loved him all the more for his flaws.

"Our common affliction," she whispered and put her hand on his cheek.

He backed up. "Take it easy," he said.

She watched him trot down the hall. Her heart went with him.

But soon another boy caught her eye. Larry Lester, a bad sort Grandma Grace would say, only wanting a girl for one thing, which Eunice gave him willingly under the bleachers after school one day. The act was stunningly brutal. He pressed into her so hard, it was difficult to breathe. Then afterward, he merely rolled off, pulled up his pants, and said he'd see her later. She felt as though she'd been mauled by an animal, and left to die.

When her period was late, she panicked, looked up the laws about getting an abortion, and cried with relief when her period showed up in the middle of the following week. The use of birth control didn't occur to her until later, when Larry had moved on to another girl, and yet another one after that.

"Well, men have their uses, you know," Grandma Grace said. "Just you keep an open mind."

Grandma Grace told a tale she'd told many times before, about being courted by her late husband. He came to her house with flowers, then sang beneath her window with a guitar he played so badly that her father chased him off with a shotgun. Only then did Grandma Grace's expression lighten, before quickly becoming dark and brooding once again.

Not long after, Grandma Grace died in her sleep. It wasn't Eunice who found her but a neighbor Grandma Grace had invited over for coffee, in a rare mood of hospitality. Eunice took it as a sign—not the death, which was inevitable—but Grandma Grace's change of heart about having people in her home. That Grandma Grace had left her house and bank accounts to Eunice rather than to Eunice's mother, proved that life contained a number of unexpected possibilities that one should be ready to embrace. Of the roughly three hundred thousand dollars Eunice received, including proceeds from the sale of the house, she gave ten thousand to her father alone, in recognition of the fact that he did truly care for her. To her mother, she gave nothing, despite being treated to a daily rant about her disgusting ingratitude and monstrous selfishness.

chapter ten

Eunice moved into a new apartment complex, where many younger professors lived. She had a spare bedroom. The living room looked out over the gorge. It came furnished. The couch and loveseat were white leather, which she found alarming. It took her over a week to sit on either, then she decided that they were deliciously comfortable.

She invited her father to come and see for himself how she was living now. He seemed impressed, though not envious. Her mother, who was not invited, continued her daily wheedling. Eunice had to admit she was getting worn down. She wondered how much her mother would accept to get off her back.

Without Grandma Grace to take care of, Eunice became bored. Her father said she should go to college and study film. Didn't she used to like old movies? The choices of higher education in Dunston were the university, which was Ivy League, and Dunston College, which offered good arts programs, but mostly in music and theater.

"What about UCLA?" he asked.

"What's that?"

"University of California at Los Angeles." He spoke proudly. He'd done his research.

"That's pretty far away."

"Wouldn't hurt to put a little distance between you and you-know-you."

Her mother would only turn up the volume long distance.

You can swing a fancy-shmancy education, but for your mother, not one red cent!

And in any case, she knew she wasn't college material.

She bought herself a car, a used Carmen Ghia. She loved it, even though it was yellow, her least favorite color. The salesman showed her how to drive a stick shift. She hoped she'd learn before she burned out the clutch. His name was Beau, short for Beauregard.

"That's 'beautiful view' in French," he said.

He was beautiful, with a very Douglas Fairbanks flair. He looked like he could handle a sword just fine. Eunice said she could see him with one. He blushed, then took her out for another quick lesson on the stick. She beamed. She was learning how to flirt! Heady stuff, she thought. She wanted to flirt some more, so she took him on a long drive around the back of the golf course. They parked on a grassy verge. He put his hand on her knee. There wasn't enough room in the car, so out they went, pawing and kissing and dropping to the ground.

It was better than with Larry Lester. At least Beau asked her, panting, how she was doing. He didn't roll off right away, but remained inert and warm, crushing her ribs. Something dug painfully into the tender flesh of her thigh. It was his belt buckle, she discovered as he pulled his pants back on.

Afterward, they sat in the car to compose themselves. Beau told Eunice he was married and couldn't get involved with her.

"What do you call what we just did?" she asked.

"Just one of those things."

"Don't you think I'm pretty?"

"Sure."

"Look at me."

He looked at her. She held his gaze. She saw him admire her hazel eyes and the paleness of her skin. The green blouse she wore went perfectly with her red hair, which she wore long and full. He took in the curve of her breasts and her flat stomach. He patted her smooth knee.

"Like I said, sure," he said.

She asked him to get out of the car.

"What? Why?"

"Because you're a cad."

"I don't think that's a word people use anymore."

"I just did. Now get out."

"Wait a second! How am I supposed to get back to town?"

"You can hitch a ride."

"That could take hours!"

"Too bad about that."

He crossed his arms.

"If you don't get out this minute, I'll say you raped me," she said.

His face went slack. His eyes filled with muted rage.

"Fine. Do your worst. Your word against mine," he said.

Eunice started the engine. She released the brake. As her hand went to the gear shift, he grabbed it with a sweaty palm.

"I don't scare easily," he said.

"How about your wife?"

He opened the door and got out. "Jesus, if it means that much to you, fine, I'll find my own way."

A school bus came slowly up the road. The children inside waved joyously at them as they went by. Eunice waved, too.

She turned back to Beau. He looked like a scared little boy wearing a suit that was too big for him. She hadn't noticed before how poorly it fit. The sleeves fell to the middle of his hands. She heard Grandma Grace.

Don't waste another minute on that poor son-of-a-bitch.

"Get in. And keep quiet," she said.

"Okay."

She stopped a block from the dealership and turned off the engine. Her eyes burned with held-back tears. She sniffed.

"Try not to take it so hard," he said.

"I'm not crying about you."

That was true. She was crying for herself, and how ridiculous she was.

chapter eleven

The man at the bank suggested an investment. Something to make her money grow.

Eunice didn't know anything about investing. She could barely balance a checkbook. When she confessed to both, the banker smiled. It was charmingly clichéd that he had a gold tooth. The charm vanished when he leaned forward and whispered, "Real estate." The banker was fond of garlic.

There were plans to build a shopping center on a wide patch of land overlooking the lake. If she were to commit her entire savings, she was certain to double her return in five years.

"What if it doesn't work?" Eunice asked. The banker smiled at her kindly, as if she'd just asked if the moon were really made of cheese.

"It's a very well-studied proposal. Baxter Bain will tell you all about it."

"Who's that?"

Again, the kind smile, the gentle acknowledgment of her shocking ignorance.

"Baxter oversaw the entire redevelopment of the Downtown Commons," the banker said. The Commons closed off the major streets in the small downtown core. The stores had hoped that with increased foot traffic, they'd prosper. They didn't. At the same time, the town's first shopping mall was built, and everyone took their business there. Eunice didn't see how the town could support a second shopping center. She raised this with the banker.

"Serving a different market entirely," he said.

How many markets were there in Dunston? she wanted to ask but didn't. He'd made her feel stupid enough.

She hadn't been home two minutes when the telephone rang. Baxter Bain had been given her number. Could they arrange a meeting?

"I don't think so," Eunice said.

"I'll keep it brief, I promise." Baxter Bain's voice was deep and boomed in her ear. He sounded like he knew what he was talking about. That confidence and ring could only belong to a handsome man, she decided. She agreed to meet him the following day.

Eunice's father was skeptical. He wanted to go with her, just to make sure Bain was on the "up and up." Eunice didn't think that was such a good idea. While her father drank much less these days, he still loved his beer and could consume it unpredictably. She promised him she'd be wary.

"Just don't sign anything," he said.

Baxter Bain was tall, blond, square-jawed, a little round in the stomach, probably in his early thirties. He was also married, given the band on his finger. Eunice didn't care. She was prepared to conquer.

He regarded her closely over the table where they were having lunch. She willed him to see inside her, to glimpse her hungry heart.

"I can tell you're an intelligent young woman, and that you know an opportunity when you see one," he said. His pink tie made her want to lunge across the table and shove her tongue in his mouth. She poked the cheese topping of her French onion soup with her spoon. She couldn't believe how dumb she'd been to order something that would make her breath stink.

They got together a number of times. She loved the way he held her chair for her, opened doors, took her arm as they crossed the street. His touch was electric.

Hers must have been, too, because he fell in love with her. At least, he said he'd fallen. Something about the flowers he sent and the late night phone calls, when he'd clearly had too much to drink, rang false. Yet she found herself believing him. She wanted to. She *had* to.

You're a fool, Eunice Fitch!

Baxter Bain wanted her money. That was the long and short of it. He wooed her to get it. She held out as long as she could. Sometimes Grandma Grace would whisper, *Watch out, girl. Hang on tight to what I gave you!* That's when Eunice wished that what she'd inherited had been common sense instead of cash.

Her obsession with Baxter Bain caused her to split in two. Her brain still worked. She knew she was being played. Her heart *wanted* her to be played. Her wise self put him off, told him she had to think the investment over very carefully. She asked smart questions about how long the project would take to construct, which national stores would lease space, and what builder would be hired. Her foolish self let him drive her out to the site every day, even in the wind and snow. He talked about their fortune, their future.

One day Eunice asked, "What about your wife?"

He waved his hand to indicate that the wife was a small matter. Eunice hoped one day to be the current wife's replacement, and even as her wise self told her to run like hell, her foolish self let him kiss her right there in the freezing wind.

Three months after Eunice gave Baxter Bain her money, spring came. The site was marked with orange spray paint and wooden stakes. A large sign with the name *Dunston Heights Mall* was clearly visible from the adjacent highway. She went there often, sometimes at night with a flashlight so she could find her way in the dark, or at sunset to take in the changing color of the lake, and seldom with Baxter Bain. He'd broken things off with her soon after taking her check. His wife was coming around, he said. Coming around to what, Eunice didn't know. He promised to keep her up to date on the progress of the development. By the end of the summer there had been no progress at all. One night he called, waking her from an uneasy sleep full of Grandma Grace, to say that the money had been lost. The contractor had swindled them both and skipped town. The authorities had been contacted. Once he was in custody, there'd be a lawsuit. The bum would pay up. She wasn't to worry about that.

Eunice digested this news and found she didn't care all that much. She was too excited by the sound of his voice.

Then she ruined things by asking, "How are things with your wife?"

Baxter hung up, and she didn't hear from him again for a long time. When he did get back in touch, it was from jail. He wanted to come clean, he said. Eunice, apparently, hadn't been the only investor in the shopping center. A number of other people—all women, though considerably older than she—had put in their life savings. There had never been a contractor, just overseas accounts in the name of Baxter Bain's wife. She, apparently, was the one who took off with all of it, and Baxter was now agreeing to testify against her in the hope that she could be found and the money recovered. Neither ever happened, and Baxter stayed behind bars.

The land was eventually sold by Baxter's real estate company to another developer who built a retirement community there a few years later. When Eunice saw that the Lindell Home was hiring, she applied. The place oozed comfort and luxury. The carpets were thick, the furniture solid and plush. The woman who interviewed her, Alice somebody, met with her in the activity room. They sat together on a sofa that faced a wall of windows.

"What makes you want to work with the elderly?" Alice asked. She didn't look much older than Eunice, then just twenty-five.

"I took care of my Grandma Grace for a long time after she broke her hip."

"I see."

"Then she died."

"I'm sorry to hear that."

Eunice focused on a little pin Alice wore at the neck of her white blouse. It was made from a slim gold bar and a blue stone at either end. The stones reminded her of Baxter's eyes.

"You seem like a very capable person," Alice said.

"I like to think so."

"Why don't we take a look around and see how you like it here."

They toured the whole building. Long, wide halls led into common areas with aquariums or bird cages. Beautiful art hung on the walls; wide windowsills were choked with healthy green plants the residents could tend themselves if they wished to, Alice explained. The dining room had arched doorways and windows. The fitness center had a swimming pool and sauna. Alice explained that there were three levels of accommodation. Independent residents lived in the outlying cottages. As an aide, Eunice wouldn't cross paths with them, unless she wanted to apply for a housekeeping position? That would entail mopping and vacuuming. Eunice didn't think so. She liked the sound of actually being in the company of someone, not working by herself. Then there was the assisted living wing. Most of the people there had suffered a recent illness or injury, and needed a little extra help before they went back to their cottages. If their recovery wasn't promising, they moved into the skilled nursing wing. Eunice would probably be assigned there.

"Now, how does all that sound?" Alice asked when they'd returned to the reception area.

"Fine."

"Good. Come in on Monday."

Eunice left the building feeling like she'd just been handed a prison sentence. She refused to be glum, however, and spoke of her new opportunity in glowing terms to her parents.

"Seems like an odd job for a young person like you," her father said.

"A job's a job," her mother said.

Eunice suspected that her mother was secretly thrilled at the loss of her fortune. She and Eunice's father still lived in the Eunice's childhood home, while Eunice had had to move out of the fancy apartment and was renting a trailer along the inlet from Lake Dunston. She still had the Carmen Ghia but couldn't afford to replace the bad muffler, so she bought a 1965 Dodge Dart Station Wagon. A car that was almost twenty years old wasn't anything exactly special. But then again, neither was she.

chapter twelve

For the next few years, the love in Eunice's heart found expression in the care she lavished on the residents at Lindell. Most weren't interested in her efforts, but a few were. Molly Moore had quite a yen for Eunice's hair, and often asked if she could braid it. Eunice let her when her shift was over because her supervisor didn't like her being on the clock for such a frivol. Eunice tried to make her see that it was good for Molly to use her hands, to have Eunice sit before her like a beloved grandchild, and to have someone to tell her stories to.

Molly was eighty-nine, which meant she was born at the turn of the century. Her mind was sharp. So was her tongue. She declared President Bush a horse's ass. So was anyone who'd voted for him.

"My mother did," Eunice said.

"Goodness! That's all I need to know about that poor woman!"

Her voice was high, yet firm. She'd had a career in business, first as a secretary after the First World War, then as a bookkeeper for a bakery, a drugstore, and a high-end store that specialized in ladies' lingerie.

"They gave me a *great* discount, though I wasn't married yet at the time, so all those pretty underthings went to waste," she said.

"Can't a woman wear frillies just for herself?"

"Sure. But it's more fun when a man admires you, don't you think?"

Eunice did. Her love life had been nil for some time. She'd gone on a couple of dates with one of the maintenance men from Lindell. He was about her age, attractive in a brooding sort of way, and looked at her as if she were his favorite meal. She decided that on the third date she'd make her move. She stopped him as they were walking across a parking lot and kissed him. He did nothing, just stood there. She asked him what was wrong.

"Our Lord frowns on such behavior," he said.

Six months later, she had dinner with the great-grandson of a resident.

He treated her to lobster at the lake, said she was beautiful, asked if she liked Italian films, then said they should go to his place and just get it over with. Eunice was fine with that, only "it" managed to last about forty-five seconds.

She took to going to bars on Tuesdays for Ladies' Night, and on Fridays for Happy Hour. Her results fell between awful and inane. One night, she crossed another frontier and brought someone home.

The man, Carson, had been charming early in the evening but got nastier with each drink. Once in the door, he looked around and said, "What a dump!"

Eunice wasn't put off by his mounting mean spirit. She decided she'd reform him, and kill him with kindness. She agreed that her orange rag rug was a little old school, as was the curved back on the sofa and the print of a little girl offering a daisy to a cow. These had all been Grandma Grace's things, which meant that putting them down upset her, but she knew that wherever Grandma Grace was, she understood. Carson dropped meatily onto the sofa, sending up a plume of dust from the ancient cushions, and told her he liked a woman who could admit that she was wrong.

Then he patted the empty space next to him, releasing even more dust. Eunice sat. He said he might be able to help her get some new furniture. He had a friend who was looking to sell a few things cheap. The friend was downsizing, moving out of state, and pretty much everything had to go. Carson leaned his head back and snored for a while. Eunice considered his offer. Carson might be the man she'd been looking for. He seemed capable, a good problem-solver. Eunice knew she was good at this, too, and that if she took up with Carson, she'd have to pretend to be inept so he could feel useful. She reflected on the stormy marriage of her own parents. Her father had been more on the ball than her mother had ever given him credit for. If she'd been gentler, more supportive, the whole family would have been calmer, with a real chance for happiness. Her mother believed in punishing people for things they couldn't help. That, Eunice decided, was the essence of cruelty.

Carson's friend, it turned out, was selling someone else's furniture. The friend had another friend who worked for a moving company. The clients were out of town, already installed in their next home, not on hand to supervise the loading of the truck and the selective culling of their possessions. A lamp, side table, and a leather easy-chair found their way into Carson's pick-up and then Eunice's trailer. She knew nothing about their true origins. She was just glad Carson had come through. She was also thrilled that the cost to her was less than two hundred dollars. Eunice invited Carson to move in with her, since the lease on his one bedroom apartment was up soon. He said it was a serious step. He didn't want her to get the wrong idea. A long-term relationship probably wasn't in the cards for him. He was open about his past with women. He'd decided some time before that he had a commitment problem, but if Eunice was willing to go with the flow, not ask too much, then he'd be happy to join her in her trailer.

Got you now!

One evening, not long after, while Carson was at his place packing, a man knocked on Eunice's door and told her that Carson needed to get rid of the hot stuff. The moving company had called the police. The friend said he was going to lie low for a while, but if things went wrong and he got picked up, he'd have to tell the cops what he knew.

"Are you saying this furniture is stolen?" Eunice asked. The man looked down at her with beady, rodent eyes.

"More like on permanent loan."

The man told Eunice to make sure Carson knew he'd been by, and to watch himself in the next few days.

"Tell him we'll go for a beer when it's all over," he said.

"What's your name?"

"I'd rather not say, you know, if the cops show up here looking for me."

If that happened, a physical description alone would have him tracked down. The guy was six foot five at least and had had to stoop to get through the trailer's doorway. He had blond dreadlocks, a few of which had been dyed black, and a tattoo of a dragon on the right side of his neck.

"I'll just call you Mr. X," Eunice said.

"Just play dumb if they ask you anything. Carson should too. He knows how."

Then Mr. X went on his way.

Eunice said nothing to Carson. The police stayed away. So did Mr. X. Eunice could tell Carson was mad about his disappearance and thought it was some selfish whim, not motivated by self-preservation. She liked knowing something he didn't. It seemed like a fair trade, given what she'd already ceded.

Their life together was a clumsy dance. Sometimes she forgot herself and tried to lead. He stepped all over her. He lost his job at the liquor store for having beer on his breath, and didn't see the humor in that at all. Then he decided he'd been granted a favor, since he never had liked his boss all that much. He came to enjoy staying home, in front of the television, and Eunice's cable package, which set her back a fair amount every month. So did Carson. He didn't contribute money. He didn't contribute time. She was expected to cook, clean, and wash his clothes when she wasn't working at Lindell.

Her days off were Tuesday and Thursday. Carson suggested that she ask to rearrange her schedule so that her days off were consecutive. That way she could get more done around the place.

"You just like having me around," she said.

"That too."

He gave her a big bear hug. He needed a shower. She didn't mention it. He'd been down lately, bored and restless.

"I got the fidgets," he said more than once.

She made his favorite dinner of macaroni and cheese with cut up hot dogs, splashed generously with hot sauce and paired with an ice cold beer. He ate slowly, enjoying it. He was her work of art, she realized. Her creation. She suggested he might look for a job, a place to put his nervous energy.

"That's just like you to throw it in my face," he said, chewing.

"Throw what?"

"That I got fired."

"I didn't mean that at all. I just thought you'd feel better."

"Don't treat me like a little boy."

"Then don't act like one."

It took her a good twenty minutes to clean up the food he'd tossed on the floor, along with the broken plate, not to mention the overturned kitchen table. Carson had taken himself out to a bar after helping himself to Eunice's wallet. She fumed. She scrubbed. She vowed not to provoke him on payday ever again; it could get expensive.

At work, Eunice had made friends with one of the residents, Elvie Sundhurst. Eunice liked talking to her. She was a widow. She'd been married sixty-two years. That sounded like an eternity to Eunice. At the time, Eunice was coming up on her thirty-fifth birthday. When she did the math, if she and Carson got married right away, she'd be ninety-seven when she'd been married as long as Elvie. She and Carson weren't getting married. He showed no signs of asking her. Sometimes she wasn't even sure she'd accept, especially after the food-throwing, table-tipping incident. Carson had come home apologetic and anxious. He said he expected to find that she'd dumped his things out into the street and changed the locks. She asked him why she shouldn't. He honestly didn't know. He knew he wasn't easy to live with, but hoped she'd give him a second chance.

Eunice filled Elvie in. Elvie listened while she played another game of solitaire. She had a small folding table in her room and wheeled herself there first thing in the morning. Eunice finished making the bed. Elvie shuffled her cards.

"I'd-a cracked his head open with a skillet, he ever tried a thing like that," Elvie said.

Carson looked for work but found nothing. Eunice suggested that he apply to the maintenance staff at Lindell, then regretted opening her mouth. If he got a job there and did badly, she'd look like a fool. Maybe she already looked like one. Her relationship with Carson was something she shared freely with the residents, most of whom didn't answer, unlike Elvie, who always had something to contribute.

"Put your foot in his backside. Take charge," Elvie said, and slapped down a Queen of Hearts.

Finally, Carson got hired on at the gun factory, not on the line, but as a custodian. He swept up after hours. He seemed to like it. He said it gave him time to think. Eunice hoped that with all that time thinking, things might improve.

One morning Eunice went to work and learned that Elvie had died in her sleep the night before. Eunice felt both sad and ripped off. Elvie hadn't seemed unwell when Eunice had seen her last. There had been no chance to thank her for her harsh but fair words. Eunice had come to feel that thanks were in order because Carson had suggested that one day they might actually consider tying the knot. He'd been so vague about it that it took Eunice a moment to realize she was receiving a proposal of marriage.

Eunice took her grief over Elvie to her father, whose health hadn't been too good of late. He suffered from a chronic cough and tired easily, yet wouldn't go to the doctor. Eunice's mother had discovered the joy of playing bingo and was usually out in the evenings, though Eunice knew for a fact, as did her own father, that bingo was offered locally only on Wednesdays at the community center. Eunice's father said he didn't mind his wife getting out and having a little fun. The question, Eunice thought and kept to herself, was with whom.

He expressed his sadness over the loss of Elvie. Eunice then spoke of Carson and the recent turn of events.

"You want to get married?" her father asked. The fabric on the arms of the chair he sat in was worn and black. Eunice thought that one of these days she might take it outside and set it on fire.

"Maybe," she said.

"That sounds like no."

"It's not that simple."

"Either you want that ring, or you don't."

Eunice realized that Carson hadn't presented her with an engagement ring. She'd seen a nice one at a jewelers in the mall. It was small but elegant. She hadn't mentioned it to Carson.

"I don't know what the big deal about marriage is, anyhow," she said. She was on the couch opposite her father's ruined chair, the same couch from her own childhood that creaked loudly when someone sat down.

"Commitment," her father said. He was sipping from a can of beer. Two empty cans lay crumpled at his feet. "Marriage is a promise, a vow."

"I know all that." Eunice's head hurt. The summer air was thick and humid. Thunder sounded dully in the distance.

"No, you don't. No one knows, until they're in it up to their eyeballs."

Eunice didn't have to ask her father what it had been like being married to her mother. Yet she remembered a sprinkling of happy moments or at least times when they were neither screaming nor avoiding one another in cold, stony silence. One winter night they had sat in front of the fire laughing. A summer afternoon had been spent working together in the garden. They both had taken her into town the Halloween she was in second grade because the houses where they lived weren't close enough together to make a good haul trick-or-treating. Eunice didn't believe in fairy tale romances and happily ever after, but she did expect that the good times would slightly outnumber the bad. Maybe that was more likely to happen if you didn't get married and just lived together instead. She didn't want to feel trapped by a wedding ceremony. It wouldn't do either her or Carson any good. She told her father exactly this.

When he stopped coughing, he said, "You're just trying to talk yourself out of the whole idea, which means you're not ready to jump in."

Eunice got him another beer, though he hadn't asked for it, then offered to stay until her mother returned. He waved his hand dismissively in a way that meant there was no point in waiting, not because he wasn't lonely, but because it might be quite late when her mother got back.

The night was thrown with stars. Their beauty helped Eunice reflect. She and Carson were a good match. He wasn't much, and neither was she. Time to face facts. She wasn't important, and she never would be.

If Grandma Grace were still alive, she'd probably say that sort of attitude was a bunch of baloney. She'd tell Eunice to get off her duff and figure out what she wanted from life, and then to go out and get it.

Grandma Grace had done a number of things with her seventy-nine years on earth. Before she was married, she lived for a while in New York City and worked as a waitress. That had been back during the First World War. It would have been hard to be a woman on her own. She also learned how to type, and got a job working for a law office until the man who ran the place set his sights on her in a way that strongly suggested the altar was not in mind. She came back to Dunston with some savings and sold baked goods from her own kitchen, which living in the middle of downtown made easy. Grandma Grace was known for her bread and rolls.

The business went under in the Depression, which she always said was just as well because she was a mother at that point, and working and taking care of a little girl was pretty hard. Eunice's grandfather wasn't drawn to the usual occupations, and fenced stolen goods. He got arrested from time to time, which always made a heavy load for Grandma Grace.

"He helped around the house, which was rare for a man in those days," she often told Eunice.

Grandma Grace got friendly with certain cops. She never specified the terms of these friendships, but Eunice was pretty sure money changed hands so that her grandfather could go on selling hot cars and radios and stay out of jail. He accumulated a little cash, but not very much, because times were still pretty hard all around, so Grandma Grace went back to work when Eunice's mother was old enough to go to school. She always felt bad about that.

"Maybe that's how come your mom turned out to be such a sourpuss, because I wasn't around enough."

Grandma Grace learned how to keep books. She got a job in a dental office. The dentist had family money, and also did well in his practice. He taught Grace about investing in solid stocks. She bought Boeing and other industrial companies that ramped up during the Second World War. Her returns were phenomenal, though she kept that to herself. She didn't want her husband knowing what she had. The stocks were all in her name. Even after he died, she lived modestly so she could keep her fortune, which came to Eunice decades later, and which Eunice lost.

But there was no point in thinking about that. Eunice had made up her mind. Carson it would be.

Music was playing inside the trailer. A woman laughed. Then Carson said, "Hey, be careful." Eunice opened the door. The woman was someone she recognized from the trailer park. Eunice didn't know very much about her except that she was divorced. She was older than Eunice by about ten years, which put her around Carson's age. She was sitting in his lap, drinking from a bottle of beer. The trailer smelled of marijuana. Eunice didn't know Carson smoked marijuana. He'd never mentioned it before. Carson stared at Eunice and stopped smiling.

"Oops," he said.

The woman looked at Eunice. She got off Carson's lap. She put the bottle of beer she'd been holding on the coffee table. She didn't use a coaster. Eunice kept a small stack on the table and always encouraged Carson to use one.

"It's not what you think," the woman said.

"What do I think?" Eunice asked.

"You remember Mandy, don't you, honey?" Carson asked.

"No."

"I should go," Mandy said. Her T-shirt had a picture of a unicorn on it. The unicorn was silver, shiny, and grinning. Mandy was grinning too. Her eyes were red and squinty. Where was the pipe? Eunice wondered. Didn't you smoke marijuana in a pipe?

"Don't rush off on my account," Eunice said. Mandy hesitated. She coughed without covering her mouth.

"Nah, hate to be a party pooper, but I got work in the morning," she said. Mandy glanced at Carson as if she hoped he'd ask her to stay. He didn't. She left.

"I didn't know she got a job," Carson said.

"Sounds like you two have gotten pretty chummy."

"We talk now and then."

"Especially when I'm not here. With her in your lap."

"Come on. She was just fooling around."

"That's my point."

"I can't talk to you when you get like this."

Eunice sat down in the stolen chair. She was glad she hadn't found Mandy sitting in it. It was a nice chair.

"Elvie died," she said.

"The cat?"

"What cat?"

"You know, that lady across the road. The one with the cat."

Was there no female neighbor Carson didn't know?

"The lady at Lindell. The one I was friends with."

"Oh. What she die of?"

"Living too long."

Carson sighed. He went and got himself another bottle of beer. He returned to the couch.

"You should get some sleep," he told her.

"You should move out."

"Why? Because I had someone over when you weren't home? I had to. You don't like my friends."

"So, you were just being considerate."

"Yeah."

Eunice leaned back in the chair. She closed her eyes. In homes all over America this same scene was being played. Whatever the circumstances, however the different actors got where they were, it always ended the same.

"This is my house, and I'm not leaving it," she said.

"You're really kicking me out?" His surprise sounded genuine. For a moment, Eunice felt herself caving in.

"Look, if it's about Mandy, don't worry. She's leaving soon," Carson said. He was leaning forward now, trying to lessen the distance between them.

"Where's she going?"

"Moving out, that's all I know. She has family in Binghamton."

Binghamton was all of thirty-five miles away. Carson's car got terrible gas mileage. He'd be asking for money, or to borrow her car, in no time.

Eunice went to bed. Carson slept on the couch. He'd stayed up late. She'd heard him moving around well past midnight. She left for work in the morning without waking him. She didn't go home right away when her shift was over. She swung by the cemetery to talk to Grandma Grace. Her advice was the same as it always was, and Eunice would take it, if she knew how.

Before she left, she asked Grandma Grace to say hi to Elvie, if she happened to run into her.

Carson and his things were gone when she returned. The stolen furniture remained, only because he hadn't figured out a way to take it along, Eunice was certain. She sat a moment, then called a locksmith to come change the lock. She thought it best that he not decide to pay a visit at some highly inconvenient moment.

Over the next several days, he was on her mind all the time, though he didn't call or come by. She had no idea where he was living. She wanted to hunt him down and force an apology out of him but knew that was absurd.

chapter thirteen

George Nash was on the way out. He had no active disease. At ninety-six, he'd simply had enough. For the past two months, he'd not risen from bed. Everything was done for him right there. Eunice came in after the nurses had checked his vitals and helped him swallow his many daily pills. Meals were always soft—pudding, a boiled egg, soup. Eunice brought the spoon to his lips and was thrilled when he took the smallest bite. When his eyes opened and he took her in, they filled with joyous light.

Sometimes they spoke a little. He asked what it was doing outside, what month it was, if the president was still a bum. One day he asked if she was married. She shook her head.

"Don't believe it," he said. His voice was deep and quiet. Speaking was the one thing that seemed not to tire him.

"Believe it."

"What's wrong with the young men these days?"

He'd been married fifty-four years. His wife had died over ten years before. Her picture sat on his dresser. She had a small oval face and a pert nose. Eunice liked to think she looked a little bit like her.

Often they just sat, hand in hand, while the television played. Eunice loved the perfect smoothness of his skin. He still had a full head of hair, and she stroked it whenever she could.

His family wanted him to spend his last days at home. Eunice didn't want him to go. She knew she had no say in the matter.

One afternoon, her supervisor, Karen, called her into her office. Alice, who had been promoted to manager of the entire home, was there, too. George's son had visited just the day before. Eunice had been off then.

"He told his father that they're relocating him at the end of the month," Karen said.

"I'll be sorry to see him go."

Karen and Alice both looked uneasy. Karen in particular. She tended to rub her nose when someone was late for work or a resident had fouled the sheets. She was rubbing it now.

"Let me get to the point. His son, Marlin, says his dad doesn't want to leave," Alice said.

"Really?"

"It seems he's formed a strong attachment to you."

"I'm glad."

"He told his son that he's fallen in love with you."

Eunice shifted in her chair. She was deliriously happy, and knew better than to show it. She adopted a puzzled, concerned expression.

"Now, sometimes residents take a special liking to someone. It's not unusual," Karen said.

"But this *is* unusual, particularly because his mental state is uncompromised, as far as we can tell. Would you agree that he's rational?" Alice asked.

"Yes. Totally."

"So, at the very least, he *believes* he's in love with you. Whether or not he actually is."

"How do you tell the difference?"

"I'm sorry?"

"Well, I mean, if you *think* you love someone, how could it ever be proved that you don't?"

Alice conceded the point.

"You see, Eunice, the thing is, well the son wonders if something inappropriate may have taken place between you and his father," she said.

"As in … sleeping together?"

"Exactly."

"Holy cow!"

Eunice asked if it were even possible for a man George's age. Karen assured her that it was. She hoped her sudden color would be taken as indignation or shock at such a suggestion, and not the truth, which was she'd thought about it, herself.

Because she loved George, too. She knew it was crazy. Obviously there was something wrong with her. She couldn't help it. Her heart always melted so easily.

"Nothing happened," she said.

"We know. But the son is skeptical. He'll get over that, I suspect, once his dad's been moved," Alice said.

"You're concerned about Lindell's reputation," Eunice said.

"Naturally."

"Well, I'm concerned, too. And I resent that son of his, let me tell you."

"Of course."

"So, just try to bring George around to the idea of leaving. Can you do that?" Karen asked.

"I'll try."

Eunice didn't try. She never brought the subject up. She hoped he might die before the son had his way, because that would fix everything, then felt terrible for thinking so.

George didn't die. If anything, he became more alert, as if gathering strength.

"They'll never keep us apart," he told her, his grip on her hand so firm it was almost painful.

"No, they won't."

Eunice touched her lips to his.

The day for George's departure approached relentlessly. Eunice thought briefly of kidnapping him, or in her words, rescuing him. It would be the end of her career at Lindell, or worse, if there were criminal charges. Maybe she could talk to the son, lay it on the line, beg him to let her care for his father for as long as he had left in the world. But approaching him would get her in trouble. Aides weren't supposed to reach out to family members. That was the job of the social workers. She could bring it up with one of the four on staff. In the end, her courage failed there, too.

Marlin Nash asked to meet with her on her next day off. Karen thought it was a good idea.

"When he hears how much you want to cooperate, he'll feel better," Karen said.

Eunice didn't care how Marlin felt.

But she put on her best outfit, a navy blue pantsuit with a blue and white striped scarf. She wanted to appear serious, in charge, someone to be respected.

He picked her up at Lindell. They went to lunch in College Town. Marlin looked around the wood-paneled, smoky room with distaste. He was in his mid-sixties, she guessed, and wore a three-piece suit, no doubt to intimidate her. He asked if she would care for a cocktail.

"Martini, very dry," she said. His mouth curled up on one side in an unmistakable smirk. He ordered one for each of them. Eunice had never tasted one before. She found it revolting, yet sipped it in a way she hoped would appear genteel and sophisticated.

Marlin looked like George—the same long face, blue eyes, and broad forehead. His manner wasn't at all the same, however. He was both domineering and furtive, as if he weren't entirely sure he was in control.

"I want to thank you for taking such good care of my father," he said.

"I'm not his only aide. Emily and Lulu are the others. I imagine you've met them?"

"You're the only one he talks about."

Emily and Lulu were both in their fifties—big, strong women with large, rough-skinned hands.

"He's a wonderful old gentleman," Eunice said. The gin had softened her voice too much, she thought. She was in danger of giving herself away.

Marlin didn't seem to have noticed. He was studying the plastic laminated menu. He put it face down on the table.

"You know he's dying," Marlin said.

"Yes. For a while now."

"We're bringing him home."

"I know that, too."

"He's putting up a hell of a fight. Didn't think the old guy had it in him."

Was that pride in his voice? Admiration? The light in his eyes said it was perhaps both.

"Then why not leave him alone?" Eunice asked.

"My sister won't have it. She needs him to die in her house."

Needs?

There was trouble between them years before, Marlin explained. His sister, Nadine, ran off with her college sweetheart. The guy was no good. Left her flat after only a month. The ink on the marriage license was barely dry. Of course, she was pregnant. Their father offered to help. She refused every bit of advice, guidance, and support. She even refused money.

"Sounds like a fiercely independent woman."

"She was a fool. She suffered. The child suffered."

In some way, Nadine blamed her father for everything, the way young women so often do.

Eunice didn't know what he was talking about. In her own life, it was her mother she blamed, never her father.

She married again. A good man, a solid man. He adopted the boy as his own. Yet Nadine always felt their father had driven her off, not been accepting enough of her. Really, it was the normal teenage stuff he'd objected to. He was never cruel about any of it. Even so, she punished him. She didn't visit often, didn't let him see the grandson. After their mother died, this absence was particularly painful. By then the boy, Benjamin, was in his twenties.

"It's hard to bring a young person that age into your life when you're an old man."

"So, she feels guilty," Eunice said. The drink had gone to her head. She felt loose and wobbly.

"Clearly."

She nodded solemnly. She wondered where the waiter had gone.

"Let me come to the point," Marlin said.

"Oh, please do."

"I—that is, we—want you to tell our dad to come home with us."

Eunice shook her head. Marlin reached into the pocket of his jacket, removed an envelope, and put it on the table in front of her.

"There's two thousand dollars in there," he said.

"You want to bribe me?"

"I want to bring my father home and have him be happy about it. As happy as he can be, at this stage of the game. If this will help you do the right thing, then it's yours for the taking."

Eunice stared at the envelope and thought about what it could mean. She cared deeply for George, but he didn't have that much more time.

Wait, what kind of person was she to even consider abandoning someone she loved?

Someone who's sick of being broke.

"Take a little time off. I'll speak to your supervisor. They can tell George you're sick," Marlin said.

"He'll worry if he hears that."

"No doubt you're correct. Then how about this? You have a family emergency. He'd accept that."

And love me even more for seeing how responsible and caring I am.

"I'm sorry, did I say something to upset you?" Marlin asked.

101

Eunice wiped her eyes.

"No, I'm fine, thanks."

They decided not to order any food, now that the matter had been cleared up.

Marlin drove Eunice back to Lindell. She sat in the passenger seat of his BMW, clutching her purse like the greedy cheater she was. She'd almost refused the money, then took it, just like that.

She said good-bye and walked around back where she'd left her car. Her head pounded from gin on an empty stomach. Someone had shoved a piece of paper under one of her wiper blades, asking her to stop by the reception desk before going home. She pulled herself together and walked back the way she'd come.

There was a note from Alice saying George had passed away only an hour before.

It was sudden, despite his condition, she wrote.

When had he gone? At the moment her hand touched the envelope? But that was nonsense. He didn't know anything about it.

George's room didn't stay vacant long. A tiny Italian woman moved into it. She had no use for Eunice, and never made small talk. Eunice was just as glad. She didn't want to spend a lot of time there.

Marlin never asked for the money back. Twice Eunice wrote out his address, obtained from Lindell, on a slightly larger envelope and slipped hers inside. She didn't seal it. She didn't even buy a stamp. Eventually she bought the Carmen Ghia its muffler, then sold the car to a collector for six thousand dollars with one condition—that he name the car George.

chapter fourteen

For her fortieth birthday, Eunice treated herself by signing up for a square dancing class at the Y. She was particularly blue. Her father had died the winter before from complications of emphysema, and her mother sang a very different tune. Suddenly, the old house she swore she'd never leave became oppressive. She begged Eunice to move back home. Eunice told her she was off her rocker. Soon after, her mother's home was foreclosed on. Apparently, they'd been behind on everything for years. She described the court proceeding with cheer, even a touch of gusto. What she admired most was how they dressed, the lawyers. Put together, you know? So calm and dignified. It gave some little proof that the world wasn't a complete mess. Eunice had some trouble with this disconnect. Rather than being furious over their role in removing her from her home, her mother was enchanted by their suits and ties.

When the sale went through, her mother took her savings, which consisted of three thousand dollars she'd gotten away from Eunice's father after his windfall, and rented an apartment downtown in a former high school that had been renovated. It happened to be the one where Eunice had suffered through four miserable years of social anxiety, in fact, and the one time she visited, she swore the tiny sitting room where her mother poured her a beer without asking if she wanted one was once the back half of her tenth grade geometry class. The view was the same: a stately Episcopal church on one side of the street, a small nicely-shaded park on the other. And the enormous elm was still there, though taller, and fuller in the trunk. Two of the branches formed a saddle that Eunice had often longed to sit in, above the world, unobserved.

The grief her mother expressed at the passing of Eunice's father seemed to be genuine.

"You're all I have left now," she said, quietly, then invited Eunice to join her weekly bingo game. For a moment, Eunice was tempted to accept, then realized that if she did, she might as well have one foot in the damn grave. Hence, the square dancing class.

The instructor was a tall, young man with stooped shoulders. His shoulder-length hair was thin on top. The frames of his glasses were heavy and black, held together across the bridge of his nose with adhesive tape. Despite all that, she found him madly attractive. His eyes got to her. They were so blue they bordered on lavender. Up to that moment, though she hadn't seen him since, Carson had still tugged at her heart. Now Carson was really and truly gone.

His name was Hamilton, Ham for short. He was twenty-six. It was clear that he didn't give her a second thought. When it was her turn to do-si-do, she kept trying to hold his hand, which the maneuver didn't call for.

One evening after class, she invited him to join her for a drink. As they sat in a booth in the back of the bar, Eunice with a schooner of amber ale, Ham nursed a cup of black coffee and explained why he'd given up alcohol. The year before, there'd been a terrible tragedy. Eleanor, his dog, had been killed. She was a cocker spaniel, young and eager, always straining forward. One night he took her for her usual walk after he'd had a few too many, and his grip on the leash wasn't tight enough. He let go. She raced into the road and got hit by a car. They'd been walking on a quiet road in the part of town where his mother still lived. It was late. That a car would come down it at that exact moment was uncanny. The driver wasn't a neighbor but someone leaving a Bible study session at a nearby home. He was a quiet little man, heartbroken over the dead animal. He gave Ham a blanket from the trunk of his car to put over Eleanor. Then he asked Ham if he'd like to pray. Ham took Eleanor and went home. Later all he could think about was how heavy she'd felt in his arms.

He had been punished by a higher authority, not God necessarily, but a spirit guide of some sort. Eunice had no idea what the hell he was talking about. It didn't matter really. With that keen light in his gorgeous eyes, and the pain in his voice, he could have been talking about the finer points of playing croquet, for all she cared.

"What got you into square dancing?" he asked.

"Oh, I don't know. Wanted to learn something different, I guess."

"Where do you work?"

"The Lindell Home."

104

"Cool."

He spooned more sugar into his coffee.

"How about you?" Eunice asked.

"Home Depot. I'm a cashier."

"Can you get me a discount?"

"On what?"

"Just kidding."

Then Ham said he had to be up early in the morning but that he'd love to get together again soon, outside of class. Maybe she'd like to come to his place next week for dinner?

Words failed her for a moment. Her heart glowed.

"You eat dinner, right?" he asked.

"What? Of course. I was just surprised."

"That I invited you?"

"Well, frankly, yes."

"Don't be. I'm supposed to."

"Supposed to what?"

"Meet new friends."

"Oh."

Ham smiled, and sipped his coffee. He returned the cup to the saucer.

"My therapist thinks it's a good idea," he said.

"Sure."

"You know, recovering from the thing with Eleanor."

"Right."

Ham asked if a week from Friday would work for her. She said it would. He gave her his address.

"Won't I see you in class before then?" she asked.

"Of course. But I didn't want to give you my address then. I mean, it might look weird with other people around."

At work, Eunice buttoned the front of Mrs. Moller's pink sweater and asked her why Ham didn't want the other students to know they were dating. Was he ashamed of her? Mrs. Moller pushed her hands away in annoyance. She didn't care for her sweater to be buttoned up, thank you.

Then she said, "Why did he invite you then, if he's ashamed?"

Eunice thought for a moment as she folded several nightgowns that had been returned from the Lindell laundry that morning.

"Maybe he thinks he'll get lucky, you know, and that's all he's after," she said.

Mrs. Moller looked up at Eunice with her brown eyes. Her wide, pink face gave her a commanding air.

"Forgive me for saying this, dear, but I don't think that's it at all. I mean, you're not unattractive by any means. You just need to fix yourself up a little."

Wasn't that the truth! For the last few years her closet had looked like the inside of a thrift store. She favored sweatshirts and turtlenecks in the fall and winter—brown, gray, or black, with black jeans. In summer, she wore tee-shirts in navy blue or forest green. The pants stayed black in hot weather but were a lighter weight. When she'd gone out with Ham, she wore her favorite sweatshirt. It was tan with pink flowers embroidered on the cuffs.

"How?" she asked.

"Makeup. Good makeup is the key."

"I see."

"I used to sell it, you know, down at Rothschild's."

Rothschild's department store was the anchor of the downtown commercial core. It wasn't as grand as it once had been, though. It was old-fashioned and fussy.

"That's how I met my husband. He was there looking for something for his sister, which I found both charming and odd because men don't know anything about makeup. I instructed him, naturally. His sister was blonde and fair, so I told him what sort of lipstick shades were best."

"Would you like me to—?"

"The one he picked was Cherry Blossom. 'Well, what do you know about that?' he said, holding it in his hand. And that silly hat of his. All rumpled in the back, as if he'd sat on it! His sister, Marjorie—she was my bridesmaid, you know, because I didn't really have any good girlfriends of my own at the time—wore that lipstick on our wedding day. Pretty as a picture, though of course, Martin—my husband—said she didn't hold a candle to me. Martin was a flatterer, all right, but he was always sincere at the same time. More of a sweet-talker, I'd say. Which was a real help when it came to business. He sold cars, you know. That was a lucky thing because I always got to drive the latest model. I remember this one time I banged up the fender of a brand new Buick, can't quite recall just how, maybe backed up too far trying to park; anyway, Martin said, 'Oh, honey, what's a fender compared to you? Doesn't make a bit of difference.' He was like that the whole fifty-three years we were married. Even at the end, when he was, you know, on the way out.

Said he didn't need any angels where he was going, on account of having had one at his side all along."

Mrs. Moller fell silent. That long sweep of time passed over her face. Her eyes were misty. Eunice had long known that old people kept all sorts of things alive inside themselves, and sometimes, those things just had to come out.

Eunice put Mrs. Moller's nightgowns away and left.

For the dinner with Ham, she bought a pale green sweater. Though she hadn't worn it for a long time, the color still suited her. The sales clerk asked what color eye shadow Eunice normally wore. Eunice never wore eye shadow, even back in the days of tearing around in her Carmen Ghia. The sales clerk complimented Eunice's fair skin and red hair and suggested that she could go pretty bold. Eunice went to the drugstore in the mall several doors down from the clothing store and stood a long time in the makeup section. She chose a hue quite close to the sweater's shade.

Ham's neighborhood was just as he'd described, quiet and stately. It was in the part of town where the better set lived. Professors, lawyers, doctors. He must have gotten a good deal on a rental or else was housesitting, probably for someone connected with the university. Some of them retired at Lindell. Eunice had learned that they often took time off to go abroad and study and needed someone in the place for a few months.

Eunice parked her car on the street, although the curved driveway was vacant. As she got out of the car, she realized that the eye shadow made her lids itch. She tended to react aggressively to any sort of irritation and assumed that before long, her eyes would swell. Even so, she took a risk and didn't wipe the shadow off. She loved the way it looked on her, and she was going to go for broke.

The walk was made of flagstone. The whole yard was tastefully landscaped and well maintained. Eunice thought briefly of her lost fortune. She had trained herself to move on quickly every time the memory occurred. She rang the bell. The door was opened by an elegant gray-haired woman in a long, lavender silk dress. At least, Eunice assumed that it was silk. The woman didn't look like the kind to wear polyester.

"You must be Eunice. Won't you please come in?"

The sound of classical music flowed from an interior room.

The woman, who stood a good head taller than Eunice, took the bottle of wine Eunice had brought and said, "I'm Hamilton's mother. Such a pleasure to finally meet you."

"His mother?"

"Yes. From your expression, it's clear he didn't mention that he still lived at home."

"No."

"I'm Eleanor, by the way."

"Like the dog."

Eleanor looked confused.

"The one that died," Eunice said.

"Hamilton never owned a dog. He's allergic to animals."

Eleanor led Eunice into a large living room. A grand piano stood in one corner, next to a pair of tall, wide windows that looked out into the yard. The dim outlines of trees could still be seen. Full night was over an hour away. On one wall were floor to ceiling bookshelves. The sight of so many titles made Eunice feel like she was back in school. More books were stacked on the coffee table, the closed lid of the piano, and a glass-topped side table. Ham hadn't struck her as much of a reader. Then she realized these were the mother's books.

"You must be a teacher," Eunice said.

"A professor."

"Oh."

"Economics."

"Money and stuff?"

"Yes."

Eleanor invited Eunice to sit down. Eunice sat. Eleanor offered her something to drink.

"Sure. What do you have?" Eunice asked.

"Everything, really. Except maybe mango juice. Hamilton can't stand mango juice."

"Beer?"

Eleanor stood still. Clearly, she hadn't expected to be asked for beer.

"Or, wine is fine," Eunice said.

"I'll just open what you brought, if you don't mind."

"What it's here for, right?"

Eleanor left the room, bottle in hand. Eunice heard her go down a hall, then into another room, no doubt the kitchen. A drawer opened. Eunice considering bolting out into the night, like the imaginary dog. Ham's miserable face came back to her as he told the story, trying so hard to be brave.

Eleanor returned with two wine glasses in one hand and the uncorked bottle in the other. She put everything on the coffee table in front of Eunice, on which glossy magazines had been neatly arrayed. *The Atlantic Monthly, The Economist, Harper's,* the same stuff that was in the reception area at Lindell.

As they sipped their wine, Eleanor seemed to relax. Her face softened. She leaned back comfortably in her wing-backed chair. Different music played then, still classical, but newer, more modern.

"Is Ham running late?" Eunice asked.

"It's just you and me this evening. This is our chance to spend a little time together and get to know each other."

"I see."

Eleanor's soft gaze grew tight, focused.

"He's quite smitten with you, you know. I can't tell you how long I've been hoping that someone older, wiser, would come along and take him under her wing."

Eunice put her glass of wine on the coffee table.

"Look, Eleanor, I think maybe you got the wrong idea about me and Ham. We're really just friends, see? Nothing more."

"You're taken with him, too, I can tell."

What would Grandma Grace say about this poor woman, playing matchmaker for her son?

Pathetic feeb.

"Let me be clear. Hamilton hasn't been well for a while. He had a breakdown a few years ago. He was in love with a woman, and she spurned him, plain and simple. It happens to young men all the time. But Hamilton is quite sensitive. He just couldn't stand the rejection, poor thing," Eleanor said.

Her eyes teared up. She didn't look like she was acting.

"Go on," Eunice said.

"He tried to kill himself."

"Wow."

"Yeah, wow."

Eleanor drank some wine. Eunice did, too.

"It was my fault, for not holding on to his father," Eleanor said.

Her ex-husband was a research scientist there at the university, she said. He fell in love with one of his lab assistants. He didn't ask Eleanor for a divorce, hoping that she'd be "modern" in her thinking.

"It's what people used to call an 'open marriage.' Very popular back in the Seventies."

Eunice helped herself to another glass of wine.

"I told him to get out. Hamilton was only five at the time. He kept asking when Daddy was coming home."

Eleanor put her glass down. She'd only had a little of it. Her eyes were troubled.

"You know, sometimes I believe he hates me. That sounds dire, I know. But, consider that he named an imaginary dog after me. An imaginary dog who died an imaginary death, apparently," she said.

She picked up her glass and held it without drinking.

"But he knows the truth about his father, that he was the one who broke things up, right?" Eunice asked.

"Truth doesn't matter much to a young person in pain."

"No, maybe not."

Eunice wiped her sweaty palms on her blue jeans. Her eyelids itched. The skin under the sweater itched. She wished she'd worn something else. She wished Ham had shown up. She wished she'd eaten more today. She was starving.

"I'll come to the point. I want you to take care of Ham. I don't mean have him move in with you. I mean take an interest in him, spend time with him, build up his confidence. He likes to square dance, obviously. He also loves going to the movies. And the theater. Bring him down to the City; take in a few shows. I'll pay for it. I'll pay for everything," Eleanor said.

Eleanor excused herself for a moment, and returned with a silver tray loaded with cheese and crackers. She began munching, then noticed that Eunice wasn't.

"Won't you have anything, dear?" she asked.

"Oh, no thanks. I'm fine until dinner."

Eleanor looked confused again.

"Aren't we having dinner?" Eunice asked.

"Well, no, actually. Ham invited you for drinks, didn't he?"

"He said dinner. Doesn't matter."

Eleanor shook her head. "That child never could distinguish between the

110

cocktail hour and the dinner hour. Probably because he doesn't drink."

"He did drink, though."

"What? No, never, not to my knowledge."

Eunice pressed a piece of gooey cheese onto a tiny square cracker and popped the whole thing in her mouth. It was delicious. She had several more. Her appetite faded. She was suffused with a growing sense of well-being. Then she recalled the situation at hand.

"Look, I'm all for hanging out with Ham, but let's just see how things go, okay? I mean, he might change his mind; I might change my mind. You know," she said.

Eleanor wiped her lips with her napkin.

"Now you have cold feet," she said.

"Well, a little, yes. See, I'm sorta used to making my own arrangements, as it were."

"Ham told me you had an independent spirit."

"I wouldn't say that. It's just I like to decide for myself when it's time to make a move."

As Eunice reflected on the moves she'd made, she had the rotten idea that maybe the best part of her life was already behind her. If that were true, that meant there wasn't a whole hell of a lot to look forward to.

"What's the matter, dear?" Eleanor asked.

"Nothing."

The silence went on. Both women felt uncomfortable.

"I should get going. It's been great, really," Eunice said.

She was out the door by the time Eleanor had put down her glass of wine and gotten to her feet.

chapter fifteen

After Eunice quit the square-dancing class, she enrolled in a fiber arts workshop.

She sat at a loom and ran the shuttle back and forth. At first, she could do no more than handle two colors—one for the warp, one for the weft. Her warp threads were never taut enough, and the entire blanket or throw tended to sag. Her back also ached. Weaving didn't seem like a good idea.

But she made a friend. Moonshine. That wasn't her given name, she explained. She'd been born Debra and came to hate it early on.

"My mother was one of the ultra-traditional conservative types. You know. Church on Sunday. No swearing allowed. Liquor was Devil's work," she said over a large mug of herbal tea.

"Polar opposite of my mother."

"You're lucky."

"Hell, you say. My mother drank till she stank."

"Great phrase! Though maybe not so much the truth behind it."

Moonshine's long black hair was kinky, out of control—a wild, extravagant mess. She wore ankle-length cotton skirts and peasant blouses. Their puffed sleeves gave her an extra touch of whimsy.

She lived in a small wooden house at the edge of campus, overlooking a ravine at the bottom of which ran a clear creek that had yielded a number of treasures. She displayed these on a wooden shelf in her kitchen: the head of a china doll, the crystal stem of a broken wine glass, and a ballet slipper that a child must have worn, given how small it was. Eunice was curious about that creek and decided to take a look one of these days.

Aside from weaving, Moonshine did all sorts of other handcrafts. She quilted, knit, and embroidered. Once, she'd learned how to blow glass at an arts school in North Carolina. The fine arts didn't particularly appeal to her, she said, which surprised Eunice. A stunning little watercolor of one of

Dunston's gorges hung shyly on the wall with Moonshine's signature in the lower right corner. Standing before it, Eunice could hear the water rush, feel its delicate spray. She couldn't believe Moonshine didn't value what a gift she had.

"It's a matter of what makes me happiest," she said. Tea had been cleared away. Two glasses now held Chardonnay. The summer afternoon filled the room with a light as golden and sweet as the wine itself.

"And it's not watercolors," Eunice said.

"My hands need to move more."

"Makes sense."

"I mean, you can't paint well with busy hands."

"Suppose not."

"I guess I like building things, in a way."

Moonshine looked thoughtful, as if this idea had never occurred to her before. Eunice drank. She enjoyed the wine.

"I'm too clumsy to make anything," she said.

"Just takes practice."

Moonshine worked in an arts cooperative on the downtown Commons that sold her stuff and other artists' too. She had big plans for that store. For one thing, she wanted to buy it and enlarge the space. The problem was being broke.

"Really? What about this house?"

"My ex's."

"I didn't know you'd been married."

"Married, kids, the whole thing."

The boys had chosen to stay with their father, Moonshine said, which was just as well, because her ex thought she was an unfit mother.

"Why?" Eunice asked.

"Pot."

"Oh."

"As in, smoking."

The mention of pot reminded Eunice of Carson. She'd seen him just the other day, driving by with a woman next to him. He'd had one hand on the wheel and his free arm around her.

Moonshine looked out over the ravine. They were on the deck, with trees everywhere. It was like being suspended in a green tapestry, safe and secure.

"What's your ex do?" Eunice asked.

"Lawyer. Chief Counsel for the university."

"Good money."

"It is. That's why I have this house."

"You lived here, with your family?"

"Oh, no. We had a place over in the Heights. He still lives there. This was just an investment—a rental property. We had some weird tenants over the years. One of them left an upside down cross on the bedroom wall. Another one broke a bunch of windows. A real pain to get those all replaced. Anyway, when things went south with us, I moved in."

"So, what happened, if you don't mind my asking?"

It was the usual story, Moonshine said. They were married too young; she didn't take to being wifey, keeping the house and cooking the meals. She was restless, sometimes desperate. Her husband didn't understand why she wasn't satisfied when he'd given her everything she'd asked for. She explained that her wants had changed. She loved her boys; that was never the problem. She just felt like they were sucking the life out of her, like she couldn't breathe. She had turned into a cornered animal, fighting for survival.

"Like a lioness about to eat her own cubs," she said.

She never thought she'd do them any actual harm, but she knew something had to give. So, she smoked a lot of pot and calmed down. Then hubby found her stash and freaked. They were heading toward a breakup anyway, pot or no pot. Seems there was also this young law student, and well, Eunice could guess the rest.

"And when did all this happen?" Eunice asked.

"Eight years ago. Boys are grown up, at this point. They like me a little more than they used to, no thanks to their father. I suppose I shouldn't be too hard on him, though. He's got problems of his own. The law student's a little loose with her credit cards. He had to take them away from her, apparently."

"You still smoke?"

"Not for a long time."

The irony, Moonshine said, was that she lost her boys because she smoked pot, and once they weren't her responsibility anymore, she didn't need it. She spoke calmly, warmly, as if praising the splendor of someone's garden. Only the pause before speaking the last few words showed that it still hurt.

"When did you change your name?" Eunice asked.

114

"Years ago. Before I was married."

"Huh."

"You're thinking that if a stuffed shirt like my husband was willing to take on someone named Moonshine, he shouldn't have been surprised at anything."

"Something like that."

The breeze came up. It held the scent of water and fresh earth. Eunice enjoyed a rare sense of hope, which quickly passed.

Moonshine continued talking about buying the arts store. She needed investors. No one would have to put in more than they could afford. What did Eunice think?

"You asking me to contribute?"

"No! I was asking if the idea made sense to you."

Eunice explained about losing her inheritance to Baxter Bain years before and why money was always a sore subject.

"I should marry a rich guy," she said. Until that moment, the thought had never actually occurred to her.

"That's what I did. Look how it all turned out."

"We wouldn't have kids."

"You might regret that."

"I'm too old, anyway."

"How old are you?"

"Forty-one."

"Me, too!"

For a moment, Eunice considered what Moonshine had experienced that she hadn't, in the same span of time.

Moonshine suggested they move inside for a while. She felt like crafting. Eunice wasn't sure she should stay, not that she had to be anywhere. It was Saturday. She usually cleaned house on Saturday.

To hell with cleaning house.

Moonshine was making a quilt. She had the pieces all cut into small octagons and spread out on the floor of the small room she used as her studio. She asked Eunice to sort the pieces by color. The fabric was sometimes patterned with leaves, sometimes one solid color, primarily blues and purples with just a few that were tones of ruby red. Moonshine sat in a shabby chair upholstered in a soft green fabric and worked her needle swiftly. Her moving hands seemed to loosen something within, and she spoke much more easily than when they'd been sitting side by side, gazing into the trees.

Everyone knew that women got a raw deal, she said. Just being born female put you many rungs down on the ladder. She'd tried to instill in her two sons the idea of parity so they'd grow up to be fair minded, seeking an equality of spirit with the female sex. She was pretty sure she'd failed. How could she make them see that women were just as important when in their very own household that clearly wasn't the case? The ditzy law student—second wife—didn't help. Moonshine's ex treated her like a little girl, which psychologically she probably was. Reflecting on her own marriage, it was only when she'd gotten her feet under her emotionally that her husband wanted out, pot or no pot. He had to call the shots, and wasn't that a typically male thing?

Moonshine was absolutely certain that her own mother's insane piety was really just another form of female subservience. Had Eunice ever noticed how all major religions treated women like dogs? Well, okay, maybe not *that* bad, but women were always behind the men. And what was this nonsense with Muslim women having to cover their bodies for fear that some random male would suddenly be aflame with uncontrollable lust?

The trouble was good old Mother Nature. Women got pregnant. Men didn't. That explained it all, really. Women were vulnerable in the sex act, men weren't. Until birth control, women were slaves to biology. And ever since the pill became widely available, men had tried to keep women firmly in their place. Oh, she knew it sounded like radical feminism, and maybe it was. But honestly, why couldn't men just chill out and let women decide when—and if—they wanted children.

Thank God her husband had left that decision squarely up to her. And what that decision came down to, because she was a pretty dumb bitch at the time, was not getting an abortion after learning she was pregnant. She knew all about birth control and hadn't bothered. She supposed she was setting herself up, backing herself into a corner. Not that she *didn't* want children, mind you, she just hadn't thought it through.

Eunice handed Moonshine the pieces she pointed to.

"Babies are cute," she said.

Moonshine stopped sewing for a moment. She looked at Eunice, trying to see inside her.

"It's just that someone brought a baby into Lindell the other day. Someone's great-granddaughter. All the residents—the ones who can still get

116

around, that is—wanted a look."

Moonshine nodded, once more bent over the fabric.

The baby had these huge brown eyes, Eunice said. She'd gotten so used to the eyes of old people. So many had thin white bands around the iris—cataracts, maybe? But this baby, the whites of her eyes were flawless, like a pearl or something. Eunice guessed that what she found so weird was figuring that transit—from flawless to old and messed up. Once, when she was young, she looked at the backs of her own small hands, and how smooth they were; compared them to her grandmother's hands, which were bumpy and veined, with brown spots, too; and thought there was no way that her hands would *ever* look like that. But now, she could see the veins distending beneath the surface of her skin just a little, and in time, that would only get worse.

"Getting old has to suck," Moonshine said.

"Beats the alternative."

Again, Moonshine studied her. Then she laughed.

chapter sixteen

Eunice's mother wondered if she should look into Lindell. Living there would be very convenient in times of need. She'd twisted her ankle. Eunice had had to buy groceries for her, tote her laundry down to the basement of the apartment building, wait for all the various cycles to complete, fold everything—even the sheets, although they were just going back on the same bed—then bring the heavy basket upstairs, and put everything away. It was a pain in the ass. She told her mother so.

"Well, it's not like I twisted the damned thing on purpose," she said.

By then her hair was completely gray. She'd had it cut short, which made her look either fierce or weary, depending on her mood.

"In a place like Lindell, there are always people around to help. And don't worry, I'd suggest they assign me someone else, to spare you any embarrassment," she said.

Eunice sat down at the little kitchen table, which for some reason her mother had covered with a piece of lace cloth. Coffee stains were numerous, also dried egg yolk. Her mother had developed a fondness for eggs, and cooked them in the middle of the night when she couldn't sleep.

"It's expensive. You can't afford it," Eunice said. She knew this from overhearing the residents and their family members talk about financial matters in front of her, as if she were invisible or deaf.

"You're just saying that."

"Check for yourself then."

Her mother's exhausted expression said she'd already looked into the matter and was just hoping for some magical solution. Eunice considered this change in her character. She used to be a fairly practical person, when she wasn't drinking, that is. But the drinking, too, had gone by the wayside, which Eunice found more perplexing that anything else.

"You're on the wagon again, aren't you?" Eunice asked.

"Says who?"

"I haven't had to hit the liquor store since you got laid up."

Her mother fixed her with an appraising stare.

"How long has it been this time?" Eunice asked.

"Four months."

Eunice whistled. That broke all previous records.

"Why did you?" she asked.

"Got bored with it."

Eunice learned the truth later, on another visit, when her mother introduced her to a neighbor, Jean. Jean was about her mother's age, mid-seventies or so, even more slightly built than Eunice. Her right hand was missing the thumb and forefinger, yet she was quite deft when it came to both pouring out coffee and drinking it from a cup. She wore her hair in a bun. Sometimes she would remove the pins and rearrange it a little more tightly on the top of her head. She managed this task as easily as if she had all ten fingers.

Jean was a Jehovah's Witness. She told Eunice so the moment they met, as if it were the most important thing that could be known about her. Eunice didn't care what she was, as long as she kept her zeal to herself, which of course she couldn't. In less than an hour, Jean had suggested to Eunice at least four times that she read the literature that her own dear mother had grown so fond of. Eunice knew right then that she wouldn't be visiting her mother too often in the future, for fear of being lobbied. Jean moved on from her beloved pamphlets to praise Eunice's mother for having found a positive and healthy lifestyle. When she said this, Eunice's mother didn't look proud or at peace, just vexed.

Eunice now understood the equation. Her mother wanted company, and Jean was the best she could get. Jean wouldn't tolerate drinking, so her mother gave in and quit.

She must be really lonely.

For a moment, she felt guilty. Then she remembered growing up. The guilt vanished.

Her mother called the following week and asked when Eunice could swing by. The carpet needed vacuuming. Eunice suggested that her mother ask Jean to do it. Eunice's mother hung up without saying good-bye.

The first snow of the season was early that year, and it took Eunice a long time to get home from Lindell. The pilot light in her trailer's wall unit had gone out again. Lighting it was hard because she'd run through the extra-long matches she kept for just that purpose. She took a piece of newspaper, twisted it into a long thing taper, and held it to the flame on her stove. Then she cupped her palm around the barely burning end, pushed it into the far back of the heater where the idiots who had designed the thing had thought to put the most essential part, and pressed the button that let the gas flow.

Better not go boom!

After four tries, the gas ignited, and warm air began to blow. She knew the heater wouldn't last the winter, so she opened the phone book and looked up places that sold used furnaces. She found the only one.

When she picked up the phone to dial the number, she saw that the message light on her answering machine was blinking. The first message was from Moonshine, wanting to know if she wanted to go sledding. Eunice hadn't pulled a sled since she was about ten, well over thirty years before. She hadn't enjoyed it much. She'd gone with a schoolmate, Mary something. Mary was bossy and had the whole system laid out. Eunice was to give the final shove downhill, and then jump on at the last moment. Only Eunice didn't make it onto the sled, which was unfortunate because Mary couldn't steer the thing to save her life and ended up in the narrow creek at the bottom of the hill, freezing, soaked, and furious. It might be fun, though, to go again and see what it felt like now.

The second message was from her mother. She was giving up the apartment and moving to a house in the country with Jean and Jean's daughter.

"They've agreed to take me in. Isn't that just beautiful?"

Good luck with that.

Winter deepened. Snow fell hard. Sometimes Eunice stayed over at Lindell in one of the guest rooms. Normally these were for family members from out of town, though staff on late shifts were welcome to them too. Eunice liked being away from home, even though the comfort level in the trailer had come up a notch. She'd had the wall unit replaced by a guy she'd known in elementary school, Billy Simms. He asked her out. She said she didn't know he'd gotten divorced.

"Who says I'm divorced?"

She gave him his check and told him to get lost. The landlord took three weeks to reimburse her. He said she should have called him first. Eunice didn't see what the difference was. The damn thing was broken, and now it wasn't.

The day after Thanksgiving, three feet of snow fell. Eunice tossed her things in a backpack, persuaded her car to start after a few slow cranks, and crawled up the hill to Lindell. The staff was taxed. The residents were restless. The deepening drifts seemed to make them uneasy. Eunice thought they might get the sense of being buried, which naturally would be unsettling, given how close to death they all were. Most lay open-eyed in bed. Those who were still mobile turned their wheelchairs to the window to watch the snow until it was too dark to see.

Eunice finished her rounds, heated up the casserole she'd brought in the microwave, and read a magazine alone in the kitchen. She was soon joined by Dean, one of the maintenance crew. He came in wearing a heavy jacket and insulated boots. He stamped his feet, leaving two small piles of snow on the floor. He took off his gloves, draped the coat on the back of the chair next to Eunice's, and poured himself a cup of coffee. He had a sip.

"Tastes like crap," he said.

"That's because it's been sitting there since dinner."

Dean took the filter out of the pot and threw it away. He obviously didn't know what to do next, so Eunice told him to sit down while she took care of it. When the coffee was ready, she poured him a cup.

She resumed eating. The food was lukewarm, but she kept on. Cold weather always made her hungry. She finished her meal, washed her bowl, dried it, and set it down on the table. Dean was staring into space.

"Something wrong?" Eunice asked.

"Woman trouble."

"Huh."

Eunice once again took her seat.

"You don't want to hear this," Dean said.

"Sure I do. Besides, it's not like I got somewhere to go."

"You holing up?"

"Yup."

"How's that?"

"Way better than driving through a blizzard."

"It would creep me out, staying here all night."

"Why? You spend most of it sleeping."

Dean considered the logic of this statement. His eyes were sad.

121

"Aren't you going to get stuck if you wait much longer?" Eunice asked.

"Nah. Got a four-wheel drive with chains."

He looked at his watch. He removed a comb from the pocket of his flannel shirt and pulled it through his sandy hair. His gesture was slow, meticulous, and not at all fussy. He put the comb back in his pocket. The walk-in refrigerator cycled on. Sometimes at night, the whole building felt like a warm, sleeping animal making regular, comfortable sounds.

"She says it's all my fault," Dean said.

"Your wife?"

"Yes."

Dean wore a wedding ring. It hadn't been much of a stretch.

"She says I'm smothering her," he said.

"Not literally, I assume."

Dean looked at her. He didn't smile.

"Holding her back, she says. Not letting her fulfill her dream."

"Which is?"

"Hell if I know. I don't think she knows either."

Eunice wondered what her own dreams had ever been. To get away. To find her own voice. To be loved. It all sounded so simple. Why did it feel so hard then?

"She must have some idea," Eunice said.

"She was an artist when I met her. Sculptor. Made these little faces that weren't quite human. She rented space from this guy way the hell out in the country, used his kiln. He let her live there. Some weird stuff happened between them, I don't know. She ended up pretty freaked out. Wanted me to take care of her, protect her. So, I did. I would have anyway, even if she hadn't asked me to. That's a man's job, a husband's job."

"And now?"

"I guess she doesn't need to be protected anymore."

"What about love?"

"Exactly."

Something clanged behind them. Maybe the range cooling off after being on for hours all day.

"She still sculpt?" Eunice asked.

"No. She works at K-Mart. Hates it."

"But needs the money."

He nodded.

"She can still do her own thing, in her free time."

"Not to hear her tell it."

"Hm."

Lillian Gish would have found a way. She was no quitter, no complainer. Eunice hadn't thought of her in a long time. All her life she'd wanted to possess her fire and determination. Sometimes she had.

"You like silent movies?" Eunice asked.

The sudden lift of his eyebrows said she might as well have asked if he liked star anise or pickled pigs feet.

"The university sometimes has a festival where they show two or three in a row. It's sort of fun. Take your wife one night. She might like seeing people fight without words. Well, not heard words, anyway."

Dean lifted his head. He looked over Eunice's right shoulder, as if the stackable stainless steel cart behind her held a bag of gold.

"You're smart," he said.

"How so?"

"You got my wife's number. She's a brooder, not a screamer."

"Clams up?"

"Says, 'If you don't know what you did, I'm sure as shit not going to tell you.'"

"Sounds like my mother."

"I feel for your dad."

"He's dead."

"Then I feel for you."

Dean watched her closely. Eunice let a certain thought cross her mind. Lillian would have looked away shyly, then back again, full force.

Those eyes of hers! If only I had those eyes!

But, she didn't. At the moment, her eyes felt empty. Dean must have seen that, too.

He pushed up his sleeve to check his watch, then stood up and said good-night. He left his coffee cup on the table.

chapter seventeen

Moonshine was desperate. The damn cat had given birth to six kittens. She had to get rid of them. The cat wasn't even hers in the first place.

"Just wandered in and stayed. I suppose I shouldn't have let her. I didn't know she was pregnant, but that's probably why she was looking for a home, right?"

Eunice didn't know anything about cats. She'd never owned a pet. She'd begged her parents for a pet rabbit once when she was about ten. Her mother made quick work of that desire when she said Eunice would wake up one morning and find it dead. Whether her mother was suggesting that she would kill it herself or that rabbits just didn't live very long, Eunice never knew.

Of course she agreed to take one, a tiny orange female she named Lillian. The routine vet bills were expensive, but she got a discount by going to the clinic run by the university. She didn't like leaving Lillian alone during the day but had no choice. She bought her a scratching post she studiously ignored, preferring to sharpen her claws on the upholstery. The sight of her frayed fabric was depressing. She got good at finding cheap slip covers to put over her sofa and easy chair, and changed them routinely.

Then there was the matter of the litter box. She cleaned it every day, sometimes twice a day, but Lillian was prolific. She was a sweet, healthy cat who seemed to adore Eunice. She slept in her bed, on her very pillow, and would knead Eunice's long hair and purr into the early morning hours. Eunice loved it. She felt connected to Lillian in a way she'd never really felt toward another human being. She supposed it was a survival skill on the part of cats to make people love them, a skill Eunice had to admit she herself sadly lacked.

The vet advised her to keep Lillian inside all the time.

"Cats live longer that way. Mother nature is full of peril."

He was young, probably just out of school, and his poetic turn of phrase made Eunice anxious. She imagined the crushed carcass of Lillian under the car wheels of a careless driver or gripped in the jaw of a huge, savaging dog.

Lillian had other ideas. She dashed out the door when Eunice was bringing in groceries. Eunice saw her furry hind end vanish through the low hedge separating her trailer from the one next door. The escape didn't last long, because it was still winter and bitterly cold. Within minutes Lillian was meowing pitifully below the kitchen window where Eunice was frying chicken for their dinner, though the vet had cautioned against feeding her "people food."

As the weather warmed, Lillian's illicit forays grew more frequent and lasted longer. Sometimes Eunice just left out an open can of cat food to lure her home. She'd reappear faithfully after a couple of days.

"You need to get that cat spayed, or you'll end up in the same fix I was," Moonshine said. She'd given away all but one of the kittens, whom she'd just had neutered. The vet clinic was so committed to controlling the pet population in Dunston that it offered to do the surgery for free.

Eunice took three days off from work to stay with Lillian afterward. She didn't need to. Lillian's spirits were as fine as ever. The worst part seemed to be wearing the plastic cone around her neck to prevent her from disturbing the few stiches in her stomach. Eunice sat with her and ran the tip of her finger along the smooth skin where the fur had been shaved. Lillian purred madly, and when Eunice lay down, wrapped herself up in her hair.

The day the cone came off, Lillian disappeared. Eunice didn't even know when she'd had the door open long enough for her to slip out. The usual cat food can didn't bring her back. Nor did standing by the door calling her name until one of her neighbors drove by and gave her the finger. She canvassed the park. No one had seen her. Many of the residents had dogs, which meant Lillian would steer clear of those particular trailers. The last one, closest to the water and surrounded by elegant weeping willows, was where Lillian had decided to hole up. The occupant was a twenty-something graduate student in photography. Her arms and legs, even her neck, were heavily tattooed.

She introduced herself as Betty Boop, then explained that she'd had a fascination for old cartoons when she was little. Her real name was Melanie, after the character in *Gone with the Wind*.

"I always thought if my mother wanted a name from the book, she could have named me Rhett," she said.

"Not Scarlett?"

"No way. I always hated that bitch. Nothing but a cock tease."

Betty had taken Lillian in more than once, she confessed. She seemed so happy to be there. And Eunice could see how much pleasure Lillian took in stretching out on Betty's spotless kitchen floor, in a band of afternoon sun.

"I didn't know who her owner was. She doesn't wear a collar. Did you get her microchipped?" Betty asked.

Eunice didn't know what that was.

"They do it the vet's office. Slide a little computer chip with your name and number under the skin. You find a stray animal, you take them in and they can scan it right there."

"Huh."

Betty offered her some coffee. Eunice didn't care for any just then.

"How about a beer?" Betty asked.

"Sure."

Betty's trailer was as exotic as she was. One wall held a number of open Japanese fans; a pink scarf was draped over a table lamp; a small wooden desk with carved feet sat under the window, its surface crowded with notebooks and photographs all in black and white; three large, complicated cameras occupied the shelves of a bookcase in the kitchen next to the refrigerator. The kitchen table was decorated with woven placemats. In the center was a ceramic bowl full of apples. Betty and Eunice drank their beers in the living room, on opposite ends of a blue velvet couch. Lillian occupied the middle and carefully cleaned her paws.

"I was never really a cat person before," Betty said.

"Me either. She's my first."

"Why 'Lillian?'"

"Lillian Gish."

"No way! You like silent movies?"

"I used to."

"I like anything that's old. Especially clothes."

Eunice laughed. She was feeling the beer. She explained that she worked at Lindell, a place Betty should check out if she liked old things. Well, old people. Betty wanted to take her cameras up there and take some pictures.

"You know, portraits," she said.

"Huh."

"Would they go for it, do you think?"

Eunice said she could ask.

"Tell them it's part of my thesis," Betty said.

"Lots of retired professors there. Might work."

Eunice collected Lillian and went home.

Alice said introducing a stranger to the residents was always difficult. The residents who still had their wits had trouble with new faces. And those that didn't obviously wouldn't care, but it didn't seem right to put them on display like that. It felt exploitative. Did Eunice see her point?

Not really, but Betty did. She was disappointed, though. She needed interesting human subjects. She'd photographed her fellow students, their friends, her friends—she even had a shot of Lillian looking out the window. She said the intent look on her face made her almost human.

Betty was dressed that day in a floral chiffon dress from the 1930's. She found it at a vintage shop downtown. Eunice suggested that she wear her hair in a matching style, with soft waves around the face. Betty's hair was dyed jet black and as straight as if she'd ironed it. Eunice thought mournfully of her thick, wavy mess, now streaked with gray. She ran her hand fretfully through it.

"Why don't you cut it?" Betty asked.

"Nah."

"I can do it for you."

"You know how?"

"I quit beauty school to go to college."

The idea, Betty said, was to cut the hair in a bob, then put Eunice in a twenties flapper dress and set her up before the camera. She'd wash the plates with sepia, to recreate the era better.

"You've got a good figure for your age," Betty said. Eunice hadn't said how old she was. Side by side, gawking in the small bathroom mirror above the tiny rose-colored sink, it must have been clear that there were at least twenty years between them. Betty was smooth under the eyes. Eunice was puffy. The flesh on Betty's jaw was firm. Eunice's wasn't.

The bob didn't turn out all that well, but Eunice pretended she thought it was spectacular. For one thing, it was longer on one side than on the other. Her felt head felt uncomfortably light. She told herself she'd get used to it. She looked at the mass at her feet and remembered the brighter curls on that black and white bathroom floor years before.

The dress Betty had chosen for Eunice was one she liked to wear herself when she was feeling particularly "jazz age." It fell to the floor when Eunice put it on. Betty was a lot taller. She said it didn't matter, because the portrait would be just her head and torso. She draped a long string of fake pearls over Eunice's neck and clipped one side of her hair with a rhinestone barrette. She put dark red lipstick on her lips, even though the picture would be in black and white.

"You'll look washed out without it," she said.

Betty moved a stool from the kitchen into the living room. She set up a lightbox she'd had in the closet, and tilted it this way and that until the amount of light that fell on Eunice's face satisfied her.

After only a few minutes, Eunice tired of sitting still and turning her head a little this way and a little back that way. Betty shot frame after frame and talked the whole time.

"Beautiful. That's right. Let all that inner light shine! Now, be mysterious. You're hiding a secret, and you want very badly to tell it. You promised not to, and it's absolutely killing you! Okay, now let's change it up. Look sad, stricken. The love of your life has gone away, never to return. You simply can't go on. Your heart has crumbled to a million little pieces."

Try as she might, Eunice suspected that her expression remained just the same. She'd gotten too good at hiding what she felt. Was it working with the elderly that had caused that? Or did it happened before, when she was a child and wanted to avoid sparking her mother's wrath?

"Perfect! A look of utter despair! I love it!" Betty said.

Lillian scratched madly at the door. Betty lowered her camera.

"Coming, my little love," she cooed and let her in. Lillian rubbed herself along Betty's legs, and arched her back when Betty leaned down to stroke her.

"She really likes you," Eunice said.

"We're the dearest of friends."

Lillian looked up at Eunice. Her tail brushed.

"She's not used to seeing you like that. I think you startled her a little," Betty said.

"Maybe so."

"Anyway, you look like you could use a break."

Eunice stretched. She moved to get down off the stool. Betty bent down, and put her lips firmly on Eunice's. She pushed her tongue in. While Eunice was processing the situation, and not really believing any of it, Betty picked up Eunice's hand and pressed it to her breast. Eunice had never felt another woman's breast. It was deliciously soft. So were Betty's lips. Eunice bolted off the stool and stepped back.

"We could make a good team, you know. We even have our mascot," Betty said.

"I think you've got the wrong idea."

"Oh, no I don't. I can always tell."

"I'm too old for you."

"Bull."

"Then you're too young for me."

Eunice went into Betty's room to change, hoping to hell she wouldn't follow and push the point. She didn't. Eunice left the clip, dress, and pearls on the bed. She rubbed off the lipstick with the back of her hand.

"I'm sorry," she said when she came into the living room.

"It's okay. It happens." Betty didn't sound all that crushed.

She's used to it.

Eunice looked at Lillian, stretched out on the couch.

"She's happier with you," she said.

Then she went home and packed up the balance of the uneaten cat food and Lillian's bowl, and left them on Betty's stairs.

chapter eighteen

Turning fifty didn't rattle Eunice as much as she thought it would. She figured she was pretty good at handling milestones by now.

Her mother, then in her eighties, had developed crippling arthritis and a severe loss of mobility. She still lived in the country with zealous Jean and her daughter. She said she was well cared for. Eunice knew for a fact that her mother turned over her social security checks to Jean, and that the money wasn't always put entirely to her keep.

She had her own room on the first floor. The heat was good. Jean's daughter had some disability that made her speech hard to understand, but her wits seemed keen enough. She did the cooking and most of the cleaning. Jean was often away, using the only car available, visiting Dunston and smaller nearby towns, pedaling her pamphlets. Sundays were spent at Kingdom Hall in Elmira rather than at the one in Dunston. There'd been some dispute between Jean and the Dunston group that she preferred not to discuss. Eunice's mother was packed up in the car, her wheelchair in the trunk, for the twenty-two mile drive along curving country roads that could be dangerous in bad weather. Eunice knew her mother didn't like these drives, that in fact they made her nervous, but she never said anything to Jean.

That summer a new resident came to Lindell, Constance Maynard. She had her own cottage, so Eunice didn't have any occasion to deal with her directly, but she saw her come and go in a new Mercedes. The clientele at Lindell was generally pretty well off, and many had high-end cars, but they drove them sedately, almost nervously, down the wide, flat road that connected Lindell to the highway beyond. Constance drove quickly, sometimes causing the tires of her car to screech. She walked quickly, too, with her head down and her purse clamped firmly below her left arm. She always seemed to be deep in thought, dwelling on some unpleasant, troubling item. She came once in a while to the dining room, though she could have cooked for herself, had she cared to. Eunice was on hand to ferry the nursing wing patients there and back and was able to observe Constance discreetly. She sat at different tables, as if trying to decide which person or group of people was most to her liking. She talked a lot, laughed a lot, and ate little. Eunice noticed right off that Constance focused much more on the men than on the women. Given that Constance was probably her mother's age, Eunice was surprised to witness such a long-lived sex drive. The men, for the most part, weren't all that interested. Constance's energy went unmatched, which she took with visible disappointment. She was known to rise abruptly from table, drop her napkin roughly beside her plate, and march off with her characteristically rapid step. Eunice didn't know why she was so fascinated by her. Then she realized it was because Constance reminded her suddenly, sharply, of Lillian Gish, at least in terms of her expressed determination and small stature.

Eunice didn't see Constance for a while, and assumed she was keeping herself busy in wonderful and entertaining ways. The thought made her unhappy because her own life was neither. She wanted to give up the trailer on the inlet and move to an apartment closer to campus where she could be surrounded by young people. Moonshine was skeptical of this decision. She still lived in the house over the creek and told Eunice she should just rent her spare room. She took her out to a seedy bar one night so they could talk about it some more. Moonshine's new boyfriend owned the place. He was their age, divorced, with a couple of citations for serving liquor to minors. Eunice expected him to be a rough sort, but he wasn't. He reminded her a little of Ham, minus the long hair and glasses. He spoke softly, moved slowly, and gave off an air of solid reliability. Maybe that's what drew Moonshine to him, Eunice thought. Though in his company she ignored him and talked only to Eunice, even when he took time to join them at their table and bring them another round of free drinks.

His name was Barry. He spoke with disappointment about his life, saying there were places he'd always wanted to see. He hadn't been able to, because his parents always needed him close. He accepted that duty, though there were two other siblings who could have been called upon—an older brother and a sister who left home and never looked back.

"Did you stay out of guilt?" Eunice asked. He removed his bifocals and polished them on the end of his sweat-stained T-shirt.

"I wouldn't say guilt, exactly. I just realized they would fall apart if I wasn't there."

Moonshine snorted. She'd told Eunice before that Barry had an over-developed sense of responsibility, which at the time Eunice had trouble reconciling with getting in trouble with the liquor board. He brought up that issue himself, as if he wanted to get it out of the way. He hadn't even been onsite either time. First one manager, later fired, then another, also let go, hadn't bothered to check IDs. Barry felt rotten as hell about it, really he did, because you had to protect young people and steer them in the right direction. And a bar was definitely the wrong direction. His own kids, three of them, had trouble sticking to the straight and narrow. That was probably because their mother didn't believe in taking a firm hand. She was too tolerant, too quick to forgive their mistakes, especially the bad ones—like getting arrested for shoplifting or being suspended for cussing out a teacher. As he talked, Eunice sat with one elbow on the table and her cheek resting in her open palm. Moonshine, meanwhile, had taken herself to play a game of darts with a guy who looked like he was all of twenty-five.

Barry asked her about herself. She told him about her parents, working at Lindell, losing Lillian to her neighbor. She couldn't tell how much he was taking in, because he was watching Moonshine across the room. When he finally turned his attention back to Eunice, he said, "The path of life is long and lonely."

Eunice was just about to laugh when she saw that he was being completely serious. She nodded gravely. His words depressed her, the more she considered them, and she had one free beer after another until she stopped thinking about it.

In the morning, Eunice didn't remember how she'd gotten home. Her car was in the driveway. That she'd gotten behind the wheel, blind drunk, struck her as very poor judgment. She had to admit that over the previous few months she'd been drinking more, and the thought that she was following all too easily in her mother's footsteps made her hangover even worse. Moonshine called to say she was having second thoughts about Barry. Eunice asked why. She said she'd met someone at the bar, one of the guys she'd been playing darts with, who seemed pretty interesting.

"Yeah? What's he do?" Eunice asked.

"Do?"

"For a living."

"Hell if I know."

"Oh. Well, what makes him so interesting then?"

"He races motorcycles."

"Sounds dangerous."

"Sounds exciting."

"Yeah, if you're into cheating death for a hobby."

"Oh, for Christ's sake. Stop being such a stick in the mud."

Just the other day, Constance had used that same expression. Eunice had come across her in one of the lounges, sitting with a magazine, looking cross. She asked if there were anything she could do for her, and Constance said she'd just had a phone call from her daughter, the details of which she didn't share but which had left her in a state. Eunice had been glad to finally talk to Constance, and Constance seemed glad for the brief company. Just as Eunice was leaving, Constance had said of the daughter, "That girl's trouble is that she's always been a stick in the mud."

When Eunice got off the phone with Moonshine, she drank a cup of very strong coffee, which helped her headache but did little to improve her morale. She took the small pad of lined paper she kept by her toaster, on which she made her weekly shopping list, and sat down with a leaky pen—the only one she could find. Her intention was to write out all the things she'd ever wanted to do or become, aside from Lillian Gish. Below each item she made a few comments.

Travel

Too expensive, unless going somewhere near, which is boring and basically stupid.

Going to college

How the hell am I going to 1) pay for it and 2) get admitted in the first place?

Starting a business and making a shitload of money

Here she paused. She didn't know how to do anything except take care of old people. What money was there in that? There were agencies that sent aides around to help those still living at home, but that couldn't pay very much. Unless you were the boss. Eunice could supervise people. She'd trained dozens at Lindell over the years. She wondered how much it would take to form her own home-care agency. Moonshine might have some idea.

She was pretty sharp, though she never did follow through on her idea of buying the studio space downtown. One day she was eager, and then she stopped talking about it, which suggested to Eunice that she'd hit her ex-husband up for the money and gotten a quick, firm rejection. He was still paying her alimony, which on the one hand was good because she didn't have to work, and on the other sucked for the same reason.

Eunice had never before considered that there was something to be said for economic adversity. When you were broke, you had to get a job. Having a job gave you at least some degree of independence. But Moonshine was pretty damned independent without having to work, so that line of reasoning was an instant fail.

Eunice put down the pen and massaged her forehead. When she saw the ink all over her fingers, she realized she'd gotten it on her face, too.

She turned on the shower, got undressed, and waited for the hot water to come up. The landlord had promised to replace the water heater the winter before and hadn't. As she stood there, wrapped in a towel, with her hand in the freezing shower stream, waiting, waiting, waiting, her phone rang just as the water turned lukewarm. She turned off the shower.

It was Barry, inviting her for lunch. He and Moonshine had just broken up, he said. He realized they had different goals, and that kind of situation never worked out in the end.

"So, you're on the rebound," Eunice said.

"In a manner of speaking."

"I'm not sure how I feel about seeing a man who just got out of a relationship."

"I'm making roast beef sandwiches. The cook had a lot left over from yesterday. No one ordered the French Dip. Can't remember the last time that happened."

"That's a non-sequitur."

"Agreed. It's also what's for lunch."

"Give me half an hour."

Eunice showered and dressed in gray stretch pants and a pink turtleneck. She was still thin, "wiry," Moonshine said. In the years they'd known each other, Moonshine had put on a fair amount of weight. She complained about it, then ate another cookie. Eunice wondered if she was doing the right thing by accepting Barry's invitation, and wanted to ask Moonshine's advice. Under the circumstances, though, that would be a really bad idea.

They ate in a separate room at the back of the bar. Sometimes people wanted to have private parties, and the noise of the front room was unpleasant, Barry said. The wooden chairs were very comfortable, and Eunice liked the soft light from the red lampshades on the wall sconces. The tablecloth was a cheerful red and white checkerboard. Barry asked if she wanted a beer, and she said an iced tea would be great. He look distracted for a moment, trying to remember if they had any tea. The guy who served them, a college kid with the name "Nick" on his shirt, assured Barry that they did.

"Of course. For Long Island Iced Tea. I must be getting old, not remembering a thing like that," he said.

Eunice picked the beef off of her sandwich, which left mustard, horseradish, and mayonnaise smeared over the sourdough roll. Barry watched her closely.

"I'm a vegetarian," Eunice told him. That had been a recent development. Coming back from visiting her mother in the country on a beautiful spring day, Eunice had stopped on the road to watch a bunch of pigs wandering a nearby sty. The piglets were charming, and her heart filled with love. She'd always admired cows, but they didn't stir her quite as much as those little pigs. She'd grown fond of chickens, too. Jean kept a number at her place, and they boldly approached Eunice, and chirped in high, pretty voices when she extended her hand.

"You want a salad, maybe?" Barry asked.

"I'm fine, thanks."

He finished his sandwich and dabbed his lips daintily on the heavy linen napkin. He wore a pinkie ring with a red stone. On the other hand was a class ring on the fourth finger, and a thick gold bracelet. His hair was thick and neatly combed. His face, though, was where age had taken hold. He had bags under his eyes, and his neck sagged into the collar of his shirt. Eunice knew she didn't look as old. She was blessed with good genes, maybe, and the fact that she stayed pretty thin no doubt helped.

"I need to pick your brain about something," she said.

His hands were around his coffee cup, which he hadn't touched.

"I'm thinking of going into business, starting a home-care agency. I could run it from my place, I think, so I wouldn't need a physical space. I just don't know what's involved—how much money, I mean. And all the hoops to jump through. I figure, you're a business owner, yourself, though home care and running a bar aren't the same at all, really."

"I take care of plenty of people right out there, every day," Barry said, nodding to the main room. "But, your point is well taken."

He looked thoughtful for a moment.

"You need a license. That would be a state thing, not federal. You have to hire people—they have to be credentialed. You need to pay salaries, insurance, and stay on top of your bookkeeping. Payroll taxes are a bitch. Then you have to file estimated income tax with the IRS every quarter, including Social Security and Medicare. And, this is probably the hardest thing about being in business for yourself, you need to fire people when it's called for, and that's not always easy. You get all kinds of sob stories, but in my experience, when someone screws up, you know in your gut if they're likely to do it again. Learn to trust that gut. I've had to fire a lot of people here over the years, and in a small town like Dunston, you run into those same folks from time to time, no getting around it. So, always keep it amicable."

"Like a divorce."

He looked at her sharply. She had no idea why she'd said that. The server took their plates away.

"You need to put up some money in the beginning, for the license and advertising. Have you thought about advertising at all?" he asked.

"No."

"Lindell might help."

"Don't see how. I'd be sort of a competitor."

"Completely different market. You take care of people in their homes before they're ready for a place like Lindell. You could become a referral source. Lindell might like that, even though they probably have a waiting list. Do you know if there's a waiting list?"

"No."

"Well, find out. If there's not, say what you're thinking of doing and ask if they'd be interested in having you spread the word, for a modest monthly fee, of course."

"Why would they help me? I'd be quitting them to do this."

"They wouldn't take it personally. At least, they shouldn't. Never take anything personally in business."

Eunice considered everything he'd said. It was overwhelming. Maybe she should forget all about it and resign herself to being a Lindell employee until the day she retired.

He said he had to go see a distributor over in Corning. Did she want to come along for the ride? Unless she had plans for the rest of her day, of course. Eunice had none.

Barry's car was huge and quiet, so quiet that the passing country took on a strange, eerie quality. The trees swayed in the brisk wind, as though filled with the spirits of an ancient race. At first, Eunice was uncomfortable and thought she should start some cheerful banter to fill the gap, but after a while, with neither of them talking, she became easier in her mind, if not exactly peaceful. Gliding through the world was always calming, and sometimes she took herself out for a drive just for that very reason, but her car wasn't in the best shape with almost one hundred and fifty thousand miles on it.

"You ever been married?" Barry asked.

"Nope."

"Ever come close?"

"Once." Only in her own mind, she told herself, since it had never crossed Carson's once.

"Any kids?"

"What is this, an interview?"

"Just trying to get to know you a little better."

"Sorry. I'm just not used to anyone…"

"Giving a shit?"

Eunice took in his profile. His snub nose was the only problem. It lent his face a childish quality she found troublesome. She supposed she could get used to it, in time.

"More or less," she said.

The road followed a creek. On one side, the land rose in a long, gradual slope. The fields were dotted with cattle and sheep. She thought about her mother, living at Jean's. For the first time, she wondered if she were happy there.

"Your parents living?" Barry asked.

"My mother. Dad died a while ago."

"What did he do?"

"Delivered liquor."

"Man after my own heart."

"Siblings?"

"Just me."

Eunice flipped down her sun visor. It had a light that went on when you slid the panel over the mirror open. She looked at herself. Her reflection was uninspiring.

"I should dye my hair," she said.

"Why would you do that?"

"Not crazy about all this gray."

"Women worry too much about how they look."

"You say these things to Moonshine?"

Barry laughed.

"Truth be told, I don't think Moonshine had much use for me," he said.

"I'm not sure how much she likes men. I don't mean that she's gay or anything, but the opposite sex seems to make her mad, more than anything else. That can't have been easy, given she's got two sons."

"She has kids?"

"She didn't tell you that?"

Barry shook his head.

"Weird."

The wind picked up, and dirt from a newly plowed field rose madly in swirling plumes. She imagine a barren plain where there was nothing to stop the wind, nothing to stop the endless dust it carried.

"You like silent movies?" Eunice asked.

"Can't say I ever saw one."

"Really?"

"How old do you think I am?"

"That's not what I meant."

Barry's smile said he was just pulling her leg.

She told him about *The Wind*, where Lillian Gish plays Lety, sought after by three different men, one of whom she agrees to marry although she doesn't love him. He lives in the middle of nowhere, where the wind howls day and night without end. He takes a job herding cattle to earn the money to send her home, where'd she be more comfortable and away from the dirt that coats everything, even the pillow where she lays her head. In the end Lety survives the madness brought on by nature's cruelty, and discovers that she loves her husband after all.

"Sounds like a tough lady," Barry said.

"I always wanted to be like her."

"Like who? The actress, or the character she played?"

This distinction had never occurred to Eunice. Though she went by many different names, in all sorts of places, Lillian was always just Lillian in her mind.

"Everyone needs a passion. That's what my mother used to say," Barry said.

"And you? What's your passion?"

She could see him thinking about it.

"I thought once I wanted to help people," he said.

"That's a worthwhile ambition."

"Police officer, firefighter. Something like that."

"And?"

"I got married, had kids, my wife wanted me to earn a living, so I bought the bar from my dad. And here I am."

Was there bitterness in his voice? Or just resignation that things hadn't quite gone the way he wanted them to? They were essentially in the same boat, he and Eunice, weren't they? Though her goals had never been quite as clear as his, life had still gotten in the way—in the form of Baxter Bain ripping her off. It didn't matter that she knew she'd been foolish and would never repeat the same mistake again. That money would have made one life possible. Without it, she'd been stuck with another.

"You ever wanted to kill someone?" she asked.

"Sometimes."

"I guess that's normal."

"Until you actually do it."

Eunice laughed. He got her, she could tell.

The road bent sharply, and he took it a little too fast. She didn't mind. He seemed to, from the set of his jaw and how he shifted in his deep leather seat. Maybe he was one of those men who didn't like making even small mistakes in front of a woman, though somehow she didn't think so.

The land was opening up now, with the steep slopes falling back and away. She told him about Baxter Bain. She left out the romance part, framing it in terms of a straightforward swindle made possible by her trusting nature. The way Barry smirked for a moment said he understood exactly what had taken place. Then his face became serious again.

"I just read something in the paper about that guy. He served his sentence, been out for a while now, and works with a developer in

Binghamton."

"You're kidding! Who the hell would hire that crook?"

"Guess he rustled up some money to sweeten the pot."

"Someone else's money."

"Good PR, having a human interest story. 'You're never too old to change your ways.'"

Eunice snorted. Barry looked at her quickly before turning back to the road ahead.

"Give him a call. You're clearly interested," he said.

"I give him anything, it won't be a call."

"My kind of girl."

Eunice considered his remark.

They were on the outskirts of Corning now, passing through a run-down light industrial area. Barry pulled into the parking lot next to a one story concrete building and turned off the car.

"You're welcome to come in and meet Joe," he said.

"Sure, if you like."

Barry reached across her, opened the glove compartment, and removed a gun that he slipped into his waistband. He didn't look at Eunice. He asked her to close the compartment for him. She did.

"Maybe I should stay here," she said.

"Come with me."

She followed him. They entered the building through a back door, went down a short hallway, and into a small office where a man sat at a desk sorting a stack of papers. He looked up at Barry, nodded, and gestured to one of two empty chairs on the other side of the desk. He glanced at Eunice and made no further acknowledgment of her. Barry and Eunice sat.

Barry and the man—Joe—exchanged a few pleasantries about the good weather, the easy drive, how well Barry's business was doing.

"College towns are always good business," Joe said, ruefully. Eunice sensed some opportunities missed out on, some chance he wished he could get back.

"Rich kids like to party," Barry said. He reached into the pocket of his sport coat, removed a thick envelope, and put it on the desk.

"Same as last time. Tell Kelly I need it tomorrow," he said.

Joe took the envelope and put it in the drawer on his side of the desk. He locked the drawer and put the key in his pants pocket.

"His mother's sick. Might not get there until the day after," Joe said.

"Tomorrow," Barry said.

Joe nodded.

Barry stood up, Eunice did, too. They left the office, returned the way they came, and got back into Barry's car. He put the gun in the glove compartment. He didn't start the engine.

"There's a reason I wanted you to see that," he said.

"To show me the real you?"

"Yes."

"I thought you ran a bar."

"I do. I sell liquor. I also sell other things in demand by a college crowd."

"What makes you think I won't tell the police?"

Barry looked tired all of a sudden.

"What would you tell them?" he asked.

"Everything."

"Did you hear us mention drugs?"

"No."

"Did you see what was in the envelope I passed Joe?"

"No."

"So you heard nothing incriminating; you saw nothing incriminating."

"Your gun."

"Purchased legally."

Eunice stewed. She was being manipulated, that much was clear.

"Why are you trusting me with such a big thing?" she asked.

"Because I like you."

"Why?"

Barry stared at her for a long moment.

"You don't think much of yourself, do you?" he asked.

"Never saw a reason to. But I don't think I'm shit either. Which is why I'm not going to get jerked around."

Barry started the car.

"You're straightforward and unpretentious. I like that. I like that a lot," he said.

"Then you must have spent time with a bunch of stuck-up flakes."

"Indeed I have."

Eunice wondered if Barry included Moonshine in that group.

They drove in silence for a long time. Eunice decided Barry was on the level, but probably not the sort of person she wanted to get close to. She'd be the first person to admit that her life was boring as hell and that she despaired often over her lousy prospects, but getting involved with a guy who could end up in jail wasn't a good solution.

"Give it up," she said.

"What?"

"The drugs. Stop selling them."

"Money's too good."

"What do you need money for? The bar does okay, right?"

"Yes."

"You got out-of-control debts or something?"

"No."

"You're just greedy, then."

Barry shrugged.

"You get used to things," he said.

"Like breaking the law."

"Like living out of the mainstream."

"Oh, so that's it. You sell drugs so you can feel like you're interesting and different and better than anyone else."

Barry shrugged again, but the twitch in his jaw said she'd hit home.

"All that guff about steering kids in the right direction," she said.

"Not guff."

"You only sell drugs to bad kids, right?"

"I'm a pretty good judge of character."

"Lives out of the mainstream and plays God, too."

It took Eunice a second or two to realize that the chirping from inside her purse was her new cell phone. She'd never had a cell phone. Lindell suggested she carry one in case they needed to reach her. She was especially good with some of the residents, talking them through irrational stubborn moments, usually about refusing to take a prescribed medication or meeting with a family member who had been long estranged.

It was Karen. She'd just gotten a call from the police up in Geneva. Seemed that Constance Maynard had taken herself on a little drive and didn't know where she was or what she was doing there. Could Eunice come in and go along with the social worker to fetch her?

"How long till we get back to Dunston?" she asked Barry.

"Hour."

Eunice told Karen she was going to be a while. Karen sighed.

Jesus, it's my day off!

Eunice was worried, however, about Constance. Karen said she'd find someone else, and thanked her.

"I'll be in tomorrow, but if something weird is up with her, I'll come in tonight," Eunice said.

"You probably won't have to. We'll get her back, fed, and give her a sleeping pill."

The magic cure. Keep them quiet.

"Everything okay?" Barry asked when she had put her phone back in her purse.

"One of our residents took off."

"Good for him."

"Her."

Eunice was aware that her tone was fierce. The events of the day had made her restless. So did Constance's flight. She watched the land, thinking all the familiar hills and fields would soothe. They didn't.

"If you could go anyplace at all, where would it be?" she asked.

Barry thought.

"Greece. You?"

"West."

"How far?"

"All the way."

Barry had nothing to say to that and kept quiet until they reached Dunston.

chapter nineteen

Eunice and Barry became fast friends. When he stopped selling drugs in his bar, he said it was because demand had fallen off. Eunice didn't believe that for a minute, nor did she believe that her pressuring him, which she did now and then, had had any real effect. She had learned that Barry did what he wanted, when he wanted.

She moved in with him, and had her own room. When he invited her, he said he was past that age, if she knew what he meant. She did, although she wasn't sure she was as past as he was, and decided that if a man caught her eye, or vice versa, she'd worry about the logistics later. So far, it hadn't come up.

His house was on the lake, about four miles outside of town. He'd renovated it from top to bottom. The bedrooms and common living spaces all had open views of water. Eunice loved it, though she knew better than to say so. Another thing she'd learned about Barry was that he didn't care for praise or compliments, or to know that someone was enjoying themselves. It wasn't that he had a negative outlook or was an old crab; he just didn't like overt displays of emotion, so Eunice kept her commentary on an even keel, and so did he, usually.

The one time he went off the rails, Eunice had been living with him for almost two years. One of his children had called on the telephone. He'd taken the call in his den, where he could sit in private. The den was in another wing of the house and met the main section at a ninety degree angle. When Eunice stood in the living room, she had a clear view of Barry at his desk, the phone to his ear, his face growing increasingly grim.

She turned away. He said nothing of the call over dinner, a meal they made it a point to share on the nights when she wasn't working. He'd cut back his hours at the bar, leaving it in the hands of a new manager who turned out to be surprisingly competent at keeping an eye on both the customers and staff. Their evenings were quiet and pleasant. That one, though, was strained. Eunice was determined not to pry. Instead, she talked.

She said her mother was leaving the farm where she'd lived with Jean to move into the Medicaid facility downtown. Eunice was keen to help Jean get her mother settled, but Jean's daughter always seemed to intrude. Eunice wasn't allowed to be useful. Jean's daughter was claiming some sort of ownership, though of what exactly, Eunice wasn't sure. All she could think was that the daughter was one of those naturally bossy women who always had to run the show. She supposed it was a useful trait, but people always ended up getting offended or downright angry.

Barry had met her mother once, when they drove out together to visit, and said bluntly that he could see why Eunice had never wanted children. She didn't know how to interpret that. For one, she'd never spoken of wanting or not wanting children. Next, in her limited experience, it was the people who'd had rotten parents who did a good job of parenting.

Some of the people she worked with at Lindell supported her theory. Dee, one of the other aides, had been beaten by both of her parents, taken away by the State, returned, and left on her own at fifteen. She had three children, all of whom were good students with easy, pleasant dispositions. Velma, the cook, had had a drunk for a father who disappeared for weeks at a time. Her son and daughter were both in veterinary school. Of course, a good partner was key. The husbands of both women were solid and stable.

She decided that Barry was imputing to her what he felt himself—the mistakes he regretted making as a father. Eunice wanted to know more about this but could only circle with vague questions. Then Fate did one if its funny/cruel things. Eunice and Barry ran into his children at a restaurant. It seemed they were there to celebrate a job offer one of them had recently received. They were polite to Barry, cold to Eunice, and dismissive when Barry asked about the job and what it entailed. That had only been three weeks before.

Barry poked at the potatoes Eunice had prepared. He'd eaten little. As a rule, he enjoyed lamb. The chops were thick cut and well-seasoned, but he'd barely touched them.

Eunice cleared, washed up, and went to her room. She worried that whatever had been said on the telephone would upset everything and she'd have to find another place to live, though that didn't seem likely. She was mad at herself for being selfish.

She went to bed. She woke to the sound of something breaking in the kitchen, a glass probably. She put on her bathrobe and slippers, and went to see.

Barry was drunk. He apologized for waking her. He said he was getting himself some water and that the glass must have slipped from his hand. She turned on the light. His face was wet with tears. His sport shirt was stained, and Eunice wondered how it had gotten that way. Then she saw a dirty dish in the sink and realized he'd been snacking on leftovers. She told him to sit down. She swept up the broken glass, found another, and filled it with water. She went down the hall to his bathroom and took the bottle of aspirin from the medicine cabinet. He hadn't told her it was there. She'd discovered it one day when she came home from work with a rotten headache.

He swallowed the aspirin and drank the water. She told him to go to bed. He stood up and went to his room. Eunice waited until she saw the light go off. She went back to bed and didn't sleep for a long time, which was too bad, because she had to work in the morning.

She arrived to find Constance in a small fury. Her daughter had requested a competency hearing. Eunice shared her ire. Constance was old, to be sure, but she wasn't stupid or fuzzy-headed, even with the nightly sleeping pill on board. She told Eunice she wanted to stop taking them. Eunice said she needed to make her request to the nursing staff and that she'd make mention of it, if she'd like her to.

Constance waved her hand to say she didn't want to think about it anymore. Eunice made her bed. Sam, the new girl, came in with a small stack of clean towels. In the front pocket of her smock was a paperback book, probably another volume of poetry. Sam had a passion for poetry, which Eunice found completely at odds with her tall, wide stature. Then she thought it was silly to assume that only petite, delicate women loved poems.

Sam went on to the next resident.

"How are things with your friend?" Constance asked Eunice when they were alone. Constance heard often about Barry. Eunice mentioned the phone call and how badly he'd taken it.

"Did you ask what was said?" Constance asked. It was mid-morning, the point during the day when she tended to be the most keen-witted.

"I couldn't do that."

"I bet you could."

Constance said being a parent was hard, and being a partner in a relationship was hard, even a platonic relationship like the one Eunice and Barry had. It all came down to instinct. Knowing when to speak, when to hold back.

"Make it a parable," Constance said. When Eunice lifted her eyebrows, Constance said, "What I mean is, tell him a story about how you were upset about something once and someone close to you drew you out. Or how you drew someone else out and knew you'd done the right thing because the person in question was glad to share, and found it...*uplifting*."

Eunice didn't think that was a good idea. He wouldn't like that he'd been so vulnerable with her. It might embarrass him to the point where he'd want her to move out.

"That's the trouble with men, isn't it? Can't talk about their feelings," Constance said.

"I know lots of women who can't do that either."

Constance nodded. She fell silent in a way that suggested the onset of a bad mood. That happened whenever her daughter was due, Eunice had noticed. Families were such troublesome things. They hurt you more often than not and didn't come through when you needed them. Except for Grandma Grace. Grandma Grace would have liked Constance. Or rather, she would have understood her, perhaps even sympathized with another example of bad mother-daughter relations. Eunice was certain that if she'd had a daughter, she'd have raised her fairly and lovingly. Of course, she'd never know for sure.

part three

chapter twenty

Sam was a large girl, big-boned, her mother would say. Others called her heavy-set. And some just called her fat. Insults were Sam's lot. Her name made it so easy.

Sam crams spam and jam.

She could go by Samantha, but that felt worse than the jiggle of her flesh every time she moved. Sam's mother was stick thin. Her father might have been, too. Any questions about him were met with shrugs. When Sam was thought old enough, she got the story from her neighbor, Layla Endicott, who made an effort to take Sam under her wing on the many afternoons when Sam's mother was still at work, and Sam's grandparents, with whom they lived, didn't want her around.

Sam was the result of a rape against her mother when her mother was nineteen and on her way home from the tacky diner where she waited tables. The rapist was Henry Delacourt, the scion of a wealthy family who liked shedding all outward signs of privilege to go slumming. He enjoyed occupying the last booth in the diner and drinking coffee into which he poured whiskey from a fancy silver flask. He pulled the brim of an ancient fedora low, so that he had to tip his head back a bit to see. His coat was torn, the soles of his boots let in the rain, and his normally smooth cheeks bristled with three days' growth.

He fooled no one.

Even in the pitch dark of a starless November night, Sam's mother made him at once from the smell of his cologne, which he felt necessary to splash on himself even under such a getup. She caught it up her nose more than once at work, when pleasantries had been exchanged.

148

"A pretty flower, you are," she said.

"Like you," he replied.

He took her for a flirt. Maybe that's why he chose her. A natural, if overly violent following up. The cologne was imported from France and had an overlay of cinnamon, a spice Sam's mother had, until that night, enjoyed on winter nights in a steaming cup of apple cider. She never tasted cinnamon again.

Henry Delacourt left town not long after the incident and settled somewhere out of state where it was said he died two years later at the hands of a jealous husband. His picture was in the Dunston High School yearbook, which Sam found online. She saw nothing of herself in his face. She didn't look one bit like her mother either. She was sure she had been cast into the water of life by some random hand, a hand that liked to turn cruel, but not always against her alone. Her mother, Flora, had been born to strict parents who looked upon their daughter's misfortune without sympathy. She was punished for being a sinner. When they died, rather than feeling free, she withered, as if she had needed the iron law of their simple morality to hold her up.

She and Sam remained in the dead parents' tall, narrow house. Three years after Sam graduated from high school, and following a string of boring, entry-level jobs, which she quit after only a few months, she escaped to southern California. She figured the time had come to feel hot sun on her skin.

L.A. was a hard place to be fat. The bodies around her were lean and tanned. Clothes were minimal. Sam cleaned motel rooms and wore black polyester pants even after work. When she walked on the beach, she cast a big shadow that bumped along in a reflection of her own awkward gait. For along with being fat, Sam had a bad leg, a birth defect, which her grandmother, Edna Clarkson, said was the Lord's retribution. Sam was glad Edna and her nasty husband, Hubert, were both dead. She had silently rejoiced at their passing.

Sam was strong. The ease with which she could lift and tote came in handy when she moved into her apartment in a mid-century building called the *Betty Lou*. Across the street, the tenants of the *Nancy Ann* were often noisy late into the night. And on the other side of a wide alley that always stank of garbage, the grandest of the three, the *Shirley Lynn* had a fountain with running water twenty-four hours a day. Who were these women? Why not the *Samantha Louise*? Sam's middle name was another misery inflicted upon her. Her last name, Clarkson, she shortened down at the courthouse. Sam Clark sounded as strong as she was. A big, solid woman needed a big, solid name.

She didn't doubt her sexual identity. She wasn't a lesbian. While she didn't find men particularly appealing, she wasn't drawn to women as love objects either. This was no doubt Fate's way of keeping her from reproducing. All she had ever really adored, it seemed, were small treasures: bits of sea glass, porcelain figurines, the tiny pearls in a hairclip a motel guest left behind. She arranged these carefully on a sill below a west-facing window that gave a clear view of the parking lot. Sam would have preferred a view of the ocean.

Stingy window, Sam thought. *But I'll wash you anyway.*

Some people might not want to do at home what they had to do all day at work, but Sam didn't mind. She didn't waste her time using spray cleanser, as she did at the EconoLodge, but white wine vinegar and a squeegee. The window was tall, the one nice feature in an otherwise bland, dingy living space. Sam didn't need a footstool. At five foot ten, the top was an easy reach. It was there, one smoggy Tuesday afternoon, with the anticipation of eating a nice pork chop and fried rice for dinner, that Sam first saw her.

Even from that distance, Sam could tell she was a tiny little thing. It touched Sam's heart to see that she was making up for her small stature by wearing ridiculously high heels. She teetered across the parking lot, a big cardboard box in her arms, which she strained to see around. She stopped some distance from the building's main door, put the box down, and removed her keys from her stylish red handbag. Then she couldn't pick the box up again with the keys in her hand, so she placed her key chain between her teeth. The effort she made exhausted Sam to watch. Sam dropped her squeegee and bottle, lumbered out the door, banged down two flights of stairs, and out into the parking lot. The little thing stared up at her. Sam lifted the box. The woman grabbed her keys with her left hand and smoothed her straight, black hair with the other.

"You downstairs neighbor," the woman said.

"What makes you think that?"

"I see you take mail from box below mine. Boxes placed the way apartments are placed."

Sam felt stupid for not having understood that arrangement.

"I am Suki," she said.

"Chinese?"

Suki shook her head. "Japanese."

Again, Sam felt stupid.

"You are?" Suki asked.

"American."

"No. Name."

"Oh, Sam."

Suki continued to stare up at her coolly. Sam asked what was in the box.

"Tea service," Suki said.

Sam didn't understand.

"Pot and cups. Also, many box tea. From Japan."

They went inside and up three flights of stairs. Sam wished the building had an elevator.

In Suki's apartment, Sam put the box on a low table in the middle of the floor. On either side of the table were a number of large cushions. A potted orchid, its petals an extravagant fleshy pink, drew light from the same tall window Sam had one floor down. The bedroom was visible though its open door. A mattress lay on the floor, covered with a blue and white blanket in an abstract pattern of flowers.

"Sort of minimal, no?" Sam asked.

"I like way of my country. American way not always better."

And then Suki asked Sam to please leave, as it was time for her daily meditation.

They balanced each other out. In fact, one dreary afternoon, when the first of the season's rainstorms had driven everyone indoors, Suki poured Sam a cup of tea that Sam would have preferred to drink standing up rather than crouched awkwardly on Suki's cushions and said, "We are yin and yang."

"That's a Chinese idea, isn't it?"

Suki laughed. Her teeth were as tiny as she was, and brilliantly white. Sam's teeth were big and sturdy, with a distinctly yellow tint that no amount of brightening toothpaste could help.

They didn't have anything to talk about, having nothing in common. The invitation to tea was Suki's payment for the kindness Sam had done her. Sam cut the visit short. A big girl like her did badly trying to sit cross-legged on the floor, especially with a bum leg.

Then certain information began to reach Sam about Suki, courtesy of

Suki's next-door neighbor. She went by Mrs. Hopp. She wore loud Hawaiian dresses and green eye shadow. Her dyed hair was more orange than red. Sam admired her stacked bracelets though. Many had small beads in tones of blue and purple. Mrs. Hopp managed to run into Sam in the laundry room every time Sam was down there waiting for some cycle to finish.

A small lace camisole was left in the dryer. Mrs. Hopp said it had to belong to "that Japanese girl." Sam agreed. Although she didn't know many other tenants by name, she'd seen quite a few from her perch at the window where she often sat in a second-hand rocking chair she bought at Goodwill. The men and women who came and went across the parking lot weren't hideous nor were they prime specimens, and almost all tended to be on the large side, with sloppy, elongated American builds. None could possibly own something so fine and delicate as the camisole.

"Shame to put a silk garment like that through the dryer," Mrs. Hopp said, and tossed the camisole onto the yellow plastic table flecked with gold that the management had graciously provided for folding.

Sam continued to sort her own things: size 10 underpants, size 18 shirts and jeans, and her trusty flannel nightgown, which she wore out of habit, though it was far too warm for the gentle climate of Southern California.

"I can take it up to her," Sam said.

"Oh, no, dear, you don't want to do that."

"Why not?"

"She has another guest."

Mrs. Hopp looked sly and held her tongue. Something rose in Sam's blood that Mrs. Hopp seemed to recognize as a threat. She quickly relented. Suki, she said, had "gentlemen callers." Young Japanese men, mostly, though sometimes an older Japanese man.

"How do you know that?" Sam asked.

"I like to know who comes and goes on my floor."

Sam had trouble seeing Mrs. Hopp get to her feet to peer out the peephole every time steps passed her door, but anything was possible, especially for an old woman with time on her hands.

Suki's bedroom was on the other side of the wall from Mrs. Hopp's, and good heavens, you should hear the ruckus sometimes! Mrs. Hopp had to actually bang her hand on the wall to say that enough was enough. She knew she was right about Suki because Suki never met her eye when they passed in

152

the hall.

"You think she's in business?" Sam asked. She wasn't naive. These things happened, particularly in a tough economy.

"Well, I hate to speculate, but it's really the only thing that makes sense."

To Sam's surprise, Suki admitted as much after Sam invited her down for a beer. Suki sat on a wobbly bar stool, which was too low for her to put her elbows on the counter.

"It not bad as you think. Men are nice men. They come here on business. Miss home. Miss their wives or girlfriends."

"You're taking money to have sex with them. It's illegal. What if the building manager finds out?"

"He seldom on premises."

That was true. Sam had trouble with her kitchen faucet, and the guy was never in when she stopped by.

Suki sipped her beer. Sam could tell she didn't like it.

"How do they find you?" Sam asked.

"Agency."

"Agency? What agency?"

Suki explained that the agency was an answering service where the caller made his request, and one of the girls there recommended Suki or any of a number of other young ladies, depending on the caller's specifications.

"And how did you find this agency?" Sam asked.

"I see ad in paper. Ask for Japanese girl to give lessons."

Sam snorted.

"*Language* lessons," Suki said. For the first time, a merry twinkle came into her black eyes. She shook her finger at Sam. Sam was charmed! Every fiber in her wanted to be Suki. Small, pert, enchanting. Life was so unfair; sometimes she just wanted to kick God in the face.

"And they offered you another position. One with greater earning potential," Sam said.

"Yes."

"Must be nice to have lots of cash."

"Most pay credit."

"Credit?"

"My phone has plug in. I swipe card."

It was hard to imagine this.

"But, don't you mind it? I mean ..." Sam's experience with sex amounted to a single encounter with Jasper Kline after school one day in her senior year of high school. Afterward, he said she should be grateful that she wouldn't have to go through life as a virgin. Then he told her not to worry about getting knocked up, because she was so fat, people probably wouldn't notice. When Sam kicked him, he howled in pain and went off limping.

"Not so much now. In beginning, I mind more," Suki said. But Sam could see her distaste in the way her shoulders suddenly seemed to harden, giving her an air of firm resistance.

She's trapped in it. She wants to get out and can't.

Suki thanked Sam for the beer and went on her way.

Sam didn't see Suki again for a little while because one of the other maids at the motel quit and there were extra shifts to be had. Sam was a hard worker. It was suggested that one day she might be promoted to head housekeeper. Sam didn't exactly see herself making a career in the motel business. But what else the future had in store, she couldn't say.

Suki went out of town for a few days and asked Sam to water her plants. Along with the orchid, she had a number of African violets that needed to be watched closely, she said, so their soil, once dry, wouldn't remain so. Sam took her time with the watering. She wanted to soak up the atmosphere and get a firm sense of Suki's private life.

What she found was evidence of a young woman with a taste for luxury and comfort. She had cashmere sweaters that would never be wearable in L.A. Hand-painted silk scarves, French perfume, fine gold necklaces that Sam didn't remember seeing Suki wear, mother-of-pearl hair clips, even her dishes were a designer name, so was her crystal stemware. There were no books or magazines, and Sam assumed their absence reflected Suki's struggle with English. There were no photographs, not of people, at any rate, only one badly composed shot of the beach. Sam wondered if Suki had taken it herself, but there was no camera in the apartment. Sam was careful to put everything back as she had found it. She stood a long time by Suki's low bed and imagined, with distress, the things that happened there. Men were brutes. Her own father. Her grandfather, who had whipped her with his belt more than once while her mother cowered in the corner and pleaded. The sports nuts who stayed at the motel when there was a football game, idiot drinkers who left vomit and piss on the bathroom floor, holes in the wall, used condoms in the bed.

Once again, as thanks for a favor performed, Suki poured tea while Sam bore the discomfort of having to sit on the floor. Sam asked where she'd gone. Suki shook her head. Sam guessed that the trip had been arranged by a client. Sam sipped her tea, which she didn't care for. She couldn't think of anything to say. Silence fell. Sam grew uneasy. Finally, Suki mentioned that she was going on another visit soon.

"Oh, where?" Sam asked.

"See family."

It hadn't occurred to Sam that Suki had a family. But that was dumb. Everyone did.

"Family very important," Suki said.

"Sure."

"You no talk about family. You tell me now."

Sam stretched her legs. What to say? Her grandparents had despised her.

"Dirty rotten seed, that's what you are!"

Her mother told her to stay out of their way, and not provoke them.

"Honestly, Samantha, if you'd eat a little less and give up all those cookies, your grandfather would have no reason to call you fat!"

Since leaving Dunston, Sam and her mother were seldom in touch. Whenever Sam had a letter from her, it was full of whining and fear about what terrible things were certain to happen to her so far away. Sam's mother had never gone more than a few miles from the town she still lived in. The larger world was full of mystery and menace.

"I have a big family. Four brothers, three sisters. That's why I booked out. Got tired of having to share a bathroom," Sam said.

"You miss them?"

"Oh, sure, sometimes. Especially Adele. She's only six."

"You oldest?"

"Yup."

"You no want to stay, help raise children?"

"Hey, I may love 'em, but they weren't my idea, if you know what I mean."

Suki's eyebrows came together, causing a line between them. "Maybe one day I marry one of your brothers. My family want me marry American boy."

"Well, I don't know about that. My brothers are all kinda nuts."

"You have picture?"

"No."

Sam didn't feel bad at all. Why tell the truth when a lie was so much more entertaining? She could go on like this all afternoon, inventing one tale after another. Suki, though, looked far away, almost sad. Sam got up to go. Suki invited her to visit a Shinto shrine over in Little Tokyo the following day.

"You're religious?" Sam asked.

"Of course. Only empty people do not believe."

"In Shintoism?"

"In anything beyond their own existence."

Sam's grandparents had been Lutheran. To her, the whole paradigm was cold, harsh, and dull as toast. She turned away from Christianity at an early age. Yet she found wonder and beauty in the world, and didn't know how to account for it.

The day was stale and hot, although Thanksgiving was only another week off. The bus was slow, crowded, and gave Sam a headache. Suki sat perfectly straight in the seat next to her, her hands, with their thin white fingers and crimson nails, clasped quietly in the lap of her blue silk skirt. Sam's hands were sweaty, as always.

They reached their stop, got off, and made their way along a wide sidewalk with flecks of mica that sparkled. Sam's shadow covered Suki's completely. Sam wore a dress, one of two she owned, because of the formality of the occasion. Her thighs rubbed together. She thought bitterly of the heat rash she'd develop later and wondered if she had any Vaseline at home.

The entrance to the shrine stood past a concrete wall, then a chain link fence. They walked through a wooden structure that reminded Sam of a doorframe, into deep, cool shadows provided by a line of poplar trees. A stone column with Japanese lettering stood just beyond. Suki stopped to look at it, then ran her fingers lovingly along the carved grooves. Sam had a sudden sense of not belonging. She didn't want to continue, and told Suki she would wait for her there, on a bench in the shade. Suki made no reply, and went slowly through the sliding wood and rice paper doors into the shrine itself.

Sam felt like an idiot. Why come all that way, on a stinky hot bus, just to plant her ass on a bench? She should get up and go inside, too. She couldn't. Her mind was in turmoil. She was on the edge of something bigger than she was, but it wasn't a higher power. It was something deep within her, completely at odds with any notions of peace.

As the quiet murmurs of the devoted reached her there, in the darkness of the trees, it occurred to Sam that she needed to fix her life. Her task list was long: weight loss, a better haircut to tame her wild dirty-blond curls, decent clothes to wear when she wasn't at work, higher education, a book club. Maybe if she met new people she wouldn't need Suki so much.

Suki returned, looking as though she'd been washed from the inside out. She strolled silently past Sam, who got to her feet and followed. Neither spoke. Around the corner, a man in an ice cream truck handed a little boy a cone with two scoops of ice cream—one white, one pink. Sam desperately wanted some and suppressed the urge. Suki looked at the small curved stone she'd gotten at the shrine. An amulet of good fortune, she said.

They fell silent again on the bus. At the door to the *Betty Lou*, Suki said, "I am ready now for journey." Sam nodded dully and went on her way.

That night she slept fitfully. The heat of the day seemed to soak into her skin. The bedroom window's small, pathetic air conditioner didn't do anything but make noise. Around midnight she lurched to her feet and turned it off. She went to the kitchen for a glass of water. There was urgent knocking at her door. Sam willed the intruder to leave her alone. The knocking continued. Through the peephole, she saw Mrs. Hopp, frantic, yet resplendent in her bathrobe and curlers. Sam opened the door, and remembered at the last moment that she was in her underwear. Her flannel nightgown was too heavy for her that night.

"There's trouble at Suki's place," Mrs. Hopp said. She was out of breath. There was something odd about the way she spoke. Sam realized it had to do with her teeth, or lack thereof. She'd removed her dentures.

"I didn't hear anything."

"Well I did. Go see what it's all about," Mrs. Hopp said.

Sam rubbed her eyes against the glare from the hallway light. Her head felt woolly and thick.

"Oh, all right," she said.

She got dressed. She slipped on the flip-flops she used when she went to and from the laundry room, which was across a courtyard that always collected puddles from the automatic sprinklers. They smacked loudly as she went up the stairs. Behind her, Mrs. Hopp huffed step by step.

The sound of wailing filled the hall. Sam told Mrs. Hopp to go back to her place and stay there.

"Should I call the police, do you think?" Mrs. Hopp asked.

"Well, if you were going to, why did you come get me?"

Mrs. Hopp didn't know. She went inside and closed her door.

Along with the wailing was a man's raised voice. He was speaking Japanese, Sam was certain, though if pressed she probably wouldn't be able to tell it from any other Asian tongue. He wasn't angry so much as desperate. His voice dropped to something softer yet more urgent, followed suddenly by the sound of something shattering. Sam thought of the lamp by Suki's bed. Solid crystal, it looked like.

One of her clients was acting up, and Suki was fighting back. Sam took three deep, slow breaths to ready herself, then pounded on the door with her fist. All noise inside stopped. She banged again. The door opened, and Suki's head appeared.

"Make no more noise. Sorry for trouble," she said. Her eyes were red, her face streaked and grimy. And she reeked of booze, gin to be precise.

Sam pushed the door open and went inside. The man was in the kitchen, filling a glass with water from the tap. He was slightly built, like Suki, but taller, though not nearly as tall as Sam.

"Get out," Sam told him.

"Sorry?" the man said.

"Bet your damn ass you're sorry. Beat it."

"Will not. I stay. I have right."

"Fuck your rights. Get going."

Suki said something in a plaintive tone. Her bad English was worse under the effects of alcohol.

Sam crossed the living room. She grabbed the man by the arm and was surprised by how thin it was. Yet he put up a decent struggle when she yanked him. Even so, he was no match for her energized bulk. She dragged him to the still open door and shoved him out. She slammed the door against him. Suki resumed her wailing, and Sam told her to shut up. Suki dropped onto one of her floor cushions and sobbed. Sam looked through the peephole. The man was still there. He shouted something in Japanese.

"If he's saying he'll call the police, tell him the neighbor already did," Sam told Suki.

"He want jacket."

The man's jacket was on a stool next to the kitchen counter. Sam took the jacket and opened the door. She dropped the jacket and told the man once more to get lost. The man tried to see around her to where Suki sat, but Sam blocked him. He said something else, and Suki lifted her head for a moment. Sam closed the door. Suki wept.

"Don't be embarrassed. One of them was likely to pop sooner or later," Sam said.

"No understand."

"You know—johns, they're not right in the head. It was only a matter of time before one of them took a swing at you."

"He no hit me. He brother."

"Say what?"

"Brother. Come to take me home. Only he say I cannot go home. They do not wish me."

Sam sat down across from Suki, forgetting for the moment how much she disliked accommodating that low table.

"He came all this way to say you can't go home?" Sam asked.

"More honorable to say to my face."

Sam gazed up at the popcorn ceiling. Her right leg cramped. She flexed her toes. Suki sniffed.

"You should not have pushed him away," Suki said.

"Yeah, guess not. Look, maybe I can go after him and explain."

"Do not. Please go now."

"Suki, look, I was just trying …"

Suki shook her head.

Sam stood. In her misery, Suki looked even tinier. Sam wanted to help her and knew that anything she offered would be rejected. Sam left her alone. As she went down the hall she hoped Mrs. Hopp wouldn't open her door. The door stayed closed.

Back in her own place, Sam listened for Suki's footsteps on the ceiling. She thought of her up there, unhappy and stuck. She thought of dragging Suki's brother across the floor. She heard a distant moan, almost ghostly. Maybe Suki was weeping again, full of remorse and regret. Maybe she was wondering how to fix things. Maybe she figured she couldn't.

And what about my own life?

The details were fuzzy, but the gist was clear. She'd had enough of the golden west. Time to head for home.

chapter twenty-one

Sam didn't read poetry in L.A., but poems were always with her. In her ear, in the beat of her good, non-lame foot. In her hand wiping clean the motel television screens. Even polishing the rim of a toilet that messy, stupid men had used, poetry was there.

In elementary school, her rendition of "The Little Ghost" by Edna St. Vincent Millay was passionate to the point of ridicule. Her teachers accused her of making fun. She was supposed to recite, so she did. She saw no reason to hold back.

She read poems on her way to school and when she returned home, unless her grandparents were in the house. They thought reading was a silly pastime. Young hands should hold brooms and dishcloths, fold towels and sheets, scrub counters and floors.

Now that she was home and the house was hers—well, technically her mother's—she read whenever she damn well pleased. Her favorites were Millay, Dickenson, Sexton, and Plath.

I made a fire; being tired
Of the white fists of old
Letters and their death rattle
When I came too close to the wastebasket
What did they know that I didn't?

Plath was her favorite. All that despair and rage! Thank you, Ted Hughes.

The first motel where she got a job was in College Town and rented by the week. The occupant of the end room was an English major, or so Sam assumed from her collection of books, particularly T. S. Eliot. She hadn't read Eliot. One afternoon, she sat down on the bed she'd just made, and did, for over an hour, at which the point the manager walked in, raised his voice, and threatened to fire her. Sam wanted to tell him where to go, and didn't, for the sake of her paycheck.

Then the motel was sold to a developer who planned to tear it down.

She held two more motels jobs before she learned that the Lindell Home was hiring. There, no one minded her carrying a book of verses and reading to the residents, most of whom were deaf as posts or disconnected from what went on around them, especially those that lay in bed, staring at nothing. Now and then one would smile in recognition of some lines learned long ago that took them back to younger selves, and happier times.

"Don't you hate being around those old folks all the time?" Flora asked.

"I grew up around old folks, remember?"

Flora looked sad for a moment. She thought of her dead parents every single day.

"They weren't so bad, were they?" she would sometimes ask.

"They stunk, and you know it."

Flora looked even sadder then, and Sam regretted saying that. She poured her another cup of coffee, though she hadn't asked for one.

"Look, I'll be getting my own place eventually, once I have a little more money saved, so why don't you sell this dump and rent one of those new apartments downtown? A change of scene would do you good," Sam asked.

"And live there alone?"

"Well, sure, I mean ..."

"I can't do that."

This was always a sticking point. Sam was more than ready for an apartment of her own. Since coming back from L.A. it hadn't been easy living with Flora. It wasn't that her mother intruded on her privacy, or made demands. It was just that she was so weighed down by her own misery! There was an air of gloom around her that nothing could lift, and Sam found it very annoying.

"You did fine without me before," Sam said.

"I did not! You don't know how lonely I was!"

Flora had a boyfriend she pretended was really only an old pal. Chuck Knight. He'd been in the picture a long time, well before the death of her parents. He never came around because they hadn't approved of him, and Flora probably got so used to keeping him a secret that she thought she still had to. It was absurd, really, because he called all the time on the telephone,

161

and Flora went out with him a lot, too, and sometimes spent the night at his house out on the lake. How he stood Flora's constant depression, Sam had no idea, except possibly by being dense and thus insulated from it somehow. The few times Sam had met him, his good cheer and lack of curiosity about anything in the larger world always gave the impression of a major dope.

Sam was late for work, and she left Flora by herself in the kitchen. As she drove, she listened to one of the recordings she'd made of herself reading Emily Dickinson. The recorder sat on the passenger seat. One of these days she might get a used laptop and burn CDs, but for the moment, an older technology was fine.

There is no frigate like a book
To take us lands away,
Nor any coursers like a page
Of prancing poetry.
This traverse may the poorest take
Without oppress of toll;
How frugal is the chariot
That bears a human soul!

Sam really got a kick out of Dickinson, especially because she lived a very solitary life. The idea was appealing.

Her co-worker, Eunice, was late, as usual. Their supervisor, Karen, never said anything to her about it, which ticked Sam off. Karen and Eunice had a lot in common. Both had disastrous histories with men. Neither had children. They often commiserated with one another, which probably accounted for Karen always looking the other way when Eunice failed to be on time.

When Eunice finally showed up, her excuse was the guy she was living with. He had problems with his kids, who were more or less estranged from him. What trouble could you have with someone who was basically out of your life, unless you wanted them back in? Sam didn't ask that question. She dusted, straightened, scrubbed the toilet in each room, and hummed.

Fannie Etheridge smiled and nodded when Sam came in. Sam recited the poem she'd listened to in the car before cleaning up. She squeezed Fannie's hand on the way out.

Sam liked the residents. She also felt sorry for them. Take Nell Morely for instance. She was often blue, and held her husband's picture in her lap hour after hour. Frank Norton, who was called "Sarg" by the staff, looked bleakly at his younger self in an Army uniform, where he smiled confidently into the camera. Then there was Constance Maynard, who'd stopped taking her sleeping pills and was, for a time, almost frisky. Now the quiet had returned, and the frequent presence of her daughter, Meredith, didn't seem to help.

That was because Meredith was a sap. Always mooning around. The way she acted, you'd think she was a resident herself, though she was a hell of a lot younger than most of them. Eunice said she'd just moved from L.A. At the mention of that huge, hot, dusty city, Sam's skin crawled.

Good old Suki. Whatever became of you?

She wheeled her cart full of cleaning supplies and fresh linens up the hall. The fluorescent lights above her buzzed quietly. A trailing ivy plant, set carelessly on a stand in a dark corner, was wilted. Some leaves were brown, and others had detached and fallen to the floor. Sam thought it was in very bad taste to leave a living thing to die in a place where everyone else was, too.

She went into the storeroom next to the nurse's station looking for a watering can or anything with a spout so she could pour water onto the soil without sending it all over the carpet as well. The carpets at Lindell were routinely abused. Incontinence was a big problem, and Sam had asked Karen why they didn't install tile floors instead. Karen looked at her as if that were a very stupid question, which was her way of saying that whomever made these decisions would flat out refuse. That seemed to happen a lot, Sam had noticed. There'd been a request for new tablecloths for the dining room, also a new coffee pot, and nothing had come through. Velma, the cook—and the one who oversaw everything culinary—told Sam the people who ran Lindell were a bunch of idiots. Sam believed it.

When she couldn't find a watering can, she went down the hall to the recreation center. There was an indoor pool and a workout room. Both were empty. She opened the storage closet and found a bunch of weighted balls, stretchy ropes, and yoga mats.

I could use this stuff.

For a moment, she thought of walking off with some of the items in front of her, but decided not to risk it.

Next, she wandered into the kitchen where Velma was furiously stirring something in a large, green mixing bowl. A lit cigarette stuck to her lower lip. Smoking was forbidden at Lindell and within twenty-five feet of any entrance, which Velma knew, of course. She also knew she wouldn't get fired. Aides were one thing, and not all that hard to come by, but someone who could make large batches of good-tasting food, which the residents and their guests praised often, was another story.

"You know where I can find a watering can?" Sam asked.

"My office."

Velma's office was right off the kitchen, next to the staff breakroom, and sure enough, in a corner on the floor was a plastic watering can. Sam realized that Velma was responsible for the row of African violets on the breakroom's windowsill.

"Make sure you bring that back," Velma said, still stirring.

"Watch your ash."

"Ash or ass?"

"Ha!"

If Velma were younger, closer to Sam's age, she'd make a good friend. Sam had a good friend, though, and one was all she needed.

Lucy lived across the street. She was twenty-seven, five years older than Sam, and had four kids. Her husband was a cop. When Sam needed a break from Flora, she went over to Lucy's and watched her kids roll around on the floor and fight. Lucy kept them in line by banging two pots together and, when silence had fallen, pointing her finger at each one in turn. Sam didn't know what unnamed threat lay behind that pointed finger, but the kids sure did, because they always stopped their mischief when it came their way.

Sometimes, when Flora was off with Chuck, Lucy and her brood marched over to Sam's. Sam cooked Sloppy Joe's for the kids. She and Lucy ate pretzels and drank wine. Lucy's husband, Glen, wanted to leave town and make a fresh start somewhere else. Lucy had talked him out of it several times already, but Sam could tell she was afraid that one day she wouldn't be able to, and that he'd quit the force, find a job doing something like driving a long-haul truck, and pack them off to someplace even colder than Upstate New York. For some reason, he had a hankering to move to Minnesota, or maybe Wisconsin. Lucy told Sam woozily over a third glass of wine if that were the case, why couldn't they move somewhere warm, like Florida? Sam pointed out that if Glen really wanted to drive trucks for a living, it probably didn't matter where they lived, in which case they could just stay in Dunston. Sam didn't want Lucy to leave. She adored her. She was skinny as a rail, even after four kids. Lucy explained her figure by saying she must have the metabolism of a squirrel.

Recalling that now, lumbering back to the nursing wing with Velma's watering can, Sam chuckled. She swung into Constance's room, which was closest to the ailing plant, filled the can with water from the bathroom sink, and was on her way out when Constance said, "Wait."

Sam turned around. She approached Constance's bed. Constance motioned that she wanted to sit up. Sam put the watering can on the floor, pressed the button that raised the head of the bed, pulled Constance forward, and plumped her pillow. She was still in her nightgown. Just last week she'd declared she didn't want to get dressed, so Sam and Eunice left her as she was but made sure to get her in a clean nightgown every third day, which coincided with her being bathed. Over the nightgown, she had a sweater knit from a light-weight wool. Her white hair had gotten so thin that patches of pink scalp showed through.

"Where is she?" Constance asked.

"Your daughter?"

Constance nodded.

"Is she coming today?"

"She comes every day."

"She's very devoted."

"She's very scared."

"Of what?"

"My dying."

"You're not dying."

"Bull."

Sam laughed. Constance closed her eyes. Her breathing was so quiet. Sam watched her chest rise and fall.

Constance opened her eyes.

"I have something to say. I'd rather tell Eunice, but she's not here, so you'll do," she said.

"Okay."

"Get that chair, bring it here, and sit down. Please."

Sam did as she was told. Constance said nothing. Sam wondered if she should remind her that she was there. In the hall, Stony Morris, another retired professor, wheeled himself past Constance's room. He was muttering. He always muttered. Sam had once asked him how he'd gotten his name.

He'd stared at her crossly and said, "From my parents, you dope, what do you think?" Eunice said the name came from a former student, about his expression, but Karen said it was because he had a particular fascination with the Confederate general, Stonewall Jackson.

"Meredith is not my daughter," Constance said.

Great. Now the old bat's gone off her rocker.

"She knows it, too," Constance said.

"Sure."

"Naturally I assumed she'd get used to the idea eventually. But now, all these years later, she still resents me."

"I'm sure that's not true."

Constance closed her eyes. She looked completely worn out.

"Tell her I embraced irony, and overlooked the human element," Constance said, her eyes still closed.

"You'll tell her, yourself."

"She's not easy to talk to."

"I'm sure she's a good listener."

At that, Constance opened her eyes, stared sharply at Sam, then closed them again. Sam asked if she wanted the head of the bed lowered. Constance said nothing, so Sam went on her way, watering can in hand.

She drenched the dried up ivy, hoping the next time she passed it would be green and strong. She returned the can to Velma's office, then went to find Angie Dugan, the Home's social worker. Her lair was just off the main reception area. She was at her desk, reading the contents of a thick file.

Sam hadn't had much contact with her but felt a connection because she was overweight, too. The staff at Lindell was disproportionately slender. Sam had instantly felt out of place when she started working there, but now, starting on her third month, she was more at home.

Sam told Angie that she'd just had a weird conversation with Constance Maynard. Angie invited her to sit.

"She says her daughter's not really her daughter. And that she—the daughter—knows," Sam said.

A line formed on Angie's forehead.

"Interesting," she said.

"Maybe she's projecting, you know. Wishing she weren't her daughter. That kind of thing," Sam said. She really didn't know what the hell she was talking about, but it wasn't a terrible notion either, as these things went.

166

"Possible."

"You think she's, you know, losing it the way they do?"

"Oh, I don't think so. She seemed pretty sharp when I talked with her last."

"Okay, then."

Sam stood up. Eunice would be wondering where she'd gotten to.

"You seem to have settled in well," Angie said.

"I guess."

"You don't feel like a fish out of water, with all the seniors around?"

"Nah. They're good people. Even the cranky ones are kind of fun."

"I hear you enjoy poetry. You sometimes read to the residents."

"Anyone complaining?"

"Not at all. I'm sure they love it. It's wonderful of you to take such an interest."

"It's sort of a thing with me. Poetry. Just wish I could write it, myself."

"'Many are called, few are chosen.'"

"Yeah, no kidding."

Sam hesitated. She wasn't ready to walk away yet.

"Well, thank you for letting me know about Constance. I'll ask Karen to keep an eye on her. You do, too, of course," Angie said.

"You know, Eunice and the daughter seem to be buddies now."

"Really? Well, maybe Eunice can shed some light on this as well, if anything gets worse."

Sam didn't know what could get worse. Saying your daughter wasn't your daughter was pretty damn bad.

"Families are tough. My grandparents—case in point. Couple of real jerks, if you'll pardon the expression. Drove my mother nuts. Though, she was probably well on her way there, anyhow, on account of how I got into the world."

Sam could see that Angie wasn't interested in all that.

"Well, I'll leave you to it then," Sam said, and left.

She thought about the times she wished she'd come from a big family, and the one she'd invented for Suki. Then she thought about all the people in the world who had a big crew and wished to hell they didn't. Sylvia Plath knew all about that. Poor Sylvia, sticking her head in an oven.

167

Against a silence wearing thin.
The door now opens from within.
Oh, hear the clash of people meeting —
The laughter and the screams of greeting:

The reception area was empty except for Janet at the main desk, reading a book, definitely not poetry, or even literature as far as Sam could tell. Probably another one of her stupid, steamy romances, the kind of thing you found in a drug store next to the cheap sunglasses. Well, to each his own. The automatic doors whooshed open to admit Laverne Welker and her granddaughter, coming back from another outing. The granddaughter was probably Sam's age. She always looked fierce, if not downright pissed off. Laverne waved at Sam.

"Great day out there, isn't it?" Sam asked, her voice overly loud. She'd learned that it was better to blare a little than to have to repeat yourself.

"Very nice, very nice," Laverne said. Her tone was high and wobbly, but cheerful. The granddaughter glared at the carpet.

"Well, have a good one," Sam said. She went out the door they'd just come in so she could cut across the field and enter the nursing wing through a back door. Fresh air kept you going. Soon, when the weather turned nasty, she'd have to keep a coat with her if she wanted to duck outside.

Her cell phone buzzed in her pocket. She wasn't supposed to have it on her at work but leave it in her locker. To hell with that, she'd thought after Karen explained the rules. She just turned the volume off. The buzz was mild, not audible to anyone else except maybe Eunice, who didn't care one way or the other.

It was Flora. She was going away for the weekend with Chuck.

"It's Wednesday. Why are you telling me now?"

"Because we're leaving tonight."

"It's not the weekend yet."

"Chuck's weekend, I meant."

Chuck worked at Greene's Nursery over in Dryden. Obviously, his days off were Thursday and Friday. Flora had probably mentioned this. Yes, Sam was sure now that she had.

"Where you guys headed?" Sam asked.

"Buffalo."

"What's in Buffalo?"

"His sister."

"Oh. She sick?"

"No. But he thought it was time we met."

Sounds serious.

No doubt her mom and Chuck would tie the knot and sell the house. Or keep it, and he'd move in. Either way, that place of her own couldn't happen fast enough.

"Well, have a blast. Don't do anything I wouldn't do," she said.

"Oh, you."

Her mother didn't hang up. Sam had reached the door of the nursing wing. She was anxious to get inside now, and back to work. She'd been gone a good twenty minutes at that point.

"Samantha, listen," her mother said.

"Yeah?"

"You know what Friday is, right?"

"Nope.

"Well, honestly! You should. It's the anniversary of your grandfather's death."

"And?"

"And I won't be there to visit the grave. I want you to go for me."

"Are you nuts?"

"Don't be rude. You don't even need to buy flowers, if you really don't want to. Pick some from the yard and tie them up with some ribbon from the drawer in the kitchen."

"Forget it."

"Samantha!"

"If it's so important to you, why don't you go yourself?"

"I told you. I'm going to Buffalo with Chuck."

"Go a different day."

"We can't."

"Too bad."

Flora sniffed. Sam gave up.

"All right. I'll go," she said.

"While you're there, say hi to your grandmother, too."

They were buried side by side. Sam remembered the discussion of how expensive cemetery plots were. There'd been some yelling about it, though she couldn't remember from whom. Maybe it was she herself who'd yelled, telling them all to shut the fuck up. Though of course that hadn't happened. She'd gotten slapped down every time she opened her mouth.

169

chapter twenty-two

When the day came, Sam's courage sagged. She didn't want to go to the cemetery alone. She enlisted Lucy to come along. They'd take the kids, make a day of it. Lucy thought that was a lousy idea. It was fine for Sam to like the thought of watching the little monsters race and tumble all over the place, because at the end of the day she could go home to peace and quiet. For Lucy, not so much. She called her mother and told her to come over. Lucy's mother was bad-tempered and strict. That, and hating to babysit, made her a great choice for keeping the kids in line.

They took Sam's car. She'd recently bought a used station wagon. She fantasized about throwing everything she owned in the back and just taking off, as she had before. She had no plan to, now that she was working. But knowing she could, if she really wanted to, was comforting.

Sam hadn't been to the cemetery for years, and had no idea where the graves were located. She expected to find someone on duty, manning the little house at the entrance, but it was empty.

"Now what?" Lucy asked. Her voice was light, full of energy. She was so happy at the change in her routine that she'd traded her brown turtleneck for a sleeveless pink one with small white buttons down the front. Sam was in her work clothes: red stretch pants and a red and white smock. She'd had time to put on something nicer but decided not to. She saw no point in making any attempt to honor or show respect to the people she'd agreed to visit.

"They're under a tree, I think," Sam said.

"Place is full of trees."

"A big one."

They looked all around and settled on the tallest tree they could see, an elm quite a ways off. Sam suggested they drive along the path that wound through the grounds, but Lucy wanted to walk. It was such a beautiful day, she said, and the exercise would do them both good.

"I saw your mom leaving with her boyfriend," Lucy said.

"Yeah?"

"I mean, I've seen him before, of course. He comes over a lot, doesn't he?"

"Lives there half the time."

"They seem happy."

"Suppose so."

"You don't like him?"

"Can't really say. He's all right."

"She's been on her own a long time, I guess."

"True."

"What happened to your dad?"

Sam slowed her pace.

"He died."

"How old were you?"

"Maybe around two."

"So, you never really knew him."

"*She* never really knew him."

They had left the cemetery road and were walking in newly cut grass, over one grave after another. Sam told her the whole story.

"Jesus, your poor mother," Lucy said.

Other people had said the same thing over the years. While Sam understood that her mother was a victim, she'd always wanted something better for her. For them both really.

"She didn't name him. She could have named him," Sam said.

"I know, but his family had money, you said. They'd have gotten a good lawyer and trashed her on the stand."

Sam stopped and stared at Lucy.

"You like Perry Mason reruns or something?" she asked.

"My husband's a cop, remember?"

"Right."

They came to the tall tree they'd seen from afar. None of the graves below it belonged to Sam's grandparents. The shade was pleasant. Sam and Lucy sat. Someone had recently placed a bouquet on one of the graves. Just as when she'd realized that no one was taking care of the ivy at Lindell, Sam was annoyed. Why underscore the fact that all things die?

171

She picked up the bouquet and brought it to her nose. The carnations were spicy and the lilies almost sickeningly sweet. They were lovely, she had to admit. Maybe it was someone's way of celebrating a person's life, or life itself, even if the irony was blunt.

"I was supposed to bring flowers," Sam said.

"Take those. But then, we still don't know where the damn graves are, do we?"

Sam returned the flowers to their original spot. She ran her hands over the grass. She picked up a fallen autumn leaf, bright red. It, too, signified death.

Lucy lit a cigarette. She offered one to Sam. Sam declined. In the distance, a lawnmower started roughly, spluttered, fell silent, then began again. The sound dimmed as the mower moved farther and farther away from where they sat.

"This is nice. Just sitting. No kids," Lucy said.

"They must keep you busy as hell."

"Damn straight."

The strain in her voice was clear. Yet, there must be good moments, too. Why else would you have them in the first place? Okay, accidents happen. Once, maybe twice, but four had to be intentional. At least Sam hoped so. A woman who didn't control her womb was an idiot, she thought. Unless it was a case of what happened to her mother.

Sam had often wondered why she hadn't gotten an abortion, not that she was sorry she was alive, of course. Only, when she imagined being attacked, raped, impregnated, and then going through with having the baby, it all seemed so monstrous. But of course the grandparents would have made the idea impossible. They were so into the will of God, they would have preached acceptance, forbearance, humility. Sam was sometimes sorry they were dead, because she'd tell them a thing or two about life that they'd chosen to ignore. Like all about self-determination. And compassion.

Lucy said something to her that she didn't entirely register.

"What?"

"I said, Halloween's coming and the kids are going nuts."

"They dress up?"

"Of course!"

Sam didn't know why she'd asked that question, since they'd trooped across the road last year and banged on her door. They all seemed to have been made up as pirates. Flora had baked chocolate chip cookies. She didn't usually bother with Halloween, but the addition of a young family nearby motivated her to be neighborly. Lucy didn't know them all that well at that point and politely declined. Flora had been crushed. Sam explained that store-bought candy was better because it was wrapped. There had been cases of tampering, and parents were wary. Flora was blue, so Sam ate many of the cookies, herself.

"You make 'em yourself, the costumes?" Sam asked.

"I do now. Glen's sort of picky about that."

"Yeah?"

"He says I've got nothing but time on my hands, I can at least make my own costumes. Besides, it's cheaper."

Lucy's expression darkened.

"He must work a lot," Sam said.

"What do you mean?"

"I don't usually see his car in the driveway, so I figure he's out working, overtime maybe."

Lucy said the truth was that her husband had a hard time being at home, what with the four kids and all, and a lot of the time he stayed over at his parents' place.

She stubbed out her cigarette against a bumpy tree root. She put the butt in her pants pocket. She looked at her watch. The lawnmower stopped. Sam suggested they get going. They were never going to find the graves unless they covered every square inch of the place.

They ambled slowly, not talking. Sam didn't feel guilty for not trying harder to find the graves. It was too bad in a way, though. She would have liked to spit on them. Flora had specifically asked her to lay her palm on each stone, first her father's, then her mother's, close her eyes, and think well of them, if only for a few seconds. That was as close to praying as Flora ever came. As a small girl, Sam got hauled off to church every Sunday until one time she pitched a fit so bad that after her grandfather finished beating her with his belt he relented and said she could stay home and read the Bible in her room. No Bible ever came her way, however, for which she was glad. She also took it as a sign that her grandparents had given up on her.

That was when she'd discovered poetry. A single volume of Tennyson was on a shelf in the living room, under a vase that held a bouquet of plastic red tulips. The book had been necessary to keep the vase from toppling, which it did the moment Sam removed it. She threw away the broken pieces and the flowers, too, awaiting her brutal punishment, though none came. She decided that the universe was rewarding her curiosity, and though the poems were a bit dense and hard to make sense of, Sam had been transported far from the peeling paint and scratched wood floors of her small bedroom.

From then on it was the library that kept her alive. She loved the space as much as what it contained: the smell of dust, the scratched wooden tables, the ceiling fan over the reception desk that spun silently, but not the women who took her card and checked out her books. They looked at her with curiosity, sometimes pity. She always wondered if they had heard the rumor about her mother and Henry Delacourt, though she also knew that her wretched grandparents had forbidden Flora ever to speak of it outside the family.

"How did you and your husband meet?" Sam asked.

"I got T-boned at a light, and he was the cop who showed up."

"Romantic."

"Not at all. I was pretty badly shaken up. The other driver was a jerk, so Glen put him in the back of the cruiser, and I had to call my mother to come get me. The car was totaled."

"Well, you got a new car *and* a husband out of it."

"Another used car, actually."

"Not a used husband?"

Lucy didn't see the humor. Sam let it go. Her parked car came into sight as they reached the top of a low hill.

"Did you always want a large family?" Sam asked.

"No."

"A surprise blessing, then."

Lucy snorted.

"Only someone with no kids would say that. No offense," she said.

"None taken."

• • •

Sam awoke to voices breaking the night. One was deep, sonorous yet harsh. The other was high, screeching, at times louder than her partner's. Sam understood that she was hearing Lucy and Glen across the street. The digital clock by her bed read 2:47.

174

"Jesus Christ," she said.

Silence came abruptly. The noise didn't resume. Sam stretched, and was glad her mother wasn't home. She'd have been up and glued to the living room window otherwise. Flora was a terrible snoop, living vicariously, drawn to all sorts of drama, especially the kind that caused weeping and rage.

The pounding on her front door woke Sam a second time. The sky was still dark. Sam didn't bother looking at the clock. She sat up and burped.

Fucking onions.

Then she put her bare feet on the floor and wriggled into her ancient bathrobe, realizing how badly she needed a new one, and then recalled some of the nicer ones the folks at Lindell had.

Thinking about bathrobes at a time like this.

Her heavy lame gait took her down the stairs, through the living room, dining room, and kitchen, to the door where Lucy's frantic face was clear through the glass.

She let Lucy in and told her to take a seat at the kitchen table.

"Let me guess, he belted you one," Sam said.

Lucy shook her head. Her hair was everywhere. She'd thrown a sweatshirt on over her nightgown. Her nosed dripped. Sam brought her a piece of paper towel.

"He's losing his mind. He says he's going to shoot himself in the head," Lucy said.

"Wait, what?"

"I took his gun and threw it outside."

"Where?"

"I don't know. In the ditch along the road."

"Where are the kids?"

"My mom's. She took them after we got back from the cemetery. I just had a feeling he might be in one of those moods."

"He's done this before?"

Lucy nodded.

Sam scratched her head. She was hungry, but her stomach still danced from the onions she'd spread on her meatloaf sandwich at dinner. She opened the front door and peered into the night. A street lamp cast a pool of yellow light to one side of Lucy's house. If she'd tossed the gun in that part of the ditch, Glen would have to pass through the light to find it, assuming he knew where it was.

"He see you?" she asked, when she returned to the kitchen.

"He was still in the bathroom. He locked the door."

"Any way he can off himself in there without the gun?"

"No."

"Pills, razors, anything?"

"I cleaned everything out the last time."

"Jesus Christ."

Lucy tore off a small piece of paper towel, then another, and collected them in her lap.

Sam put the teakettle on to boil. She always put a kettle on when she had to do some hard thinking. The night she decided to go to L.A., the kettle's steam coated the windows until she couldn't see out. Before she wiped the glass clear, she wrote her name, *Sam Clarkson*, then wiped the away the *son*.

It had made so much sense; she didn't know why she hadn't seen it before.

"I should go," Lucy said. She didn't move. She went on tearing the paper towel.

"He ever do any counseling?" Sam asked.

Lucy lifted her eyes for the first time since Sam put her in the chair. They were full of rage.

"Not Glen. Glen's too good for that. Too smart, to hear him tell it, and I heard him tell it over and over and over. I wish to hell he'd get fired or something, so he'd have to face the fact that—"

He's nuts?

"Getting fired would only put a financial strain on you and the kids. The man needs help."

A swift kick in the ass is more like it.

Lucy shook her head and cried. She used the paper towel to wipe her nose. Sam was at a loss. Seeing her cry was the worst yet.

"You know, it really would be better if he just died," Lucy said.

"Come on!"

"He's so miserable. And when he's miserable, he's mean. The other day Benny said, 'Mommy, Daddy's meaner than Oscar the Grouch.'"

"Who the hell is Oscar the Grouch?"

"From Sesame Street."

"Gotcha."

Lucy was weeping now, and put her head down on her folded arms.

"Wait here," Sam said. She turned off the stove and padded across the street in her bare feet. A small stone cut sharply, and she cursed under her breath. She'd have preferred to yell but figured there'd been too much of that already tonight.

She entered by the back door. The kitchen smelled of fried food, yet was spotless.

Lousy ventilation.

The dining room was tiny. Sam had been there before many times, but then—in the dark, silent, almost empty house—it was unfamiliar and sad. The living room was large, with plastic bins full of toys stacked tidily against one wall. The wood floor creaked. The house was old, like Sam's, built in the twenties when wealthier townspeople thought it was stylish to live in the country and have farmers for neighbors.

"Glen, it's your neighbor, Sam!"

The hallway leading to the bathroom was also dark, and Sam wondered if Lucy had had the presence of mind to shut off all the lights before she ran out or if they'd been carrying on in the gloom, which seemed more likely.

A dim light seeped from beneath the bathroom door. Sam put her ear close. She heard nothing. Then there was a brief movement within.

"How you doing in there, Glen?" she said in the same overly cheerful voice she used to address the residents at Lindell.

"Leave me alone."

His voice was heavy.

"Open the door, Glen," she said. To her amazement, he did. He sat on the closed lid of the toilet. The room was small enough he could have turned the doorknob without getting to his feet. He was in his officer's uniform, even down to the thick-soled black shoes. The holster on his hip was empty. The collar of his undershirt was stained with sweat. He stank of it, too. His black hair was thinning on top and looked greasy. So did his skin. Sam had never seen him up close. When they'd first moved in, she'd waved at him across the road. He'd nodded in reply. Sam remembered that nod. It was dismissive, cold, hostile. Or maybe he was just shy.

"What say you and me go sit where it's a little more comfortable?" Sam said.

"Where's Lucy? Do you have her?"

"She's at my place, but I don't *have* her. Now, come on, up you go."

"Get out of my house."

"Can't do that, Glen."

He lifted his head and stared right into Sam's eyes. The anguish in them was chilling.

"What did she do with my gun?" he asked.

"I have no idea."

Sam wondered then how Lucy had managed to get it away from him. Glen wasn't particularly tall—in fact, Sam was sure she was taller than he was by a good couple of inches—but he was wiry. Maybe he had just let her have it. Maybe he just gave up.

"Look, you can't sit on the can all night. Come into the kitchen. I'll make coffee."

"I need a drink."

"A drink's the last thing you need."

Glen put his face in his hands and sobbed. She'd never seen a man cry.

Well, they're not any better at it than we are.

"Look, you got a lot to live for. Those kids, for one thing. They're enough to keep anyone going, right?"

Sam regretted her words when Glen cried harder.

She went into the hall, lined with framed shots of the kids. She took down two and brought them into the bathroom.

"Glen, look at these precious faces. Come on, look. You really want them to grow up knowing their dad didn't love them enough to stay alive?" she asked.

Glen looked at the pictures without seeming to see them. Sam put them on the small counter.

"Glen, you don't come out of this bathroom, I'm going to have to haul you out. Now, don't give me the rap about being a big strong cop and all that. I'm big and strong, too, and you're in no shape to argue, so what do you say you stand up and come with me, okay?"

Glen didn't move. He wasn't crying then.

Sam put both hands under one arm and pulled. She got him on his feet. He leaned on her as she shuffled him slowly across the hall and back the way she'd come to the kitchen, where she loaded him into a chair. She turned on the overhead light. Glen's face was blank, his eyes glassy.

Christ, I hope he didn't get his hands on something and took it after all.

But then he straightened up and focused.

"Go tell Lucy to come home," he said.

"Not until you and I have a little talk."

"Nothing to talk about."

Sam sat down across from him. The surface of the table was covered with one of those thick pads that protects the wood underneath. The thought of Lucy trying to keep her furniture from getting scratched moved her. That woman worked her ass off, and for what? To listen to this slob bitch and moan?

"What's got you so down on living, anyway?" Sam asked.

Glen stared at the surface of the table for a long time, so long that Sam was about to ask him again.

"She doesn't love me," he said.

"Of course she does! She's frantic with worry this very minute."

"She just feels guilty."

"About what, for God's sake?"

"Being in love with someone else."

"Who?"

"Someone she used to know."

"And she told you this? 'I'm in love with so and so.'"

"I can just tell. I see it in her face. I feel it every time I touch her."

He pounded his fist on the table, toppling the saltshaker and causing some dried rose petals to fall from the aging bouquet leaning in a vase. Sam had seen Glen get out of his car with the flowers in hand and thought maybe it was their anniversary. Then she'd recalled that Lucy had said they'd been married in the summer, and it was fall, then. In that moment, watching Glen carry the flowers along the stone path to the back door, Sam thought how nice it would be to have someone in your life who brought you something pretty, just because, just to remind you that you were loved.

Except these flowers were a plea to be loved in return.

Sam righted the saltshaker.

"I'm no expert, believe me, but there's got to be a way to work things out. You've got four kids," she said.

"You think I don't know that? I begged her to break it off. Time and again."

Sam was exhausted. She went into the kitchen and took a plastic glass from the cabinet. She knew where they were kept. She'd helped Lucy with the dishes more than once. She poured herself some water, drank it, rinsed the glass, and put it in the dish drainer. The glass was decorated with several laughing dinosaurs, green and yellow.

"I'm going to go home now and talk a little bit with Lucy. You have to promise me not to do anything stupid," Sam said.

Glen said nothing. She stood, put her hand briefly on his shoulder, and left.

Though the sky was still dark, the presence of light was near. Sam sensed it in the stillness, the deeper quiet of the hills whose gentle tops would be the first to warm.

Lucy was where Sam had left her, at the table, staring through the window into the night. Sam sat. Her stomach was on the warpath again. The folks at Lindell sometimes complained about heartburn, so she figured it was basically an old person's problem. If true, she'd aged decades in that one evening.

She waited for Lucy to ask how Glen was. She went on sitting, looking out. Then she turned her head, and Sam saw in her eyes the same blank expression she'd seen earlier in Glen's. Whatever the bullshit was between them, it was killing them both.

"Who's the guy?" Sam asked.

Lucy's face tightened.

"There is no guy. There never was."

"Glen said—"

"I know what Glen said. He's been saying it for years. Every time he messes up and I call him out, he starts talking about the guy who doesn't exist, deflecting onto me his own crappy behavior."

"Huh."

"You don't believe me?"

"I don't know what to believe."

Lucy put the pile of torn bits of paper towel on the table.

"Well, it doesn't matter, one way or the other. It's my problem," she said.

So why the fuck did you wake me up in the middle of the night?

Sam took a deep breath. No point in going down that particular road at the moment.

Lucy got up and let herself out. Sam stood and went to her front window to watch her go slowly across the road. She didn't retrieve the gun from the ditch. She'd have to before the kids came back. Maybe Sam should go remind her, because she might not remember in the morning.

"Fuck that," Sam said, and took herself to bed.

chapter twenty-three

Flora demanded to know why she was so down, if something had happened at work, if one of the residents Sam was close to had died. Sam said she was fine. Everything was fine. Flora let it go but watched her in a way that was long-standing and deep between them.

Sam hadn't talked to Lucy since that night, two weeks before. She saw her come and go, with the kids and without, returning with groceries or not, just living her life as if nothing had happened.

At work, Eunice was in the dumps, too. She was worried about Constance Maynard lying in bed all day, though it was fairly common at this time of life. On top of that, her mother had fallen at Lakeside, Dunston's Medicaid facility. She'd broken her hip. That signaled the beginning of the end for her, too. Eunice told Sam about her Grandma Grace, who'd suffered the same fate. She went on and on about her, how great she'd been, how she alone had been the person in Eunice's young life who'd given a damn about her.

When Sam's interest in Grandma Grace, or anything else except the specific chore right in front of her, failed to materialize, Eunice asked her what on earth was wrong.

So, Sam mentioned Lucy and Glen, and Glen's failed suicide attempt.

"And this guy's a cop. That's super scary," Eunice said.

They were cleaning Katherine Foley's room. She was one of the few residents in the skilled nursing wing who'd put her own touch on the place. Her dresser was crowded with crystal figurines, which Sam was very careful not to break. The giraffe was her favorite, though the seahorse dangling from a gold wire was also sweet.

Suki and her little treasures.

The thought made her even sadder.

Katherine was propped up in bed, working on a crossword puzzle. She'd had polio as a young woman, which meant her mobility was very limited, otherwise she wouldn't be in that wing in the first place. Her mind was sharp. She liked listening to Sam and Eunice talk.

"Very scary. Very scary indeed. Though I have to believe that emotional stress of all kinds is very common for first responders," she said.

"Goes with the territory, I expect," Eunice said.

Sam stuffed Katherine's dirty clothes into a drawstring bag.

"My brother was Sheriff of Tioga County. The things he saw! Now this was years and years ago; the country was much more rural than it is today. A farmer's pig got loose. Dug herself out, or someone left the gate to the sty open, I don't rightly remember. But this pig, she had such personality, such wit. Pigs are witty creatures. Never forget that. Anyhow, this pig, Beulah, was pregnant. Don't know why she took herself a notion to go roaming when she was expecting and her teats were practically dragging through the dirt, but she did, and so off she went. The lane the farmer lived on never got much traffic, being way out, and all, but this one driver was going along, drunk as a skunk, right at the moment Beulah decides to cross the road. And of course he runs smack into her. He ends up in the ditch, Beulah ends up dead as a doornail, and her piglets choose that moment to be born, right there on the road, in the middle of a starry summer night, crawling out of the tear in their mother's stomach. My brother gets the call, made by the fellow who lived by the ditch the drunk slid into, and gathers up the piglets before he even checks on the driver, who turned out to be just fine and didn't remember a thing about it! My brother was an animal lover, and the sight of Beulah put him in a bad place for quite a while. Then there were all the dead deer over the years, and people's dogs. Really took a toll on him. After a while, he said he couldn't take it anymore, and asked for a desk job. He was dead the next year. All that stress had just built up inside him with nowhere to go but his heart, and that was that."

Katherine picked up her crossword puzzle. Sam threw the laundry bag onto the cart. Eunice emptied Katherine's trash basket.

"That's quite a story," Sam said.

Katherine looked up from her paper and over the top of her glasses.

"I was trying to make a point, what was it?"

"About the stress of being in law enforcement?" Sam asked.

"Yes, yes. Exactly. Though it sounds to me as if your friend is a little more than stressed out if he's threatening to kill himself. He needs serious help."

Sam thought Glen would benefit from spending some time with Katherine and her firm words. So could Lucy, who seemed to have taken Sam's efforts completely for granted. Sam had expected either an apology from her or an expression of gratitude.

I don't know what I would have done without you.

But nothing came, and Sam realized that their friendship had passed some wretched frontier from which it was unlikely to return.

At four o'clock, when Sam's shift ended, she looked in briefly on Constance, who lay in bed as usual and might have been asleep. It was impossible to tell. Meredith had been by recently, judging by the faint aroma of perfume she'd left behind. Sam had heard nothing more from Constance about her. Their last exchange, however, was still fresh.

She's not my daughter.

She thought of the evening ahead. Flora would cook, Sam would do the dishes, Chuck would watch television with Flora by his side on the ancient couch. Chuck would tell her to buy a new one, and she'd shake her head. Her part-time job bagging groceries, plus the remains of her parents' insurance policy, didn't stretch very far. They left Sam alone, didn't make demands, yet she felt like an outsider in her own home.

Before things got more serious with Chuck, Flora's attention had always been on Sam. Usually that attention was negative, informed by anxiety, layered with criticism, and surely reflecting her own frustration, but now Sam wondered if maybe all the time it had been informed by guilt.

Rape victims carried a lot of guilt, or so she had heard. They wondered if they'd done something to invite the attack or misled the attacker before the fact, pretending an interest that wasn't really there. Sam had tried to imagine her mother thinking these things, suffering from them, being accused of them by her parents.

How had it all come about? Not the rape itself, about which Sam had given considerable thought, but afterward? Flora would have come home in a state of bruised disarray, and would have tried hard to hide it. She would have been shaken, terrified that she would run into Henry Delacourt again, and then relieved when he left town. She would have begun to recover, to heal, to feel as if there was a life almost worth living from then on, until she discovered that she was pregnant.

Then, even if she had managed to hide the rape from her parents, the results of it would be impossible to conceal. There would have been fury, beatings, too, accusations about her wanton ways rather than support, understanding, and love. Some women in that position had been known to take their own lives rather than live with such monstrous shame. But Flora survived. Sam survived. Layla Endicott, to whom Flora must have confided everything at some point, surely in whispers and tears, took it upon herself to make Sam aware of why her father was a phantom.

At the time, Sam was eleven years old. Layla's words were shocking, naturally, but even more shocking and disappointing was that Flora hadn't come to her with the truth herself. Sam confronted her at a strategic moment when the grandparents were out of the house. Flora denied nothing, and when Sam forced her to explain why she'd kept quiet all that time, Flora said, "I just wanted to think it never happened."

Flora was alone in the house when Sam returned after work. She stood at the stove, stirring a pot of chili from the smell of it. Chili was an important dish in their family. When Flora made it, something big was in the wind, such as the day before Sam left for Los Angeles or the evening after it was confirmed that her own father was terminally ill with lung cancer, caused by decades of cigarettes whose smell Sam could still detect in the small bedrooms upstairs, including hers, though the walls had all been repainted since.

Sam got herself a bottle of beer from the refrigerator. She'd recently started drinking beer on the advice of Caroline Boone, who declared that a serving a day was responsible for her still being alive at the age of 97. Although alcohol was not served to the residents and was actively discouraged, Caroline's grandson kept her supplied with a weekly six-pack (Caroline abstained on Sunday), which she was allowed to keep in the kitchen. When some of the bottles went missing, Sam knew one or more of her fellow employees were helping themselves. She suggested that Caroline's grandson provide a small refrigerator, the kind that had a key like in fancier hotels—though Sam had never seen one herself, she remembered Suki mentioned them, calling them "mini-bars." The suggestion was taken; the refrigerator now sat in a corner of the closet, and the key hung on a string around Caroline's neck, which she refused to remove, even when bathing. The chronically damp string caused a rash, so a thin silver chain was found somewhere to replace it.

Flora tasted the chili and nodded to herself in satisfaction. She put the lid on the pot, the spoon on a plate by the stove, and took off her apron, one that Sam had given her for Christmas with an image of a smiling reindeer holding a cocktail in its cartoon hoof. She ran the water, filled the sink that held a number of utensils she'd used to make the chili, poured a stream of bright orange dish soap in, and watched a mound of bubbles rise.

Seeing it, Sam was suddenly taken back. She was eight years old. She and Flora and the grandparents were at Lake Placid, in a cabin, on vacation. They'd never taken a vacation before. Her grandfather worked on a dairy farm.

"Cows don't take time off," he said.

But then, they had, apparently. Later, Sam learned that her grandfather had been fired. They'd all gone away so the adults could confer about a plan of action, which seemed more complicated than just his looking for a new job.

Sam's chore was to wash dishes. She had made a mass of bubbles, too. She loved them, loved washing, even loved drying.

She broke a cup, or a plate, she couldn't remember which. Her grandmother swept the shards into a rusted dustpan, threw them into the metal trash container out back, propped the broom in the corner of the kitchen, and then hit Sam hard enough to make her head ring. Her nose bled down her white, sleeveless shirt, which her mother told her not to wear because it emphasized her fat arms. Dirtying the shirt enraged the grandmother further, and as she raised her hand once more, Sam picked up a heavy wooden stool and said, "I'll beat the crap out of you if you touch me again." Her grandmother was so surprised she just stood there with her hand still raised until Flora got between them and hauled Sam out, still holding the stool. A couple of years later, Sam was taller than her grandmother. They took to avoiding each other from then on.

Flora turned off the water. She took a pitcher of iced tea out of the refrigerator. The refrigerator was yellow. So was the stove. She sat down. Her black sweatshirt was stained with tomato sauce.

Flora drank iced tea. Sam sipped her beer. Flora's brow was knit; the lines in her face were deep. She was only in her mid-forties but looked considerably older, something about which she occasionally complained and then once sought to correct by dyeing her hair raven black.

"Remember all that junk we threw out a couple of weekends ago?" Flora asked.

"Sure."

"We kept that box of pictures. You want to go through them with me?"

Sam wasn't interested in old pictures. At work she was surrounded by them, always black and white, of husbands and wives who were long gone. She supposed they were useful for keeping the mind alive, but the wear and tear on the heart must be terrible.

Unless with time, love and longing faded. Was that possible? Could the heart's fire dim and go out altogether?

If so, then it was Nature's mercy, bestowing inner calm before meeting eternity.

"You've been in the dumps for days," Flora said.

"And you think pictures will cheer me up."

"They can be fun to look at. Makes you imagine life back then."

"I prefer poetry."

From across the road, the sound of car doors being slammed reached them. Sam had left the back door open when she came in, making the noise audible. There were three slams, which meant that Lucy had returned with at least two of her children. Sam missed them. Maybe she should invite them all over for chili. She put the idea to Flora.

"Really?" Flora asked.

"Oh, I guess not. She probably doesn't want to see me right now."

"What did you do?"

Sam put her beer bottle on the table and wiped her mouth with the back of her hand.

"What's that supposed to mean?" she asked.

"Nothing."

"Don't give me that. You think I did something to Lucy, and that's why I haven't been seeing her, right?"

"I don't think anything of the kind." Flora's color was rising. Sam rinsed out her bottle in the sink. She took another from the refrigerator. She sat back down.

"Why do you assume I'm to blame? What if I'm not to blame at all? What if all I did was try to help?" Her voice was firm and even, not a hint of rage.

"I don't think you're to blame for anything."

"The hell you don't. Let's consider the case of your dear departed parents. You always told me not to piss them off, to do what they wanted so they wouldn't get mad. You know what? They got mad anyway because they were a couple of crazy fucks. And you made me think it was my fault. It wasn't. It was their fault for being intolerant, uptight pains-in-the ass. I could have been Miss Goody Two Shoes and they'd have hated me, because I was a reminder every single day that you'd been raped."

Flora put her face in her hands and for a very brief moment Sam was glad she'd wounded her. When her mother looked at her again, Sam wasn't glad.

"I've been wanting to talk to you about this for a while. In fact, I wanted to bring it up just the other day."

"Bring what up?"

Flora said nothing. She was quiet so long, Sam finally said, "Well?"

"It's hard."

"Quit stalling!"

Again, Flora just sat. Sam put her palms on the table, ready to stand up and leave the room.

"I wasn't raped. I only said so because I didn't want my parents to think I'd let him," Flora said.

"Wait."

Flora raised her hand to say Sam should be quiet and listen.

She'd been in love. He said he was in love with her. Such an old story, she couldn't believe she fell for it, but she had. Had Sam ever considered that the history of the world could be written on the hearts of deceived women? Her mother's poetic turn of phrase was new—a part of her, like the truth about Sam's origin, that she'd kept to herself.

He said he wanted to get married, and though Flora wanted very badly to believe him, she was worried that his family would never approve. He said they'd be won over by her in an instant, then never brought her home. She came to see that he had no intention of marrying her, that he probably wasn't even in love with her. When she told him she was pregnant, he bolted.

"So, little Flora gets herself knocked up, passes herself off as a rape victim who bravely keeps her child, and raises that child on a fat, fucking lie," Sam said.

Flora looked grim.

"Did you tell Layla Endicott the truth, or did you lie to her, too?" Sam asked.

"I lied. I hadn't meant to. I mean, I didn't want to tell her anything, but she saw me come and go, my stomach growing all the time."

Lucy's children were playing outside. The eldest, Alice, had a high, bossy voice. She was only eight, but Lucy relied on her to take the others in hand. Sam thought of her as Little Lucy, a name that had made Lucy smile, and Alice frown.

"And your parents bought the whole story, no questions asked," Sam said.

"Yes."

"And didn't report it."

"No."

"Why the hell not?"

"I'd brought shame on them."

"So they didn't care about seeing justice done. They just wanted to sweep it under the rug."

Flora said nothing.

"How did they explain me to their friends?"

"They didn't have any."

Sam couldn't remember anyone coming to the house for dinner, a cup of coffee, a game of cards.

"What about *your* friends?"

"I only had one. I told her what I told everyone else."

"Who was it?"

"Mayva Barns. You met her years ago, before she moved south."

A tall, skinny woman with wispy hair came to mind. She'd worn clogs that made noise on the wood floors. She took Sam to the lake once, without Flora or the grandparents. Her car had a strong smell of dog. She told Sam the dog's name was Eloise, which Sam found funny. She decided that Eloise was pretty, with white fur and a black nose. She wanted a dog, and Flora said she couldn't have one. The grandparents were firmly opposed.

"Why didn't you move out?" she asked.

"I didn't think I could manage by myself."

When Sam's grandmother wasn't busy at her church, she cooked, cleaned, laundered, all in a state of silent fury. She'd been a small woman with bright blue eyes, and held herself taut, as if wrapped around a steel cable. Sam's grandfather wasn't much taller than his wife, and he carried himself in the same stern way, until he fell ill, when he seemed to soften and shrink.

There had been other kids at school who didn't have fathers. Divorce was most often the reason. Sam told people her father had died, which was what Flora had told her many times with an emphasis that now rang false.

"He's not really dead, is he?" Sam asked.

"No."

"And never actually left Dunston?"

"Right."

"You know this how?"

"I looked in the phone book."

Flora rose and stirred the chili. She put the spoon down, and didn't return to the table. Sam finished her beer. Lucy's kids must have gone inside. It was getting on dinnertime. Soon Chuck would lumber through the door with his inane good cheer.

"Does he know all of this? Chuck, I mean?" Sam asked.

"Some."

"What part?"

"That I was involved with someone and we didn't get married."

"Doesn't take a fucking rocket scientist to figure that out, Mom."

Flora looked at her with a blend of fear and despair.

"Why are you telling me now? Why not before?"

"Because his father died."

Franklin Delacourt's death had been in the paper that he owned along with two radio stations. His wife had died years before. His house was up for sale, which meant Henry could cash it out. It was a big property. The whole estate would be hefty. Sam should go and stake her claim.

"Hold on," Sam said.

The idea was nuts, yet she couldn't overlook that she'd been poor all her life. So, obviously, had Flora. The only asset Flora had was the rickety house she was standing in. Sam was no genius at real estate, but she was pretty sure it wasn't worth a whole lot. The assessed value had dropped for the last few years. Flora would have been thinking about that when she put two and two together.

"Why don't you go and stake your own?" Sam asked.

"I might get something, if you were still a minor, but you're not."

"You've really given this a lot of thought."

Flora shrugged.

"You're hoping I'll reward your good advice, which I'm sure as shit not likely to do, given what you put me through with your lying bullshit, unless you made the case that I owed it to you, like a, what's that called, a finder's fee."

Sam could see that this was exactly what her mother had had in mind.

"What makes you think I'll get anything, anyway?" Sam asked.

"Because you'll hire a lawyer and insist on a DNA test."

"Aren't you the clever one."

Flora sat down. She seemed wrung out. But then, she always seemed that way. As long as Sam could remember, her mother had been as drab and dismal as the brown plaid wallpaper on the kitchen walls. Once, though, she must have been bright and shiny, back when she was falling for Henry Delacourt.

Chuck's car rolled up the driveway. He came through the door humming. He was deeply tanned from working outdoors. His hands were dirty.

"Hello, lovely ladies!" he said. He went right to the sink and washed up. Sam didn't understand why he never did this before leaving work. It was as if he needed to mark his territory by leaving grime. He wiped his hand on the dishtowel Flora kept folded on the counter. He tossed it back down, without refolding it. He helped himself to a bottle of Sam's beer. He took a long, eager drink.

"You two look like the bill collector's been banging on the door. What's up?" he asked. He touched the back of Flora's neck.

"Just girl talk," Sam said.

Chuck nodded solemnly.

"Whatever you got cooking smells awful good," he said.

"I'm going for a walk," Sam said.

"Samantha—" Flora said, just after Sam went out the door.

chapter twenty-four

Eunice asked her to come for Barry's birthday. Sam didn't know why Barry would want her there. Eunice said new faces were called for. She'd invited Angie Dugan from Lindell, and told her she could bring someone. Sam said she'd have to see if she were free, though of course she was. These days, all she did was go to work and go home, where Flora made herself scarce, thank God, by spending most of her time at Chuck's.

Sam went through the box of pictures Flora had suggested she take a look at the day she spilled her news. They were all of Henry Delacourt. The man must have a huge ego, to give away so many shots of himself. There he was, on a sailboat, rowing with his college team, standing under the Eiffel Tower, on a cobblestone street. He was tall and fit. Sam decided that she looked a little like him, after all.

As her curiosity about him grew so did her rage. He got Flora pregnant, then just walked away. Did he know she kept the baby? Had he ever wondered?

She drove along the lakeshore to Eunice's house. Their place was hard to find because the white post with the address was set back from the road. Sam had to circle around twice. Eunice should have put up a sign or tied some balloons to it. The driveway was long and descended a good sixty feet before leveling out in front of a modern-style property where a few other cars were already parked. Sam put her station wagon where no one could pull in behind her so she could leave when she wanted.

Eunice had said not to bring a present. Sam didn't feel right showing up with nothing. She'd never met Barry before and knew nothing about him except that he owned a bar, but figured she couldn't go wrong with a tastefully decorated coffee mug. The one she chose had an image of the Dunston University clock tower. She'd climbed it once, several years before. One hundred and sixty-one steps had winded the hell out of her on the way

192

up. Then, coming down, her knees strained and burned.

The front door was open, and no one was in the entry hall. A wooden table along the wall held a small bouquet of white flowers. Sam put her gift there. The sound of mellow jazz led down a hall and into an open room with a wall of glass windows looking right out over the lake. The sky was restless, and the rushing clouds cast moving shadows on the water. It seemed like a beautiful place to live, and Sam felt a pang of longing.

Voices in the kitchen were light and pleasant. Eunice was there, removing a baking sheet from a wall oven. She wore a dress. Sam could see that she wasn't used to dresses from the way she kept tugging at the hem after she placed the sheet on the counter to cool. When she turned and saw Sam she smiled a tense, anxious smile. It was strange to see her outside of work, as if Lindell was their only world. For a moment, they were like aliens landing roughly on a new planet. The moment passed quickly. Eunice said she was so glad Sam could make it.

Eunice introduced Sam to Barry. He shook her hand weakly. He, too, looked tense, as if he'd rather be sitting down, watching television, or out of the house altogether, maybe back at his bar. When the invitation came, Sam asked why Eunice wasn't hosting the party there. Eunice said it wasn't the nicest atmosphere.

Angie Dugan was present, too. Her olive pants were drab, though her silver top gave her a festive air. She had two orange bracelets, obviously plastic, on one wrist. The other had a modest silver bangle. Beside her was a tall, black-haired young man who instantly caught Sam's eye. He wore black jeans and a white T-shirt under a light-weight leather jacket. Even his shoes were stylish. He reminded her of the guys in L.A. He nodded to her, though said nothing.

"This is my brother, Tim," Angie said.

"Timothy," he corrected her.

Even his voice was pleasing, low, gentle. Sam wished her clothes were nicer. She had on khaki pants and a blue knit top to which she'd added a necklace with blue stones she'd gotten for herself in L.A. right after the fiasco with Suki's brother. A reward for her bravery and resolution, she'd told herself.

Two more people arrived, one of the bartenders from Barry's place and his girlfriend. Looking at everyone, Sam realized that Eunice and Barry were the oldest people there.

Eunice directed everyone to a table where glasses and beverages had been arranged. Timothy grabbled a bottle of beer from a tub packed with ice. He offered one to Sam. Sam took it. She inspected the end of the table where food had been laid out. There were crackers with cheese and some nasty-looking red stuff that Eunice said was roasted red bell peppers. Sam chose a baby carrot from another plate and shoved it into some dip, which to her dismay turned out to be onion-flavored. She used a pink cocktail napkin to receive the partially chewed carrot, looked around for a trashcan, then shoved the napkin in the pocket of her pants.

"Not a fan?" Timothy asked. Sam hadn't been aware that he'd seen her. They removed themselves from the group and occupied a window seat covered in white leather.

"Great view," Sam said.

"It would have taken some big bank to level the lot like they did. Most of the houses around here are built to accommodate the slope."

"You're a contractor?"

"I work in retail."

"Where?"

"The GAP."

"Their stuff never fits me."

"You have to go a size up."

"They don't have sizes for fatties."

"You're not fat."

Sam drank her beer.

"Big-boned, then," she said.

"Does it matter?"

"No, I guess not."

They sat in silence. The others had remained in the kitchen. "Such a wonderful time of life really," Angie said. Laughter followed. The telephone rang. No one answered it. The mellow jazz that had ushered Sam in changed to classical.

"How do you feel about Mozart?" Timothy asked her.

"It's all right."

"You mean, 'he.'"

"Yeah, he."

They laughed. Sam didn't like feeling ignorant, though she knew she was, about many things. Timothy, though, didn't seem ignorant at all.

"Let me guess. You went to college," Sam said.

"Right here at Dunston University."

"Ivy League. That's pretty rad."

"Took me five and a half years."

"Why so long? Working on the side?"

"No. Had a little trouble getting focused."

Sam could see him drop into himself at the memory. Then he lifted, and said it was his mother who'd wanted him to go to school. Angie was already in college over in Cortland. It was his mother's plan that all her kids benefit from higher education. Sam asked how many kids there were.

"Five," Timothy said.

"Wow. That's a lot."

Timothy's face drew into a small passing frown.

His mother hadn't gone to college, herself, he said. Nor had his dad. She left him for a rich guy, a real bonehead, in Timothy's opinion, though he had to give the guy credit for improving his mother's life, at least in a material sense. At the time, though, he'd thought she was just a greedy jerk, but then he realized that not having money is a huge pain, and while having it doesn't guarantee happiness, it makes life a hell of a lot easier.

Sam wanted to ask him why he worked if he was so well off, which made her think. If she got money out of Henry Delacourt, would she quit Lindell? Obviously, that depended on just how *much* she got, but yes, she'd probably quit. And do what? You had to spend your time somehow, even if you didn't need a paycheck. Which is no doubt exactly what Timothy figured. Also, the step-dad's generosity might not extend to him, but just to the mother.

"And do you like it? Selling clothes?" Sam asked.

"No."

"What would you rather do?"

"Draw."

"Draw?"

"Cartoons."

He pulled a folded up piece of paper out the pocket of his jacket. He opened it and handed it to her. It had an image, done in pen, of a penguin playing an accordion. The penguin was smiling. Its head was perched at a jaunty angle on its little round shoulders.

"Very good. Does it have a name?" Sam asked. She gave the paper back to him.

"Not yet."

"Patty, the penniless penguin."

"Playing for her fishy supper."

Angie approached them from the kitchen. She asked if they needed anything. Sam said she was fine. Timothy did, too.

Timothy said Angie always did that, play hostess in someone else's home. He said she wasn't being bossy—though God knew she used to be, when they were young—she just had a keen sense of responsibility to other people. Sam suggested that such a trait would be necessary—and highly valuable—in a social worker.

"You thinking you want to sell your cartoons?" she asked.

Timothy put his empty beer bottle on the carpet.

"More like write a children's book."

He said it quietly, not meeting her eye, as if the statement were embarrassing. Or maybe Sam was the first person he'd shared that ambition with. She hoped it was the latter.

"And if it sells a lot, then you quit the GAP, right?"

"Something like that."

He looked at her then and didn't seem embarrassed.

Then he turned toward the water. The wind was up. The surface was all choppy. He stared at it a long time, until Sam asked what he was trying to see below the surface. He apologized if he looked like he was brooding—hardly appropriate for a birthday party. It was just that back in college he'd stood at a window once, looking down at the lake when it was gray and full of white caps, just like today.

"Is that what you meant about trouble focusing? Nature was more fun than the inside of a book?" Sam asked.

Timothy smiled for the first time since meeting her.

"No, not more fun."

He'd rushed a fraternity—against his mother's wishes. He saw later that she'd been right about the culture, but at the time it was very important to him to belong to a group of people outside of his family. Sam had no doubt heard about some of the really stupid things pledges did just to get accepted. Usually these involved alcohol and running around half-naked soaked in shaving cream, that sort of crap. His assignment had been more subtle. There'd been a girl, a student, who belonged to some Christian group that preached abstinence until marriage. In that day and age? It was all positively medieval, which made the idea of seducing her all the more intriguing.

"Wait. You had to seduce someone you didn't even know?" Sam asked.

"Well, I got to know her, obviously, by joining her group, pretending to care about it."

He took her out on a few dates, played it cool. She saw through him at once. She'd been down that road before with at least one other guy, though not from the same frat. He apologized and said he'd leave her alone if that's what she wanted. She didn't. One evening, she had him up to her place and made him dinner. That was where he'd stood, watching the water, though from a different direction, obviously, since she lived in College Town.

Well, to make a long story short, the reason this girl preached abstinence was to diffuse all the sexual tension around her. She was pretty—beautiful, actually—and guys were always hitting on her. But that wasn't the whole story. She'd been raped when she was a teenager, by one of her father's business partners. Her father didn't believe her.

"That's rough," Sam said.

"The partner assumed she was interested in him, so he might not even have felt he was forcing her."

"She say that?"

"No. But that's what it sounds like to me."

"You're saying she gave the impression of consenting."

"She said they were friendly, sometimes a little more than friendly. He might have gotten the wrong idea."

"Maybe she claimed rape for the sake of protecting her own reputation."

Timothy looked at her closely. Her cheeks warmed.

"So what happened?" she asked.

"With what?"

"You and her."

"Nothing. We went our separate ways."

His voice carried a tone of regret. Maybe he'd been in love with her.

She stared at the water, longing to be in a sound boat heading for the far shore. She'd been on a boat only once, when she was quite young. Her grandfather was there, and someone else, not Flora or the grandmother. The sun had been in her eyes; the motion of the waves threw her off balance. She almost went over the rail. For an instant, there had been fear in her grandfather's eyes, something she never saw again, even when he knew he was dying.

Sam looked at her empty beer bottle. More laughter flowed from the kitchen. Eunice called out that they were cutting the cake. Sam and Timothy went to see. The bartender was patting Barry on the back, which Barry didn't look like he cared for. There was a big space between them, and the bartender stopped patting. Then he put his arm around his girlfriend, who stood on his other side. She didn't warm to his embrace, and Sam decided, watching all this, that they weren't going to be a couple long.

"Shall we sing?" Angie asked.

"No," Barry and Eunice answered in unison.

"No candles?" the bartender's girlfriend asked.

"Too many to count," Eunice said. Then she seemed to regret her words, but Barry was unperturbed. He looked less tense than he had at the outset. He held a full glass of wine, which was no doubt the reason.

Eunice cut the cake. She did it badly. Sam offered to help. Eunice handed her the knife.

"I never could slice a cake properly," she said.

"Nothing to it," Sam said.

People handed her plates, and she filled them until everyone had a share.

"Forks?" the bartender's girlfriend asked.

"Oh, right, so sorry!" Eunice spun around and yanked open a drawer. She dug out a handful of forks. Sam and Timothy still came up short. Sam helped herself to the same drawer, and was amused to find that along with utensils it held a lot of rubber bands.

The cake had a lemon flavored frosting, which Sam recognized at once.

"Velma made it, didn't she?" she asked, her mouth full.

"She did. She even offered. I think Velma secretly yearns to be a pastry chef," Eunice said.

"Who's Velma?" the bartender's girlfriend asked. Her eyes were brown, almost beady, and looking at them, Sam disliked her all of a sudden.

"She's the cook at Lindell," Eunice said.

"This is pretty damn good," Barry said. He'd had to put down his drink to manage the plate of cake. He looked around for it, though it was on the counter directly in front of him.

"Lindell? The old folks' home?" the bartender asked.

"Retirement community," Angie said.

"Same dif."

Angie smiled warmly, to hide her annoyance, Sam thought. Angie turned away and helped herself to a glass of something from the drinks table.

"Happy birthday," Sam told Barry.

"Thank you, dear," he said.

Dear?

Sam and Timothy returned to their perch in the living room. Sam took a second slice of cake along. She was enjoying it a lot. The sugary flavor reminded her of a birthday party for one of Lucy's kids several months before. Balloons, shrieking, wrapping paper in shreds on the floor. The cake Lucy made hadn't been as tasty as Velma's, but then Velma baked from scratch. Thinking that, Sam decided that she must be moving on if she could recall something without sadness that only a short while ago would have made her ache.

She found Timothy studying her.

"What you said before, about a woman making a false accusation," he said.

"Yeah?"

"Where did that come from? If you don't mind my asking."

"Get me another beer first. Please, I mean."

Timothy did as she asked. He didn't bring another for himself. Sam put her dirty plate on the floor and accepted the beer. He hadn't opened it for her, but the cap twisted off easily. She put the cap on the plate and drank. She could see tension in the way he held his shoulders. He sat forward, elbows pressed to his knees.

She told him about her mother and Henry Delacourt.

"Jesus. That's a hell of a lie, isn't it?" he asked.

"Just a little."

"You think it's true, what she's telling you now?"

"I thought about that. She has no reason to lie now. She had a reason before. So, yeah, I guess I believe her."

Then she added that her mother thought she could make some financial claim against Delacourt. Provided she could prove they were father and daughter. She'd need to find a lawyer, one who was willing to take her on with the promise of a cut of the money later.

"A contingency fee," Timothy said.

"If that's what it's called."

Footsteps fell from the front door into the kitchen. Whoever it was walked slowly, almost hesitantly. Words of greeting were made. Then Eunice led Meredith into the living room where Angie was sitting with the bartender and his girlfriend on a blue velvet sectional on the other side of the room from Sam and Timothy. Sam hadn't realized they'd left the kitchen, which meant Eunice and Barry had been in there by themselves.

Not too sociable, now are they?

She wasn't surprised to see Meredith. Eunice had mentioned that she might come. She looked woeful, and Sam wondered if Constance had died. But if she had, Meredith wouldn't be there, would she?

She was elegantly dressed, as always, in a lightweight, boat-necked sweater and a pair of pressed linen slacks. She put her leather shoulder bag on the table in front of the sectional and shook hands with the bartender and then with the girlfriend. When Eunice led her over to the window, she shook Timothy's hand, and nodded politely to Sam.

"How's your mother?" Sam asked.

It was a stupid question, because Sam had seen her just the day before, but she couldn't think of anything else to say.

"The same."

Eunice stood with her arm looped through Meredith's. She was claiming her somehow. Or protecting her.

"You should try the cake," Sam said.

"Yes."

Then Eunice led her away, as if she just couldn't navigate the room by herself.

Sam drank her beer and enjoyed the scudding clouds. She didn't feel like she had to keep the conversation going, and neither, apparently, did Timothy.

Then after a moment, he asked, "So, aside from working at Lindell and needing a lawyer to slam dunk your biological father, what else are you into?"

"Poetry."

"Yeah?"

"Mostly Sylvia Plath, these days."

"That's awesome."

"Hang on."

Sam went into the kitchen where she'd left her purse on the counter. Eunice, Meredith, and Barry were seated at the table, drinking, speaking quietly. An untouched slice of cake sat before Meredith. Sam took the book she carried with her these days and returned to Timothy.

"Here," she said, handing it to him. It was *Ariel.*

He opened the book to the page she'd turned down.

"Read the last paragraph," she said.

There's a stake in your fat black heart
And the villagers never liked you.
They are dancing and stamping on you.
They always knew it was you.
Daddy, daddy, you bastard, I'm through.

"I didn't mean aloud," she said. She turned to see if the others had taken note. They hadn't.

"She sounds angry."

"Well, sure, but she's also taking charge. At least, that's how I see it."

"I find poetry hard to understand sometimes. Not that I read it all that often. Not since college, anyway."

"It *is* hard to understand. And when I can't figure it out, I just concentrate on how the words make me feel."

She told him about the tenant at the motel who'd had poetry in her room, and how Sam had been found sitting on her bed reading a volume of T.S. Eliot. Then the motel closed, and Sam didn't know her name. She had no way of finding out. If she had, they could have gotten together to discuss the greats. It was so hard meeting people who shared your interests.

"Unless your interest is drinking, or watching football," Timothy said.

"Good point."

Angie laughed at something. She was joined by the bartender's girlfriend. The girlfriend slapped herself hard on the knee. The bartender, sitting between the two women, laughed, too.

Poor Eunice, Sam thought. Here she'd gone to the trouble to invite people to make Barry's birthday a success, and they weren't talking to him all that much. Why didn't he have any friends of his own? And why didn't Eunice?

"You have friends?" she asked Timothy.

"Sure."

"Lots?"

"I wouldn't say lots. People I go out with sometimes."

"Girls?"

"Not really."

He blushed.

"I was just thinking about this party, and the other guests, and why none of Barry's friends are here. I mean, that guy he works with doesn't seem too chummy, if you ask me. Which you didn't, of course. Just saying," she said.

Some people had trouble making friends, Timothy said. His own mother was a good example. She got married young. Her life was all about her kids and keeping things going for the family. After she got married again and had time to do what she wanted, she still didn't make friends. Sam said she must be lonely, then. Timothy said he never had that impression of her. But she'd always been hard to read, so it was entirely possible.

"What about your dad? Are you guys close?" Sam asked.

Timothy took a moment to consider.

"More than we used to be. I didn't like him much when I was young."

"Because?"

"He drank all the time and sat on his ass, basically."

Sam said Timothy's dad would have gotten on great with her grandparents. Not.

"Hardasses?"

"Rock hard."

Eunice had entered the living room and was insistently tapping her glass with a fork. Silence fell. Barry was on one side of her, and Meredith on the other.

"I, that is, we, would like to make an announcement," she said.

Sam and Timothy swung around, so the lake was behind them now. Timothy leaned close to Sam and quietly hummed the wedding march. Sam jabbed him with her elbow.

Eunice gestured to Barry, inviting him to speak.

He rocked onto the balls of his feet a couple of times. He stopped.

"Go on," Eunice said.

"Okay. Well. First. Thanks for coming to my party. You get to be my age, birthdays don't mean so much. Except when you can share them, with friends." He paused. Sam could see his mind go somewhere else. He looked distressed. Then he recovered himself.

"So, now's a good time to let you all know that I'm giving up *The Caboose*. Jax, you already know about this. We've been talking about it for several weeks," Barry said.

202

Jax—the bartender—nodded solemnly.

"I'm looking for a buyer," Barry said.

"Because you won't let me have it for fifty K under asking," Jax said. There was no edge in his voice, but Sam sensed some bad feeling there.

"But you're in complete charge until that time. All I ask is that you don't run her into the ground," Barry said. Jax's girlfriend looked cross.

"You're retiring?" Angie asked.

"Moving on to a new venture. Which brings us to announcement number two. Eunice and I are going into business. Starting an elder care service that lets people stay at home longer."

Angie clapped. No one else did.

"What's it called?" she asked.

"Lillian's Angels."

He talked on. Life is a funny thing, he said. You never knew what doors were going to open. There he was, all settled in this house, and in *The Caboose*, thinking he'd reached the top, or maybe not the top, but a plateau, a nice comfortable place where he could look back on things with an even perspective. And then you meet someone who changes things for you, only you don't see at first what those changes are, exactly. You just go with the flow. You have to be *open*, he said. You have to *trust*.

As he continued to delve into matters of the heart, Sam watched Eunice listen. She stood, hands clasped, gazing up at him with a soulful expression, especially in her eyes.

Then Meredith was talking. It seemed that she, too, had news to share.

"I've agreed to donate a little seed money to Lillian's Angels." There followed soft murmurs of approval. "And, out of respect for my mother's wishes, I'm also going to turn her childhood home into a community center for women wanting to better themselves," she said.

"Oh, how wonderful!" Angie said. She stood and put her hand on Meredith's arm.

She and Angie took a seat together on the couch. Barry and Eunice sat, too, signaling that the party might now resume.

"How about you? Any announcements?" Timothy asked Sam.

"I need to use the bathroom."

"Ground breaking."

"Earth shattering."

She asked Eunice where to go, then went down the hall she'd indicated on the far side of the kitchen. The floor was slate. Framed pictures of children, clearly taken decades before, hung on both walls, and Sam was unpleasantly reminded of Lucy's home and the night she put two of them before Glen in the bathroom.

Assholes.

Come on, be fair.

They were just a couple of fucked-up people, in over their heads.

As she washed her hands and examined her reflection in the large mirror, she wondered if she were capable of love. She'd always believed it of herself, though events with Suki and Lucy now caused her to doubt. She had needed them both, cultivated them, and then become disappointed, which raised another question—could you still care for someone who let you down?

She returned to the party. Timothy looked up immediately, as if he'd been watching for her. Something about him suggested an accustomed anguish, which along with how he'd described his parents meant he might have asked himself the same question.

chapter twenty-five

She ordered herself not to be nervous.

Pull yourself together this instant!

Her stern resolve was fleeting, and gone altogether by the time she reached the genteel brick building on the far side of campus. This was a part of Dunston she'd never been to before, which struck her as strange given how long she had lived there.

He was a therapist, specializing in children and young adults, according to the small brass plaque mounted by the front door. Sam hadn't known that beforehand. All he said on the telephone was to please come to his office. She realized, as she climbed the short flight of stairs to the door, that he might have thought her a prospective patient when she'd said the matter was urgent and couldn't wait.

She entered the foyer of a converted house. A pair of French doors, lined with fabric, were just to her right. She knocked. When there was no answer, she opened one and stepped inside. There she found a large desk with a computer monitor on it and some papers. Beyond the desk was another door, which is where Sam assumed she'd find him.

What kind of doctor has no one out front?

Her unease grew rapidly. Once again, she gave herself a firm rebuke.

Oh, go on, get in there!

She didn't have to, though, because he came out to greet her. He was tall. His hair was dark, thick, and streaked with gray. The tweed jacket he wore reminded Sam of some of the people who came to visit at Lindell. His slacks had a sharp crease. The hand that gripped hers was warm and dry. Sam knew hers was damp with anxious perspiration. He ushered her into the room he'd come out of, and gestured to a large leather chair across from an elaborately carved desk.

He waited until she sat, then he took the chair behind the desk.

He watched her calmly for a moment, waiting for her to speak.

"So," she said.

"Why don't you tell me what brings you here today?" he asked. He seemed like a nice person. He'd have to be, right? You couldn't be a therapist and be mean. You'd go out of business in no time. What she couldn't figure out was why a guy like him would go into that line of work in the first place. Maybe he was working out his own guilt complex.

"You're my father," she said.

He leaned back in his chair, as if to take her in from a different perspective.

"Yes, I know," he said.

"How? You've never met me. And I sure as hell have never met you."

"Because you bear a striking resemblance to my late mother."

From the top of the bookcase behind him, he removed a leather folder containing two pictures, side by side, of a man in one half and a woman opposite him. He handed the folder to her across the desk. Sam wasn't sure what decade the picture dated from, but she guessed the 1950s from the woman's flowered hat and pearl choker. And there she was, Sam in an earlier day, the same broad forehead and long nose. The fleshy lower lip was pretty much exact, too.

"Wow. What was her name?"

"Edith."

"Edith Delacourt."

"Edith Langley, before she married."

She gave the pictures back. She didn't know what to do next.

"When you called to make the appointment, you sounded angry. Were you?" he asked.

"Sure. Why not? I mean, wouldn't you be?"

"I suppose so."

They went on looking at each other. Sam tried to see him being involved with her mother, dating her, making love, telling lies.

"I just want to know why," Sam said.

"Why ...?"

"Why you bailed, why you never tried to find me, why you never did a damn thing for me."

Again, the long look from the leaned-back chair.

"Are you absolutely sure of your facts?" he asked.

"What do you mean?"

"One, I didn't bail. Two, I did ask to see you a number of times. And three, as to not doing anything for you, it was clear that my efforts would be highly unappreciated."

Sam rubbed her forehead with the tips of her fingers. A dull ache had begun there. Also in her stomach because she'd had no breakfast.

"You're having trouble knowing what to believe," he said.

"Something like that."

"Let me begin at the beginning then."

They'd been in high school together. They met in the Drama Club, to audition for the roles of George and Emily for that year's production of *Our Town*.

"I thought you met in a diner," Sam said.

"A diner?"

"Where my mother worked."

Henry shook his head.

Just another fib.

He resumed. Neither of them were chosen, but they continued to attend rehearsals because they each had a friend in the cast. And they liked spending time together. He found Flora lively and full of mischief. Did Sam know that her mother had once coated the seat of a lunchroom chair with glue, at the table where the cheerleaders always sat, and it just so happened that the lead cheerleader chose that particular one to plop herself down in, on a day when she was in uniform, no less? Flora had confessed the prank not long after they met, and he assumed she was trying to prove that she was the kind of girl he should be interested in. She struck him as vulnerable, though at the time, being a boy of eighteen, he wouldn't have used that word.

It soon became clear to him that she was two people, or to put it in terms that made more sense, she lived two lives—one at school and the other with her family. During the day, she laughed, teased, and spoke of the future optimistically. But on the weekend, when he picked her up for a date, she came out to his car downcast, quiet, and brooding. She never invited him into the house. He never met her parents. He understood, from the few references she made, they were strict, old-fashioned even, suspicious of people.

"She said she was in love with you," Sam said.

"And I was in love with her."

He was going away to college. She wasn't. He said he'd marry her when he'd finished his first year at Yale. She said that if they did marry, he must take her away from Dunston forever. He tried to get to the bottom of it. Something changed in her then. She became defensive, almost irrational. He didn't bring it up again. When she told him she was pregnant, he offered to marry her then and there. She agreed.

He bought a ring, got the license. He told his family nothing; he assumed she told hers nothing as well. They were to meet at the courthouse. She never came. He called and was told she wouldn't speak to him. He went to her home, and the father, a mean, angry-looking man came to the door with a baseball bat in his hands and told him never to come back. He assumed that the parents were holding her captive, refusing to let her leave the house.

He consulted a lawyer, a friend of the family who would keep the matter in the strictest confidence. Unless he had good grounds, it would be unwise to go to the police. The lawyer suggested writing a letter, though given their past behavior, it was likely that it would be destroyed before ever reaching Flora's hands. He wrote anyway, sometimes sending pictures of himself, begging her to contact him. To his immense relief, she did, also by letter, in which it said she had changed her mind about marrying him and to please leave her alone.

"What could I do?" he asked.

"I don't know. Assert your rights."

He sat, hands folded on the smooth surface of his elegant desk.

"I thought it would be harmful to you both if I got in the way," he said.

"Because …?"

"Her parents were capable of doing harm."

"All the more reason to have saved us!"

"It was a difficult choice. I made the one I felt best."

He offered money; it was always refused. By the parents, not by Flora. He was pretty sure they had stopped passing on his messages.

"She told them you raped her," Sam said.

For the first time, his eyes registered a sudden, sharp look of surprise.

"Hoping to protect herself from them, no doubt," he said.

"Except that they punished her anyway. They treated her like shit."

He shook his head. Then his gaze left her face.

"What I don't understand, though, is what her parents made of a

208

presumed rapist wanting to have contact with his victim, and then offering money for the support of the child he fathered," he said.

"Maybe they thought you were trying to lessen your crime by making amends."

"Then they didn't know much about human psychology."

"All they knew about was cruelty."

"They were hard on you, too?"

"Of course."

"Making you pay for your mother's sins."

For a moment, he looked truly sad. Sam thought about the kinds of things he must hear in that office. The fear and rage of ordinary people. She bet he hadn't heard anything quite so strange as what she'd just told him. Her thoughts turned then to Flora, the lie to her parents, Sam herself, Layla Endicott, and her one good friend, Mayva Barns.

"She told me you were dead," Sam said.

"And you decided to look for me anyway?"

"Just the other day she came clean about not having been raped. When she told me that, I figured the rest of it was crap, too. She admitted you were alive and well, right here in Dunston."

"I wonder what made her decide to share the truth now, after all this time."

"She read about your father in the paper. She said you'd probably come into money, and that I should try and get some."

Now he looked amused.

"You don't mince words. I wish more of my patients were like you," he said.

"Is there any?"

"Money? Not much. My father wasn't a thrifty man. In his youth, yes. But as he aged, and after my mother was gone, he spent freely. Then there were the stupid schemes he invested in—real estate developments that went nowhere, principally. He had this friend from school who talked him into all kinds of nonsense."

Sam thought he sounded like an idiot, but kept that to herself.

"I invested something for you, though, years ago. In case we ever met," he said.

"What if I had never looked you up?"

"It's in my will that you're to receive it when I die."

Sam asked the sum. Just about forty-two thousand dollars, he said.

That was worth almost two years of working at Lindell. All those days of freedom. Or a new car. A car and a trip. A trip somewhere new.

"That's not chump change," she said.

"No, it's not. Which is why you want to be careful with it. I can help you weigh your options, if you like. But, that's up to you, of course. If you'd rather I not interfere, I won't."

"No, it's not that."

He stood, came around to her side of the desk, and gently put his hand on her shoulder.

"It's a lot to take in, isn't it?" he asked.

She nodded. Rather than brimming with joy, she felt drained and empty.

"It'll take a couple of days to get the money from the brokerage firm, if that's all right," he said.

"Sure. You have my number, right?"

"You left it when you called."

That had been only three days before. Now, if felt like a much longer time.

Sam stood. She hoped he wasn't going to embrace her. He didn't. He took a step back, leaving a wider space between them. At the last minute, she thought it appropriate to shake his hand, though when she did, she didn't meet his eye.

chapter twenty-six

Sam said nothing to Flora about meeting Henry Delacourt. She spoke only of bland, neutral things—the weather, if they needed to buy more laundry soap, and how late in the day the new mailman swung by their place—which caused Flora to watch her with concern and suspicion. Those moments of scrutiny were short-lived, though, since she and Chuck had decided to marry.

"I finally gave in," Flora said.

She beamed. At times she was giddy. Sam had never seen her that way, and was reminded of how Henry Delacourt had described her back in high school. The thought of an outwardly cheerful young woman who was in fact lonely, browbeaten, and mistreated gave her pause once again. She still fumed over the deceit she'd been handed, but it was tempered by seeing more clearly than ever before the emotional hardship Flora herself had suffered.

Flora and Chuck were going to live at his place. That meant for the time being, Sam would have the old house to herself.

"What do you mean, for the time being?" Sam asked.

"Chuck thinks I should put it on the market."

"Does he?"

"You said you wanted to find your own place, didn't you?"

"I suppose so. But, the house is in pretty bad shape. I don't know how easy it'll be to find a buyer."

"Chuck says for the right price, it'll sell in no time."

The old farm two lots down from Lucy and Glen was for sale. Sam had seen in the paper that a developer had proposed a slew of new homes but was having a little trouble with the zoning board. New housing was in hot demand in and around Dunston, something to do with a small technology company that had been founded by a couple of graduates of the university. The company was growing, and people were moving in.

"I should probably start looking, then," Sam said.

"Oh, take your time. There's no hurry."

Sam went to her room and sat at the same desk she'd used all the way through school. The desk was placed in front of a window that looked out over the rear of the property. It was a three-acre parcel, and since no homes had ever been built on the back of the adjoining plots, the view was uninterrupted. Sam couldn't deny that it was peaceful. She'd always found it so, even when nursing her bruises, inflicted on her by angry hands.

To one side was a stand of trees and undergrowth that had never been tended. Sam had often thought of it as belonging to her alone because no one from the family ever went there. She walked its quiet seclusion when she was troubled, which she often was. One day, she offered something to the woods that she'd since searched for but never found.

She made a friend in the third grade, Missy Thomas. Missy was everything Sam wasn't: petite, stylish, well cared for. Missy liked Sam for her brash nature and for being impossible to embarrass. When boys teased Sam, she just moved off. Sam became not only a friend but a protector. Missy had an older brother, a tall, handsome boy in the sixth grade, whose verbal abuse of his little sister was constant and merciless. One day on the playground, the brother, Davy, called Missy "ferret-face," and Missy's flawless blue eyes welled. Sam walked over to Davy and punched him hard on the arm. He was so surprised, he did nothing but gape. Missy invited Sam to go home with her that afternoon. Davy had Boy Scouts and wouldn't be there to bother them.

Missy lived closed enough to walk. Her neighborhood was as charming as she was. The road she lived on followed a creek. They stopped to lean on the railing above and look down into the gentle rush of water. Missy told a story of being very young, maybe four years old, and having a passion for toothbrushes. It must have been their bright colors that she had liked. Her father bought her one whenever he visited the drug store. She took the newest toothbrush with her everywhere, and one day, walking with him by that very spot, she accidentally dropped it into the water. He went down the path by the creek's edge and looked for it, with no luck. As she watched him climb back to her, she decided to be brave and not cry anymore. Sam loved that story. It was thrilling to think of Missy as someone with passions, wanting to possess things that made her happy. She liked the image of her father trying to recover her lost treasure.

Missy's house was empty because both her parents worked at the university. Every day she returned to find a cupcake on a plate on the kitchen counter by an empty glass. The glass was for milk, which she could pour herself. Her mother set these things out before she went to campus in the afternoon. She was a professor, Missy said, and was only teaching one class that semester because she was going to have a baby. Missy hoped for a sister, not a brother. She didn't know where she'd fit in with another boy in the house. Sam asked if Davy had a snack prepared for him, too, and Missy said no, he was old enough to take care of that himself.

Missy shared the cupcake with Sam. It had a luscious chocolate filling. They ate at the table in the formal dining room. Sam's house didn't have a formal dining room; they took their meals in the kitchen. Missy's table and chairs were painted white. The seat cushions were red velvet. When they were done, Missy put the dish and glasses in the kitchen sink. Then they explored her parents' bedroom. Sam was drawn by the large jewelry box on the dresser. It was made of wood and had three drawers, each with a gold-tone knob. Missy opened the lid for her. Sam looked down on a sea of glitter. Necklaces, bracelets, and rings lay carelessly jumbled on a bed of dark blue satin. The drawers were loaded, too. Missy said her mother had gotten a lot of her stuff when she was married before, and that her dad didn't mind her keeping it, though she didn't wear it very often, probably to avoid hurting his feelings. To Sam, they sounded like nice people, which made her feel a little awkward when she stole a yellow topaz pendant from the middle drawer while Missy was in the closet, pulling out a number of brightly colored scarves and lining them up on the four-poster bed.

Sam was sure that Missy's mother would never miss the pendant, and nothing was ever said about it later. She kept the pendant safely hidden in her room, in the pocket of a homemade dress at the far end of her closet. Sometimes, she took it out and held it to the light, adoring its warm honey glow. Then she put it away, and let weeks pass before she looked at it again.

The following year, Missy's dad took a job at another university, and the family moved away. They said their good-byes on the playground. Missy's mother was there, with Missy's baby brother in a stroller. She was a tall, elegant woman with a fine, slender throat, perfect for displaying the jewel Sam had pinched. That was the first time Sam felt guilty, and the feeling never left her, even after she took the pendant to the dark stand of trees, closed her eyes, and threw it far away.

With the property going to strangers, the pendant might be found and celebrated with delight and wonder.

"How did it get here?" someone would ask. "Oh, what a lucky thing! Here let me put it on you."

How odd that what bound her most strongly to this place had never really been hers at all.

That afternoon she got a call from Henry Delacourt saying he'd like to mail her a check for the sum they discussed. She asked him to hold off for another two weeks. Flora's wedding would take place then, and until that time, she'd be "in and out," as she put it. Seeing his name on an envelope would force a discussion Sam wasn't ready to have. Would she prefer to pick it up at his office? No, that wouldn't be convenient. She wanted to tell him about the stolen pendant, and realized that would sound weird. Maybe, if they became friends, she'd find a good moment to bring it up.

chapter twenty-seven

For Eunice's last day at Lindell, her supervisor, Karen, held a tea in the common room. She set the time to fall during the afternoon quiet time so the staff could be free to come and wish Eunice well. Sam arrived forty-five minutes in to find Eunice and Meredith at a large table, an untouched plate of cookies before them, and two empty teacups. Because the saucers each had a spoon, it was clear that the tea had already been consumed. By the sink on the other side of the room were other cups, waiting to be washed. At least a few people had stopped in to say good-bye, Sam thought. But why did Eunice look so sad?

Sam joined them. Up close she saw that her eyes were wet.

"Her mother died last night," Meredith said.

"Oh, no! I'm so sorry!"

"They said it was coming, after the broken hip and all. She just never seemed to bounce back," Eunice said.

"That's what I call rotten timing," Sam said. She took a chocolate chip cookie from the plate and was annoyed to discover that it was actually oatmeal raisin. She ate it anyway.

"So funny to think of her being gone. I mean, we weren't on the best of terms most of the time, but still," Eunice said.

"She was your mother," Meredith said. Then it was her turn to look glum. Constance had slipped into a coma the day before. Her time was coming, too, maybe that very day.

"I'm tired of all these people dying," Sam said. Those words surprised her. The sadness around her had pulled something out she hadn't known was there.

"I don't mean *your* people—your moms, that is. I just mean everyone here, at Lindell. I know it goes with the territory—it's a retirement community, right? But still, don't you ever wonder sometimes what it would be like to work around younger people, or even kids? No one getting old and feeble, no one passing on."

Eunice pushed her empty teacup further away from her and said, "I used to feel that way, back when I first started."

That had been almost thirty years before. She couldn't believe how long she'd been a part of the Lindell family. One of these days she should sit down and figure out just how many people she'd taken care of in that time, and try to remember them all. In the beginning, not long after she came on board, she was certain the job would only be for a little while, until something better showed up. Then she found that she really did have a knack for talking to old folks, and keeping them engaged. That was something her Grandma Grace had often said about her—she'd mentioned her before to both of them, right? She'd been a great old lady, full of piss and vinegar, if you'll pardon the expression. Sam would have liked her, and Meredith too. And now, all these years later, Eunice realized that the one thing she'd done her entire life was take care of other people. That wasn't a bad way to spend one's time, was it? There were worse ways to make a living.

What Sam heard in her voice wasn't exactly regret, but an acceptance of something that hadn't always been easy, or made her happy. Eunice stopped talking.

"Do you want to take it with you now? Or come back later, when the room is being cleaned out?" Meredith asked her.

"Oh, I hadn't really thought about it. Whatever's easier, I guess. Now then, I suppose."

Meredith explained that she was giving Eunice the needlework Constance had begun again with great energy, and then had to give up when that energy failed. She knew Constance would have approved. Eunice said she had no idea what she'd do with it, because she had no skill with that sort of thing at all and, in fact, couldn't even thread a needle. But once she got *Lillian's Angels* up and running, there might be any number of old ladies who'd be glad for a little project like that. Her face softened when she said it would be a fine tribute to Constance's memory, wouldn't it?

Meredith agreed. And she'd do her part with the community center. She already had a good idea of what classes to offer and who would teach them. She'd put out her feelers and had gotten quite a good response. People were so willing to offer their time, it warmed her heart, it really did. The tenants would be gone by the end of the year, and then the house could be seen to.

There was a lot of furniture from Constance's childhood that Meredith had absolutely no idea what to do with. She didn't want any of it herself. Of course, it could all be sold, but there were some nice pieces that should go to a good home.

"You should come by when the time's right and take a look around. I'd be glad to let you take your pick," Meredith said to Sam.

"Me? Oh, well, thanks. I could use a good dining room table, though it should be on the small side. I'll be moving into an apartment after my mom gets married and we sell our house. She said I could take anything I wanted, but our stuff is all junk. And when I say junk, I mean junk."

One of the nurses entered the room quietly and whispered in Meredith's ear. Meredith's face froze. Sam had seen that look before. Meredith was most likely thinking what a shame it was that she hadn't been at Constance's bedside when she went. If she got the chance, Sam would tell her it was often that way, there at Lindell. Family gathered to watch and wait. Then they took a break, got a bite to eat, a cup of coffee, a breath of fresh air, and bam, that's when it happened. As if at the end, the dying preferred to pass on in the company of strangers.

chapter twenty-eight

Flora was off on her honeymoon with Chuck in Old Orchard Beach, up in Maine, when Henry Delacourt called Sam. She'd received his check four days before, and had yet to deposit it. She explained that she was heading to the bank later that day, but that wasn't why he'd called her.

"We didn't get a chance to talk much about my life since your mother left it," he said. "It's not that I'm so fascinating, believe me, but I wanted you to know that I'm married and have two children, a son and a daughter. I've told them about you. Naturally, it was a bit for them to take in, but they're sturdy, compassionate souls. And they've expressed a lot of curiosity. So, to get to the point, I wonder if you'd like to meet them?"

Maybe that fake family I made up for Suki wasn't so fake after all.

Sam said she'd think about it and would let him know. He said they were about her age. The daughter was twenty, and the son was twenty-one. Sam had just turned twenty-three. Henry hadn't wasted much time putting his life back together after Flora's parents slammed the door in his face. But then, why should he have gone on waiting for something that would never be?

"Which makes me think," Sam told Timothy over a beer at her place.

"Of what?"

"If maybe I'm doing the same thing, waiting for stuff that won't happen."

"Like?"

For one, success at something. She didn't have any solid goals. She said this plainly, no trace of despair or self-pity.

"Go to school. Study poetry. You'd be great at it. You probably know most of what they'd teach you," Timothy said.

"And then?"

"You don't have to map out your whole life. One thing at a time."

Snow was on the way. The air smelled of metal. Sam hoped the old furnace would hold up just a few weeks longer, then it would be someone else's problem.

"I need to find a place to live. The house is on the market," she said.

Timothy took in the yellow wall oven with its missing knobs, the stove, also without a complete set of knobs, and the yellow refrigerator that leaned because of a dip in the floor.

"Well, not to be a downer, but it might take a while for someone to fall in love with it," he said.

"I'm not waiting until it goes. I want to move now."

"Move in with me. I've got room."

"House or apartment?"

"House."

"Will the landlord mind?"

"I'm the landlord. My mother bought the house for me. To promote stability in my life."

Sam took a moment to imagine someone buying her a house.

"What do you want in terms of rent?" she asked.

"No rent. Just help with the utilities."

"Where is it?"

"In the Heights."

"Of course."

That was the nice part of town. She'd have professors for neighbors. Maybe a lawyer or two.

She couldn't deny it would make things easier. She just didn't know how she felt about living with someone she might become romantically involved with, not that things showed signs of going that way. They were friendly, nothing more. Yet sometimes she found him looking at her in a strange, almost hungry way. She had more or less assumed that men weren't interested in her because she was chubby, and now wondered if she'd sold herself short. As far as Timothy himself, she found him very dashing with his mop of dark hair. He reminded her a little of what Ted Hughes must have looked like, but then Ted Hughes had been an asshole. He was the reason Sylvia Plath killed herself, Sam was sure. She didn't hold to all that history of depression stuff. When you found out your husband was cheating on you, and you were stuck with two young kids, the despair from that alone would have been enough to get your head in the oven.

The other day Sam had told Timothy about meeting Henry. Now she went over his phone call, her extended family, and not being sure she wanted to meet them.

"You should. Why not? Nothing to lose," Timothy said.

"What if they hate me?"

"Then to hell with them."

But what if they were good people, nice people who were interested in her? Maybe they were like her in certain ways. Maybe they could be friends.

"Well, it's not like I'm up to my armpits in close company," Sam said. She thought ruefully of Lucy, who was still estranged. Now, with Sam moving, there'd be no reason for them to ever see one another again.

"You have me, and at some point I'm sure you'll meet the rest of my family. But, only if you want to," Timothy said.

"Won't they assume, you know, that I'm your girlfriend?"

"They can think what they like. Who cares?"

"You're awfully nonchalant, Mr. Dugan."

He'd had to learn to be that way. Growing up, he'd been hyper vigilant, always on the lookout for the next flare up between his parents. He felt responsible when they didn't get along, though even then he knew it wasn't his fault. He just always felt guilty about things, a sentiment that was helped along a lot by his mother's criticism, though many of her remarks were true. He'd been lazy as a child and teenager, then resentful and self-destructive. He wouldn't have wanted to have himself for a son either.

"That's a little harsh," Sam said.

"Maybe."

She asked his advice about quitting her job, now that she had this money. He said unless the work was driving her nuts, she should hang on a little longer, until her plans were more clear.

"How old are you?" she asked.

"Thirty-one. Why?"

"Just curious."

He looked amused.

"Making sure you can trust my judgment?" he asked.

"Something like that."

She put their empty bottles in the sink and said that if it were okay with him, she'd like to go and take a look at the house.

chapter twenty-nine

It was actually more of a cottage in terms of size, and also because of the lead windows in the living room, which made Sam think instantly of a picture book she'd once had. She wasn't used to feeling nostalgic, though the emotion wasn't altogether unpleasant. Her room was in the back. She was delighted to find that she had her own bathroom.

A two-sided stoned fireplace separated the living room from the TV room, and with the weather now miserably cold, Timothy kept the woodpile stocked. Their work schedules were such that they didn't see a lot of each other. Sam didn't mind, because she knew they'd cross paths often enough to keep a connection alive. She assumed Timothy felt the same way.

Flora was glad Sam had new digs. As for herself, she was happy, and even described her state of mind as being "over the moon." Chuck was no great catch, she said with a laugh, but she'd found a home in his heart, and that was a good thing. Sam didn't begrudge her her happiness. She still hadn't told her about being in touch with Henry Delacourt, though. She had to admit her reluctance stemmed from her entrenched anger at the depth of Flora's lie.

For the holidays, Lindell was resplendent with garlands and bows. On the door of each resident's room a small decoration had been attached—a silver star or a candy cane, sometimes a few strands of tinsel. Constance's old room was vacant. It wouldn't be occupied until the first of the year. Sometimes Sam stood in the doorway, remembering the fierce soul that had lived within.

With Eunice gone, Sam worked with a new aide, Stell.

"Not Stella?" Sam had asked. Her response had been a weary sigh. Stell was fifty if she were a day, and from the few remarks she'd made, she'd taken the job because of a recent financial misfortune involving her husband.

"Probably lost his job," Timothy said, after Sam filled him in. It was a

Thursday, the one day both of them had off. It was also the day Sam had agreed to visit Henry Delacourt and his family. She was a wreck. She'd already pulled out her phone twice, ready to call with the excuse of being sick or that her car wouldn't start.

Watching her fret, Timothy said he'd go with her.

"Don't do that," she said.

"Then stop me."

She'd learned that he could be like that, forceful and kind at the same time. She asked him what she should wear.

"You look nice in purple," he said.

She paired her purple sweater with black pants. The black ankle boots were new, an indulgence made possible by the money. She wasn't used to spending on herself and found it glorious. It was something she'd have to be careful with. She was starting to think seriously about school, just as Timothy had suggested.

She hoped her outfit would convey strength and spirit. She hoped they were small people, over whom she could tower. Henry was tall, though, so they probably would be, too.

"You want a drink before we go?" Timothy asked her.

She shook her head.

"Might steady you."

"I'm fine."

He kissed her on the cheek. For luck, he said.

The Delacourts lived in the same neighborhood as Timothy, though their house was considerably grander. It had a brick walkway that led from the street. The door was framed by tall arches, and through one of the huge windows on either side of it a Christmas tree dressed with round silver and red ornaments was visible. Smoke rose from the chimney. Sam had the same nostalgic sense she'd had when she first walked into Timothy's place, as if something from a childhood story had come to life.

Only this story was now hers.

END

View other Black Rose Writing titles at www.blackrosewriting.com/books and use promo code **PRINT** to receive a **20% discount** when purchasing.

BLACK ROSE
writing™